ECSTASY OF THE DEEP

A VENORA MATES NOVEL

OCTAVIA KORE

Editor: LY Publishing

Cover Artist: Sam Griffin

An enticing savior, an old love, and one deranged alien hell-bent on destroying it all.

The seemingly endless war with the Grutex has caused many inconveniences for Amanda, but none of those have been as bad as losing funding for the project she is working on that's supposed to help save humanity. When she foolishly risks her life to continue her research, Amanda is thrown into the path of an alien the likes of which she has never seen, who claims she's his mate. The problem is, he isn't the only one making that claim.

As an ambassador for his people, Oshen is used to handling delicate situations, but he has never been in one quite so delicate as this. Instead of enlightening Earth's government about the existence of Galactic Law and their right to seek aid, he finds himself face to face with the one being he's waited his whole life to find: his mate. But the little human is in trouble and he needs to convince her to leave Earth or he risks losing the most important thing he has ever had.

Damned. Cursed. Gulzar has been called many things over the course of his life. Many in his tribe refuse to even look at him, and who could blame them? The only light in his life has been his little goddess, the only being in the entire world who looks at him without judgment. When he gets a vision of her in distress, Gulzar knows he will do anything he can for the female he loves.

A note from Hayley:

While we try not to veer too far into darkness, I feel like there are some things that need to be talked about before you dive into this novel. In this novel, you will read about miscarriages (not the main character). This is something I have been through, so I know some people need to know before it pops up in a book. You will also read about a condition I personally suffered while pregnant called hyperemesis gravidarum. While in this book most of her sickness is not on the page this is a very real and sometimes deadly condition. I tried to water it down so that the book is still readable. After spending four months hospitalized with my oldest, I decided that if I ever became an author, I would write a character who suffers from this. While I wish that a simple rattle would cure me, there is none of that for humans!

The character Amanda goes through a lot, and there are many ways a person can react to these events. One way a woman reacts to sexual assault is to become hypersexual. A lot of the time this is because she wants to get control back that was taken from her, or because she wants to replace a bad memory with a good one. Due to this not being widely known I really wanted to write a character who also reacts this way. A lot of what I write are things I have been through, though the circumstances are different. As with anything you can read about this online. These are not all the triggers in the book, but they are ones I wanted to talk about. We tried to still make the novel light enough that it won't trigger others.

Please take care, and enjoy the story.

Glossary

Adamantine (ad-ah-mahn-tINE) - A metal used by the Venium in the construction of their ships and buildings.

Allasso (ah-lah-soh) - This is the beast form spoken of in the ancient lore of Venora.

Brax (brah-ks) - A Venium curse.

Brutok (BrOO-tok) - Close friend.

Dam (dam) - Mother.

Daya (dai-ah) - A nickname (like mom) Oshen's family uses for his mother.

Feondour (FEE-ehn-dOOR) - A small duck-like creature native to Venora.

Fosalli (foh-sah-lEE) - A plant native to Venora that resembles many types of Earth coral. Mainly grows in the shade of trees within the forests on the planet.

Fushori (foo-shOOR-EE) - The glowing stripes that run along the body of the Venium.

Gleck (gleh-k) - Curse.

Grutex (groo-teks) - Alien species loosely allied with the Venium.

Gynaika (gI-nAY-kah) - Wife.

Hisar (hEE-zah) - A reptilian species allied with the Venium.

Kokoras (koh-kOOR-ahs) - Cock.

Mia Kardia (mEE-ah kAR-dEE-ah) - A Venium term of endearment "my heart."

Mikros/Mikra (mEE-kroh-s/mEE-krah) - Little one or little ones.

Mitera (mEE-tair-ah) - Nickname for mother used by Kythea.

Mouni (mOO-nEE) - Venium word for cunt. Name of Oshen's AI.

Okeanos (oh-kEE-ah-nohs) - Venium term for the ocean.

Plokami (ploh-kah-mEE) - Large aquatic creature native to the oceans of Venora.

Sanctus (saynk-tuhs) - A nearly extinct rainbow species of alien.

Sire (seye-ur) - Father.

Syzygos (sEE-zEE-gohs) - Husband.

Tachin (tah-chin) - An insectile species working with the Grutex.

Tigeara (teye-gEER-ah) - Predator native to Venora. Feline in appearance.

Venium (veh-nEE-uhm) - Alien species native to Venora.

PROLOGUE

AMANDA

SIX YEARS EARLIER...

*A*n angry yowl echoed from the carrier at her feet as she glanced around the nearly empty waiting room of her veterinarian's office. More and more people were holing up in their homes, and it was starting to feel as if the whole country was under some sort of self-imposed quarantine.

"Almost time," Amanda cooed at the disgruntled cat within the carrier. Soon Hades was going to absolutely hate her, and she couldn't say she would blame him.

"I'll take him back if you want." Jun chuckled, shaking her head and rolling her eyes. "You can't even take your own cat into the room to get neutered."

"He'll hate me!" Amanda pouted.

"Why? It's not like you are the one chopping off the jewels." Hades hissed, and her best friend stuck her tongue out in his direction. "Oh, hush, you. The vet recommended it so do not go getting nasty with us."

"Will you really take him back there for me?" Hope welled up inside her chest and she turned pleading eyes on Jun. Amanda was a major softie when it came to animals, and the thought of her cat, who was basically her baby, being in any sort of pain tore at her heart. Even though it was for his own good, it still didn't sit well with her.

"If you do it, you will cry again, and you know the staff hates when you get emotional. It upsets all the animals." She wasn't wrong at all; Amanda was a crier. The staff here practically groaned anytime she walked into the building, but she couldn't help it. "You are twenty-four years old. You would think this would not be a problem."

"Age has nothing to do with my feelings, Junafer." Crossing her arms over her chest, Amanda sank down into her chair and turned her face away.

The TV that sat up in the corner of the room was tuned in to the news, and they were showing yet another dark, unfocused video of what people were claiming were alien abductions. The scrolling text along the bottom of the screen talked about how there had been a couple thousand reports filed across the globe of missing persons, both men and women, and strange ships in the sky or aliens roaming around cities.

"Can you believe this?" Amanda asked, watching as the footage stopped on a blurry outline of something the witness swore was a massive alien.

"They are all *baliw*, all of them!" Jun huffed as she scrolled through her phone.

It *did* seem like everyone was going crazy. "Hard to believe that so many people are buying into all of this. It's like Bigfoot sightings. Nothing is really visible in any of the videos."

It wasn't that she didn't want aliens to exist, or even that she didn't believe they were out there, but to think that beings who were advanced enough to travel through space were dumb enough to be caught on camera just didn't seem right. This had to be the work of a bunch of enthusiasts.

"We had a couple come into the hospital last night who swore up and down they saw one of those things." Her friend's dark brown eyes rolled up toward the ceiling dramatically. "They ran into the waiting room screaming about the end of days and that we should be running for our lives."

"Yikes. People are losing their minds."

"It made me feel like I was back home. Just a bunch of superstitious nonsense being spread by people who want to believe in every conspiracy out there. Panic over anything and everything."

Amanda couldn't help the snort that left her. As a very proud Filipina, Jun had told her many stories about where she had been born and raised, many of them included far fetched tales of creatures meant to scare children into behaving. The current alien panic reminded her of the Aswang stories she had been telling her since the day they met in the emergency room of the local hospital. Jun had been the nurse taking her vitals after a very unfortunate incident with a horseshoe crab.

Contrary to popular belief, horseshoe crabs didn't use their tails, or telson, as a weapon, and they were normally about as far from dangerous as you could get, but Amanda was a master klutz. While attempting to flip one of them over as it struggled in the surf, she tripped and managed to impale herself on the upright telson. Luckily, both Amanda and the little arthropod managed to come out mostly unscathed. A quick cleaning and a little stitch had gained her a lifelong friend.

"Hades?" The vet tech called from the doorway as she walked out. When her eyes landed on Amanda, she sighed. "Do you have your tissues?"

"I'm going to bring him back for vitals and the hand-off." The poor tech's shoulders sagged in obvious relief. "I'll be back."

With a quick goodbye and boop to Hades' nose, Amanda held back the tears as she watched the three of them disappear down the hall. Her big Maine Coon might be an absolute jerk to most people, but he was her snuggle bug and she would always worry about him when he was away from her. It wasn't long before Jun came back out into the waiting room looking a little disheveled. Obviously, Hades hadn't wanted to go along with the plan.

"Bad?" Amanda attempted to hide her grin behind her hand.

"Well, I don't think I have any holes in my clothes, so this might be a win." A few clumps of hair fell to the ground as Jun brushed herself off. "We need coffee."

Amanda nodded, slinging her purse over her shoulder. "We definitely need coffee. My treat." The nectar of the gods made everything better.

~

The light of the Florida morning warmed her skin as they exited the small coffee shop, turning back toward the vet clinic where Hades should be recovering. Each step along the uneven concrete sidewalk made her feet feel heavier and brought on an unexplained anxiety within her. Maybe the extra shot of espresso had been too much? Probably, but she shrugged and blew into the hole on the lid of her to-go cup as they continued on, the muffled sounds of distant cars and voices floating down the street.

Tampa had always been a busy city, full of tourists bustling around, filling the small shops and restaurants. You never needed a reason to be out here, but there was far less traffic now. Sure, there were still spring breakers littering the beaches, but the usual cast of Tampa's characters had all but disappeared. A scream sliced through the quiet and Amanda whipped her head around in the direction it had come from, expecting to see some college age students messing around, but what she saw had the cup slipping from her hand.

A massive hulking figure had its arms clamped tightly around a young woman on the other side of the street. Her blonde hair was tangled around her face as she struggled against the creature's chest, calling out for someone to help her.

"Are you seeing what I'm seeing or was the coffee too strong?" Jun breathed in disbelief, but Amanda barely heard her.

She was too focused on the alien, the real life, honest-to-gods alien that was currently abducting a woman in plain sight. Its face struck her as eerily familiar and she gasped. She knew those features and would never forget them. They were so similar to the creature she had been dreaming of since childhood, that she could have sworn she glimpsed during her dives into the gulf as she pursued her dreams of becoming a marine biologist.

While this alien was slightly different than the one she remembered, he was no less fantastic. A circle of blunt-tipped protrusions sat regally on the top of its sloped head like a crown. All six red eyes, three on each side of the alien's long skull, suddenly narrowed on Amanda, its flat nostrils flaring wide, and the fleshy tendrils that hung like vines from the sides of his face wiggled as he took a terrifying step forward.

That one step was enough to snap her out of whatever trance she had been in.

Reaching down, Amanda snagged Jun's hand. "Run!" Their feet pounded the pavement, and neither one of them dared to look back to see if the creature was following. When the pair reached the vet clinic, Amanda shoved Jun inside and slammed the door, pressing herself against the metal and wood as she fumbled with the locks.

This couldn't be happening. These weren't some gray aliens

with big heads and eyes beaming people up. That alien had been far too similar to the creature she had grown up calling her imaginary friend, and imaginary friends were not real.

"This isn't happening. This can't be." But even as Amanda whispered the words, she knew everything was about to change.

CHAPTER 1

OSHEN

PRESENT DAY...

The planet below them was similar in appearance to their own, he reflected as he peered through the gazer on the ship. But on their homeworld, Venora, there was only one large landmass surrounded by the massive okeanos. This world, in contrast, had multiple landmasses, both large and small, dotting the expanse of its own blue waters. Unlike the humans, Oshen's species was not land dwelling. The Venium preferred the safety of the water and the dome that had been erected long before Oshen had been born.

"Meatface, you have a ping," his AI interrupted his observation. "Commander Vog is requesting that all crewmembers report to the main common area."

With a shake of his head at the name, Oshen huffed. It was obvious Brin had been tampering with his AI again. The Havaker was his best friend, but he was a constant pain in his tail when it came to his tech pranks. Oshen was an ambassador and not tech savvy at all so fixing what had been done to the AI was going to be a long process.

"Thank you. Send confirmation."

Honestly, the request didn't come as a surprise. After orbiting the planet called Earth for weeks, the crew aboard the mothership was fast becoming restless. No one had been allowed to venture down to the surface, and the walls of the ship had begun to feel as if they were closing in around many of them.

Humans, the primitive inhabitants of the planet, were not used to outside interference. Other species had visited, but no official contact had been made. Not until recently, when the Grutex happened upon them. The large, troublesome race had made contact with the council and claimed that Earth might hold the solution to a growing problem the Venium and many other species were facing.

The database that the Grutex had provided them with offered little information on the humans and how they would be helpful, which was just one reason they were here. The Venium government was not going to simply trust a race that had lied and schemed its way to power.

"Confirmation sent."

Tail snapping in annoyance, Oshen turned away from the gazer and walked out of the viewing room, stepping around a few of the benches that had been pulled out from the wall. The metal beneath him vibrated with his sure gait as he made his way through the halls of the mothership.

One of the things that had excited him most from the database was the extensive amount of life on the planet, particularly those that resided in the waters. His favorite animal so far was the shark, since it reminded him of his own species with its sharp teeth for tearing into prey and streamlined bodies for cutting through water.

If the gods were good, he would be allowed to explore the okeanos of this new world soon. His species believed in many gods, but their most important deities were the two moon gods Ven and Nem. Both had fallen in love with the sun goddess, Una, and had formed the sacred three. They loved the waters of Venora so much that they chose to birth their children within it and had provided them with the means to prosper for generations. It was believed that the children of this triad brought forth the very first Venium.

Pups were taught from a very young age that if they earned the favor of the moons, they would guide you to your bondmate, the one Venium you were destined to be with for all times. Although a trio had made up the first mating bond, very few had presented since the old times. It was a very rare and special occasion, one that Oshen had never witnessed in his lifetime. With any luck, the moons would turn their favor on him and grace him with a bondmate to settle down and raise a brood of pups with.

"Nice of you to join us, Ambassador Oshen." The sneer that crawled across Vog's gray face tugged at the scars that covered nearly half of it.

"And a pleasant sol to you as well, Commander."

The violet glow of Vog's fushori was there and gone so fast that he may not have noticed if he had not been paying attention. If he were going to compare the Venium to a shark, Vog would be a Great White.He was large and grey and was not willing to take any nonsense. Vog was someone most of the crew respected and all of them feared. With a quick nod, Oshen moved to take a seat next to his brutok, Brin, locking tails for a moment as a sign of friendship before he let his fall to the floor near his feet.

Vog's voice resonated through the room. "It has been decided that there will be no exploration of the planet or its waters until the council gives us permission. It seems that we have stepped into a war between the humans and Grutex."

Oshen's growl vibrated within his chest. "You know that many of us are being called down to the world and yet you would deny us our chance to see why?"

Vog's eyes narrowed threateningly. "You know the protocol as well as I do. We are not allowed to interfere without first being asked. For now, we will wait for a call of distress or until we see a violation of Galactic Law. Is that understood?"

Jaw clenched tightly, Oshen managed to ground out a respectful reply. "Of course, Commander." But just as Vog turned to address the room once more, Oshen raised another question. "How do you expect humans to know Galactic Law? Are we assuming the Grutex handed over the terms so that the natives of this backwater planet could report them? How many violations do you think have been committed so far?"

"I cannot change the law merely because you do not like it. In fact, I do not have the authority to change it at all. If you do not agree with the way the Venium handle conflicts and interventions, then you should move to have it changed when we return to Venora... Ambassador." Vog's tone was icy, and Oshen knew better than to push him further. "The Sanctus females have offered their service to those of you who have the need." He waved his hand as more males began to speak. "It is not up for discussion. Dismissed."

"Ridiculous," Oshen mumbled as he and Brin strode side by side down the hall, their frustration palpable. There was no way he was going to let the commander keep him from going where his soul told him he needed to be. Not when he knew that whatever the gods had in store for him was waiting on the planet below.

"I know that look, brutok," Brin said with a grin, his shoulder nudging Oshen's.

"Which look is that exactly?"

"The one that tells me we are about to do something stupid and exciting."

"I have no idea what you are talking about." Oshen lifted his chin in mock offense.

"Oh, please. When we were young, that look always told me we were about to get into some trouble." He rubbed his hands together, his ears twitching in excitement as he bounced on the balls of his feet. "What have you got planned, brutok?"

~

*B*rin cursed as another shot from the plasma cannon caused the craft to pitch. Bringing the small shuttle to the planet's surface probably had not been their brightest moment, but they had felt such a strong pull that stopping to assess the risks had been something they neglected to do. The Grutex ship chasing them fired again, barely missing as Brin jerked the controls to the left. Lights flashed on the console, and warning sirens blared through the small space as the craft made an ominous creaking sound.

"Brin!" Oshen hissed as he tapped at the keys in front of him, silencing a few of the alarms.

"One moment." Brin evaded another shot, dropping the shuttle close to the surface of the okeanos.

They should have anticipated this welcome. The Grutex weren't exactly on friendly terms with most species. They were secretive, cunning, and untrustworthy, taking what they wanted without remorse, dominating unsuspecting worlds. The Grutex used and destroyed whatever they pleased. Though they had a tentative agreement in place, they certainly were not going to be okay with the Venium getting wind of whatever they were doing here.

Oshen growled as he watched two more ships join the one already in pursuit on the monitor in front of him. Brin's jaw was clenched, his fingers flying along the buttons as more shots struck the hull of the craft.

"This is not good!" Oshen shouted over the renewed blaring of alarms.

Brin glanced at the display. "Uh, no, this is definitely *not* good."

There was no way they were going to be able to escape this many Grutex. His friend was pushing the machine to its limits and they were still barely keeping their lead. Smoke billowed from somewhere behind the cockpit, the acrid smell burning his lungs and making his eyes tear up.

"This isn't going to hold together much longer." A loud explosion punctuated his words, followed by the chaos of even more alarms that seemed pretty unnecessary at this point. "We need to get out of here!" The roar of the flames and the shriek of the alarms were becoming deafening.

There was nothing more either of them could do to save the craft. Brin slammed his palm down on the red button and hit the code to start the emergency ejection process. The ship's comm made the announcement moments before Oshen was launched from the ship, his body flying through the hatch as it sprang open.

"Brin, no!" The breath was ripped from his lungs as he left the ship, and the world around him went dark.

The cool sensation of saltwater pressing in on him was the first thing Oshen noticed as he came back to consciousness. He allowed himself to drift limply with the current for a moment as his jumbled mind worked to piece together what had gone wrong. He'd been on the shuttle, hadn't he?

Oshen cracked open one gleaming golden eye and peered into the murky darkness around him. *Definitely not the shuttle.* The gills on either side of his neck flared open as the unfamiliar okeanos filtered in over them, and his mouth pulled into a grimace. *Definitely not the okeanos of the homeworld.* This water wasn't as clean as he and Brin had hoped when they first looked upon it.

Oshen's eyes flew open in alarm. *Brin!* Where was the other male? He whipped his head around, searching desperately for any sign of his brutok, but the movement only brought his attention to a large, painful wound on his side. He bared his teeth as he gazed down at the torn flesh. Oshen was lost and compromised in uncharted, alien territory. *Fantastic.*

"Meatface, you survived? Lucky me." The too-sweet, feminine voice of his comm's AI made his jaw clench in annoyance. "I'll be here to assist when you are done with your napping."

"Mouni." He sneered down at the wrist his comm was embedded in. When he found Brin, he was going to give him a thump upside the head for reprogramming the unit only to answer to the word for a female's genitalia. "Make yourself useful for once and run a full body scan." He heard the soft chime that indicated the program was following his command and filtered more water slowly through his gills, trying to calm the racing of his heart.

"Scan complete, Meatface. I have found a problem. Do you still wish to have a kokoras?"

"Excuse me? What does my kokoras have to do with anything?" The damned AI. hadn't stopped commenting on his phallus since its last "upgrade" from Brin.

"It is my recommendation that you have it removed before we find dry land."

"Oh, for the sake of the gods! What is the extent of my injuries, you malfunctioning piece of scrap?" Gills flaring in annoyance, Oshen moved his legs through the water.

The AI actually laughed at him. "You'll be fine. Quit acting like a pup."

Oshen moved his fingers along the deep gash in his side, trying to gauge how bad the damage was. *What's the point of having the AI if I have to do this myself?* If Oshen had just listened to the commander, he wouldn't be dealing with this right now. He could have stayed in his cabin, requested the company of a Sanctus female, and had a good night.

Lies, his mind chided. He didn't want the Sanctus females; he wanted whoever was calling to him.

"Wishing you had stayed on the ship instead of stealing the shuttle yet?"

Oshen glared at his device. He definitely planned on having her reprogrammed the moment he was back on the ship and would get one of the other Havackers to do it for him. "We didn't *steal* the craft." He pressed his hand against the wound, wincing at the sting. "It was tactically acquired." The AI made a noise that sounded suspiciously like a snort. "And I'm not interested in the Sanctus."

Though the rainbow-colored females were very beautiful, they held no appeal for him. Oshen wished to find his gynaika, the female that would call to his body to start the reproductive process, the only female he could ever have a family with.

Finding one's bonded, however, was becoming increasingly difficult on his homeworld. Many Venium had taken to settling for pleasure mates, but Oshen didn't want that for himself. He had spent time in the company of a few pleasure mates, and while they were lovely females, he just couldn't see himself giving up on what he truly desired.

"I should have stayed home instead of accepting this mission," Oshen said. He absolutely preferred the company of his family to the AI program.

"Ah, yes, I'm sure staying behind to care for an entire brood of pups is far more exciting than this."

He admitted that time away from his siblings had been something he looked forward to at first, but Oshen wasn't used to being alone. His parents had blessed their failing species with fourteen healthy pups over the course of their mating. As the second-born, Oshen had naturally grown up looking after his younger siblings.

This assignment would allow his people to gather more information on the Grutex and had the added benefit of a vacation of sorts. Helping to raise his siblings while learning to become an ambassador from his sire was oftentimes exhausting.

Pain throbbed through his side.

The gash was deep and jagged and would probably leave a decent scar. The salt in the water surrounding him stung his wound, and he gritted his teeth as he addressed his AI. "Mouni, any word from Brin?"

Oshen knew the male was capable enough to look after himself, but worry clawed at his stomach when he thought about how badly damaged the shuttle had been. They hadn't planned for the Grutex to find them so soon, or even at all, considering the fact that the Venium thought they had arrived undetected.

Their simple craft was not built for the strain of battle, and it was lucky for them that the okeanos on this planet was capable of sustaining their kind. There was little hope of finding an underwater city like the one on his homeworld since the dominant species here dwelled on land.

"Still unable to locate the most handsome man in the verse."

Oshen growled, his tail flicking in disbelief. *Really, Brin?* Pulling the salty water across his gills, he turned his wrist over and looked at his comm. The screen projected onto his inner arm and he tapped on the display, sending out another ping to try and locate the wily male.

The reception here was disturbingly spotty, and he had to try multiple times before he got anything to work. Relief raced through him as an answering ping and a request to talk flashed across his arm. Oshen accepted the call and he grimaced as Brin's bloodied face filled the screen. Cuts mangled the gray skin of his cheeks, and his black braids sat in disarray around his head.

"Brin! Where are you? Are you okay?" he inquired as he coddled his own wound, trying to prevent more of his lifeblood from escaping into the water surrounding him.

"Fine, fine." Brin grinned in his usual annoyingly charming manner. "Don't act so worried, brutok. We've been in more challenging situations."

"The shuttle?"

"Blown to bits." Brin waved his hand through the water in a contemptuous manner.

Oshen winced over the loss of the craft, knowing it had most likely cost a fortune, but he was thankful they were both still alive. In the okeanos, there was no way to know which direction to go. It seemed to spread on for as far as the eye could see.

The depths he would have found comfort in on Venora felt ominous on this planet. He could feel his gills flutter in the polluted waters and hoped that his comm would work long enough to help him find the other male. The injuries on Brin's face tugged at his conscience. He wished that they hadn't followed through with this insane plan.

"Do you know where you are, brutok?" Oshen felt disoriented as he looked around once more. There was no moon in the sky tonight, and the surface of the water above him seemed to be calm.

"I think I've found a place for us to get some land under our feet. I'm sending you my location now and I've already sent out a distress signal to the mothership. Hopefully, reinforcements should be here as soon as you make it." Brin's hand moved up to swipe some blood from his brow just before the comm abruptly ended.

A moment later, coordinates flashed across the projected

screen on his arm and he set a course for them. Soon they would both be back on the mothership and in a mess of trouble.

~

*O*shen moved as close to the shore as he dared, glancing around at the abandoned dock that jutted out into the water. This was where his comm had indicated that he needed to be, but he saw nothing aside from the floating vessel at the end of the dock and the building a little further inland.

The loud clang of metal drew his attention and he watched as a figure darted from the building. A human, and a small one at that. *A female?* Venium females were slender and willowy, but this human one was curvy and voluptuous. The movement of her chest had his lifeblood heating and a tingle shooting through his body. As she got closer, he could see her dark hair flying wildly as she glanced behind her.

From the shadows at her back sprang the familiar form of a Grutex male. Oshen growled, lunging forward as the large male tackled the human, bringing her to the ground beneath his body.

There was no way he was going to stand back and allow this. She needed his help.

CHAPTER 2

AMANDA

A FEW HOURS BEFORE …

*T*oday was just not going to go as planned. She could feel it in her soul. Somehow the universe was going to fuck it up, and she wasn't looking forward to finding out what it had in store. Amanda hitched her bag higher up on her shoulder as she hurried down the empty hallway toward the gear room, glancing down at her watch.

Only a couple hours late. Thank you, unreliable alarm clock.

Trashing that old piece of junk was going to be so incredibly satisfying when she got back home. Her footsteps echoed through the space as she sprinted the last few feet to the door and flung it open.

"Amanda?"

She squealed in surprise and spun toward the voice. Standing off to the side, clipboard clutched to his chest and thick-framed glasses sliding precariously close to the tip of his nose, was her supervisor.

"Jim," she wheezed. "I was just grabbing my gear and heading to the docks. Running a little behind."

"A little?" His face twisted into a frown as he watched her heft the bulky scuba gear from the shelf. "It's almost evening."

With a wince, Amanda smiled apologetically. "I know, and I'm so, so sorry. Has the boat already left?"

"You didn't get my message? I could have sworn I sent it to everyone on the project."

Anxiety spiked through her. Amanda had been so concerned about making it there in time to catch the boat that she hadn't even stopped to check her cell before running out the door. She patted her pockets but didn't find its familiar shape. "Uh, message?" Dropping into a squat, she unzipped her bag to rummage through the mess of notebooks, loose paper, extensive collection of pens, and snack wrappers. No phone. *Crap, I probably didn't even take it off the charger.* She ran a nervous hand through her dark, tangled mane and huffed out a sigh of frustration.

Jim scratched at his short, graying beard before tucking the clipboard under his arm and shifting uncomfortably from one foot to the other.

"Seems that the guys upstairs have decided it's too dangerous to proceed with Project Alpha for the time being."

Ah, cue the universe and its fucking everything up.

"Too dangerous? How is it any more dangerous than it's been in the last few years?" She stood, raising her brows as she waited for an answer. Men and women were still being taken, but not as often as before. Even so, the restrictions had only gotten worse, with some of the larger cities implementing curfews and limiting the amount of people allowed in public areas. "What does that mean for us exactly?"

"Unfortunately, it means no expeditions until we get the go-ahead from the investors. Their funding, their call." He sighed when he saw her shoulders sag in disappointment. "I know this is a setback, but there's nothing we can do about it. It's a waiting game until this ridiculous war ends, and God knows when that will be at the rate we are going."

Amanda looked down at the bag and gear lying at her feet, squeezing her eyes shut to stop the angry tears that threatened to spill. Disappointment flared in her chest as she mourned the loss of her favorite retreat. As a marine biologist who studied deep sea ecology, much of her work was spent in the depths of the oceans. She loved discovering new things, and even with the precarious situation at hand, she found herself wanting more and more to go out and explore. This was her project, something she had worked tirelessly on for the last few years. She couldn't and wouldn't lose this.

Jim turned back to his clipboard, effectively dismissing her.

"All right then, guess I'll see you when we have the green light to proceed." Amanda grabbed her bag and put the gear back but didn't plan on leaving anytime soon.

～

*H*iding out in a utility closet had seemed like a great idea hours ago when she first ducked inside, but now her legs screamed to be stretched and her stomach rumbled its disagreement.

Probably shouldn't have eaten my emergency cheese puff snack ration in the bathtub the other night.

She rolled her head from side to side to work out the stiffness that had settled in after her nap, but she couldn't risk leaving just yet. Jim was still doing his inventory of the gear room, and she wouldn't be able to explain why she needed to borrow the expensive equipment if the project they were working on was currently shelved. It was still hard to believe the investors had decided it was suddenly too dangerous to continue their research. That was the whole reason they needed to continue working. Something about this whole thing just didn't seem right.

It wasn't like they were doing anything top secret. Her team was studying deep sea animals in the Gulf of Mexico to find a way to make ocean dwellings a possibility in the future—the near future, with any luck. The war with the Grutex was getting out of hand, and many people feared what would happen if the alien invaders won. Hiding out in the vast oceans might be the only way to escape enslavement or whatever it was they did with the humans they had already taken.

Amanda perked up at the sound of a door opening and smiled wryly at the pitchy rendition of a rock ballad echoing through the hall as Jim made his way out of the building. *Finally.* Her joints ached as she stood, opening the door and poking her head into the empty hallway. *Coast seems clear.* She slung her bag across her back and hurried back to the room to grab her gear. Jim had only left a small floor lamp on, and it cast a meager light around the open space. She was thankful they hadn't gotten around to installing security cameras in the new facility just yet. It wouldn't do for her to be caught skulking around when no one else was there.

She grabbed the equipment she had shelved after her talk with Jim, double-checking that she had everything she would need for a solo excursion, and groaned under the weight as she swung her load up onto her shoulder. The loud thud of something slamming into the door startled her, causing her to drop the gear and stumble back into one of the dark corners of the room to hide. Her equipment sat forgotten on the floor not far in front of her. Eyes wide with fear and pulse pounding loudly in her ears, Amanda stood as still as she could.

Adrenaline flooded her system, forcing its way through her and trying to escape. When it came to fight or flight, she was firmly in camp flight, but there was nowhere to run. She was caught, fear rooting her to the spot. The door on the other side of the room burst open with such force that it bounced off the wall behind it and splintered.

The hulking figure that stood in the doorway was the stuff of nightmares. *Grutex.* The alien's crown still reminded her of a dragon fruit. This male, like all the others of his species that had come in the last six years, had six glowing red eyes set into the elongated slope of his head, framed by numerous blunt-tipped protrusions. His exoskeleton was a deep mauve, and vine-like tendrils of varying sizes curled around his neck.

Many people had compared them to plants, since some of the males sported leafy-looking vines. The holes she assumed were his nostrils sat high up between his first four eyes and flared slightly. The Grutex male tossed his head back as he sucked in a deep breath, almost like he knew she was there.

Don't look here, Leafy. As if hearing her thoughts, his head swung in the direction of the corner where she had taken refuge. Heavy footfalls vibrated the floor, the thundering sound shaking her body.

I need to leave! Get up! Get up! But where would she even go?

"Female, drop the device and put your hands up." He growled, staring down at her menacingly.

Device? Amanda looked down at her hand and noticed she still had her bag clutched in a death grip. She wanted to tell him that it wasn't anything dangerous, which is what she assumed he meant by device, but she couldn't seem to find her voice.

"I don't like repeating myself, human." The Grutex reached for her, his hand shooting out with lightning speed.

Amanda's throat filled with bile as the large male fisted her blouse in his clawed grasp and lifted her off her feet with hardly any effort. The fabric ripped beneath his hold, no longer hiding her body from his view. All of his eyes seemed to narrow on the flesh that he exposed, a rumble of appreciation vibrating his torso before his eyes focused back on her face.

"I have found you." The words were whispered, as if he were in awe. "She was weak, but you are not, are you? You will succeed where she failed."

As he pulled her closer, Amanda struggled against him, kicking and clutching at his forearms. The sudden shifting of the plating that covered his groin made her body seize with alarm. She stared down in bewildered horror as a thick, black appendage sprang free and grazed along her jean-covered hip. It was hooked, the tip pointing back toward his pelvis, where a smaller protrusion wiggled stiffly in a circular motion. She had seen one of these before on a dead Grutex, but now that she was seeing it in its erect form, Amanda couldn't help but gape in fascination.

It looked like a giant version of a bee penis. *Thank you, National Geographic, for that fun little tidbit of information.* The alien crushed her against him and buried his face between her breasts, all of the hard ridges and sharp points scraping against her soft skin. She was so startled by the warm, wet stroke of his tongue that she didn't notice when he pried the strap of her bag from her hand.

"I have searched for you for so long, female. It will be my greatest pleasure to finally breed you, to hear you scream for me as I fill you with my seed."

Amanda reared back in disgust and felt his sharp teeth graze the flesh of her chest. His words made no sense to her. "Let. Me. *Go!*" She screamed as she swung one leg forward, connecting with his unprotected cock.

The Grutex male grunted loudly, dropping both her and the bag to the ground as he curled into himself. Amanda didn't waste any time. She ran, not even feeling bad about the whimpers echoing around her. She dashed through the empty door frame, not sparing a glance at the crooked door that lay against the wall. Every step was another one closer to freedom, and she knew that her kick wouldn't keep the male down for very long.

A loud roar bounced off the walls and labored breaths followed her down the halls, tipping Amanda off to the ever-decreasing space between her and her assailant. She made it out the front door and bolted toward the first place she saw. The dock stretched out in front of her and the large boat at the end rocked in the water.

If I can just get to a boat, I might be able to escape!

The moonless night didn't aid her at all. Her feet slid on the loose gravel, refusing to find purchase, and she managed to scramble on to the boardwalk just as the Grutex slammed into her back, pinning her to the weathered planks.

"You're mine. I will not lose you again." The feeling of the male grasping her hair and pulling her head back before sliding a hand up her thigh sent icy rage through her.

"No!" Amanda screamed, wrenching her body violently, but it was no use. The male on her back was massive, and she had no hope of throwing him.

Please don't let this happen, she pleaded desperately to the Universe just before hot liquid sprayed across the back of her neck. She gasped when the heavy male was suddenly torn from her body. A sharp crack penetrated her shocked mind, and she rolled to the side. Struggling to her knees, she prepared to run but hesitated when she caught sight of the scene unfolding behind her.

She had expected to find two Grutex locked in battle since it was something she had seen on television too many times to count. The large males would challenge one another for the rights to a human before abducting them. Instead, Amanda watched with wide eyes as the Grutex reeled backward from the force of the blow that the tall, lean male landed to his midsection. Her stomach heaved at the sickening crunch the exoskeleton made when it shattered, and she turned away, squeezing her eyes shut and slamming her palms over her ears.

This can't be real. I'm dreaming. I'm obviously still asleep in the closet waiting for Jim to leave.

The muffled sounds of fighting stopped just as suddenly as they had started. Amanda hesitantly opened one eye and steeled herself for what she would find as she slowly turned her head.

A bright gold glow filled her vision. It radiated from the exposed body of the stranger, who was crouched over the broken, twitching form of the Grutex, its blood soaking the boards beneath it. She watched as the lights raced angrily over the new male's face in the same way she had observed in comb jellies. They followed the path of small barnacle-like growths that started over his large yellow eyes and swept across his brow, disappearing behind long, pointed ears. His chest rose and fell with each labored breath, the slits in his face where a nose should have been flaring as he looked her over.

"Are you injured, female?" He swayed on unsteady legs, stumbling forward before collapsing.

Amanda lurched forward in an attempt to catch him before he could hit the boardwalk, but he was heavier than she expected and they both tumbled to the ground. She carefully pillowed his head against her upper thighs and brushed back the ends of the black dreads that had fallen across his face. The harsh black suit he wore looked a lot like a wet suit and was torn. Blue liquid seeped from what seemed to be a decently sized wound on his side. His limp arms were tipped with long, blood-soaked claws.

As the lights from his body faded, his skin seemed to transition to a deep gray, and gills on either side of his neck flared slowly as his muscles relaxed into unconsciousness. She wasn't sure who he was, or even *what* he was, but he had risked his life to save her. Leaving him here to possibly die wasn't any way to pay back the sacrifice. She needed to get him somewhere safe so she could clean him up.

"Looks like you're coming home with me, big guy." First, she would retrieve her bag from the floor in the gear room, and then she would figure out how to get her unconscious savior out to her car.

CHAPTER 3

GULZAR

"Do you think it is safe to be out so far from the village, Gulzar?" Kythea turned her anxious face in his direction, the light of the early dawn glinting off of her xines as it filtered down through the trees above them.

"Ky," Gulzar whispered, sighing in exasperation, "if you were so concerned about being outside of the village, why did you beg to join me on my hunt?"

A twig snapped beneath her feet as she took another careless step forward, wincing when the sound bounced off of the trunks of the trees around them. "Sorry."

With an agitated huff, he searched the forest floor for signs of his prey. Considering the amount of noise Kythea had already made he wasn't sure that today was going to be fruitful at *all*. Anything with even the most basic survival instinct had probably fled the area by this point. Gulzar turned to see his childhood friend scrunch up her short nose as she inspected the bark on a nearby tree, the gills on the side of her neck flaring as the aqua lines of her fushori glowed with her lingering embarrassment.

How Kyra had ever thought they would make a proper mated pair was beyond his knowledge. Her daughter, unlike Gulzar, wasn't the least bit curious about the world around her. Instead, Kythea was content with staying in her dwelling, learning daily tasks like cooking, mending clothing, and rearing children. Perhaps these were traits that other males sought when courting a female, but not him.

It wasn't that he didn't care for Kythea, or even love her, but he would never choose to have a family with her. Somewhere out there was a female for him and he refused to settle. In recent years, his existence had been filled with solitude, days upon days alone in the forest searching for something that wasn't there. No matter how many times he found himself standing among the trees or lying on the soft, mossy ground to stare up at the green, swirling sky, Gulzar always came away feeling empty. His little goddess had been so distant, and where he had once felt her love and acceptance, he now felt her absence. Most days, he wished death had taken him when it had stolen his mother away.

Gulzar the Damned.

Damned to spend his miserable life within a tribe that hated him, to spend his life alone as an outcast among the people who should have cared for him when he needed them the most. In their eyes, his curse could never be lifted. Kyra had spent so long telling him there was no curse, that it was all nonsense, but he had seen the way she looked at him each time she lost one of the young she carried, like she was trying to keep herself from blaming him. After all, Kyra had nursed him after his mother's death. Surely she had not escaped without some sort of retribution.

Today marked his first accompanied hunt, but it wasn't necessarily by choice. Ky had made such a fuss about going with him that he had agreed just so she wouldn't draw attention to them. He couldn't say what had possessed her to make the decision. Maybe she thought spending time alone with him would convince Gulzar to strengthen their bond. He knew she wanted that, but no matter how hard she tried, he was never going to allow it.

When he was old enough, the elders had insisted that he go through a 'reeducation' so that he could safely live within the tribe. They believed he needed to understand what he had done so that he might spare more lives, but all it had done was to point out how much of a threat he was to any female he came into contact with—and that included Ky. Even with her losses as evidence of the dangers they faced by associating with him, Kyra had held out hope for so long that he would find a mate with her daughter.

He had insisted from a young age that he had a bond with a goddess, a special connection that allowed him to communicate with her anytime he wished, but when it wasn't ignored by the elders, it was seen as a desperate attempt to be accepted. Despite the ridicule, Gulzar had continued to see her, to experience her emotions, to grow with her. In truth, his little goddess was the only being who had never judged him. She had never seen Gulzar the Damned, only Zar, as she had called him. They couldn't understand each other's languages, but she learned his name, or at least a portion of it, long ago when they were young.

There were days when even Kyra and her family had given him the same looks, the same wide berth that the other villagers had, but did his little goddess? Never. He loved her. She was the reason he could never bond to another, could never mate and create a family with anyone other than her. Gulzar might be damned, but he wasn't ignorant. He knew this was impossible because goddesses didn't fall in love with mortals. In all of the stories Kyra told him when he was young, the deities never gave up their existence for someone like him.

His xines wriggled restlessly on the broad expanse of his

shoulders and chest as if they were reaching out to his goddess. He longed to feel her, to touch her pale skin, her dark mane that looked so soft. A shiver ran up his spine as he tried to turn his attention back to the hunt.

When he had awoken this morning, it had been with the feeling that today was going to be special, and he didn't believe Ky insisting on coming with him had been what that feeling was predicting. Gulzar reached up to scratch at the tingle that danced along the back of his neck. The forest had gone quiet and when he looked around, he no longer saw Ky. Where had she wandered off to? When he tried to call out to her, he realized he couldn't hear himself. He couldn't hear anything. A jolt of fear speared through him and he stumbled forward, his shoulder slamming into the trunk of a nearby tree. This fear wasn't his own.

Little goddess.

A scene played within his mind, and what he witnessed made his body go rigid with rage. She was fleeing from someone and the same fear he had felt moments ago poured off of her as she pushed herself forward. Gulzar's mouth opened on a silent roar of rage as she was knocked to the ground, her body pressed beneath the bulk of her attacker.

No! Clutching at the tree in front of him, Gulzar tore at it, shredding the bark with his claws, slamming his hands into the splintered wood. When the face of her assailant was revealed, he felt the rage grow tenfold. A tainted offspring of Nem. What were they doing anywhere near a goddess?

He needed to get to her, but how? Unlike the tainted offspring of Nem, he had no means to travel the skies. Anger at his inability to aid her, at the absolute helplessness he felt, rolled through him, and he felt the young tree give beneath his hands. Dirt fell from the roots as he pulled it from the ground, sending it tumbling through the bushes and underbrush. The darkness at the edges of his vision began to close in and he stumbled forward, trying to reach his little goddess even though he knew his efforts were in vain. The last thing he saw was the ground rushing toward him as darkness closed in.

~

*W*hen he woke, he found that he was no longer in the forest where he and Ky had been hunting. Instead, he was lying on his back, staring up at the high ceilings of his childhood home. The exposed timbers that ran from one side of the room to the other brought back nostalgic memories of when he used to climb them as a young one, his claws digging into the wood as he pulled himself up higher and higher. Kyra had often stood beneath him, pleading for him to come back down, to stop being so daring, but it had only made him laugh.

A grin tugged at his lips at the memory just as something else wiggled back into his mind. *The little goddess!*

With a gasp, Gulzar shot up, almost slamming his face into Kyra's in the process. "Calm, sweet one. Shh, you are safe."

"She is not safe!" He felt the older female's hand press against his chest as she tried to push him back down.

"Kythea? She is in the main room. She brought you home."

A growl tore from his throat. "Not Ky. The little goddess needs me. She is in danger."

"Gulzar…" Kyra sighed.

He knew that tone. His adopted mother might love him, but she had never truly believed in his visions. "I know what you think, but this is not something I have made up. I saw her in the forest. She was being attacked by a tainted offspring of Nem."

The frown that crossed her face told him that she, like the rest of the village, found the name disturbing. "This is something that should be brought before the elders and the goddess herself."

"You know they will never allow that." The deep voice that rumbled from the doorway belonged to Kyra's mate, Viseer.

"It is a bad omen." Kyra's hands twisted anxiously in her lap. "He must seek the knowledge of the goddess."

Viseer nodded, his eyes coming up to meet Gulzar's. "I agree, but the elders have shown us time and again that they will not listen to him. If he wants an audience with the goddess, he will need to seek her out himself."

"Viseer," Kyra narrowed her eyes on her mate, "what are you suggesting?"

"That I speak with her directly," Gulzar answered. Viseer was right; the elders would never give him an audience with her, not even an accompanied one.

"If they catch you—" Kyra began, but Gulzar wrapped his arms tightly around her.

"They will not." His xines wriggled anxiously. "All will be fine."

~

All will be fine.

Gulzar nearly snorted out loud at the lie as he ducked behind one of the dwellings nearest to the temple. The darkness of night wrapped around him, the shadows shielding him from the few villagers who made their way to their homes. As fast and as silently as he could, Gulzar rushed up the steps of the temple and cracked the large, heavy doors. Slender candles covered nearly every table and their flames chased away the darkness within the open space. With a deep, steadying breath, he pushed the doors open just enough to squeeze in and then softly shut them.

His mental bond sparked to life, searching, reaching out to the goddess that resided here, but he felt nothing. With a frown, Gulzar stepped further inside, eyeing the statue of the goddess,

Una, and her mates, Ven and Nem, that stood in the center of the main room. He knew there was a certain way the others reached out to her, but because of his status, Gulzar had never been allowed to witness it.

The sound of the large temple door hitting the stone wall behind it had Gulzar jumping and spinning around to face whoever had walked in on him. Instead of the elders or even the Chief, Trakseer, Gulzar saw Kythea's shocked eyes staring back at him.

"Sorry!" she whispered, grabbing the door and softly closing it behind her.

"What are you doing here?" Gulzar hissed in annoyance, stomping over to the female.

"You took off without even knowing how to speak to Una." Hands planted on her hips, the female who had been like a sister to him his whole life raised a brow ridge. "How did you think you were going to accomplish this?"

He hated admitting she was right. "Fine," he grumbled. "Show me." He silently begged the goddess for patience, fighting off the annoyed rattle that threatened to spring from his chest as she moved to the base of the statue, placing one delicate hand on the foot of the goddess.

With wide eyes, Gulzar watched as a blue glow sprang from between her fingers, splashing the walls with its colorful rays. "Goddess," she began, "we ask for your wisdom."

"Your request has been acknowledged. You may speak," a soft, feminine voice said from within the stone.

For a moment, Gulzar could only stare in awe. This was the first time he had ever heard Una speak.

"Goddess?" There were so many things he wished to ask her, but only one thing was important enough to sneak in here. "How can I help the little goddess who reaches out to me?"

"I do not understand your request. Please reword."

With a frown, Gulzar huffed. "There is a goddess who has reached out to me. She was being attacked by a tainted offspring of Nem, and I seek your guidance with how to assist her."

"More information is needed to resolve your request. Please reach out to the goddess in question."

"Reach out to her? I already have."

The sound of distant footsteps approaching from somewhere within the halls of the temple had Kythea jumping back and snatching his hand. She tugged at him, her fushori pulsing with her anxiety. "We need to leave, Gulzar!"

"I have not gotten an answer—"

"Now! If you are caught here, the punishment will be severe."

With a soft curse, he followed her through the doors and down the steps. They didn't stop running until they were within the walls of Kyra's courtyard.

"I am sorry you did not get the answer you were hoping for." Ky panted as she caught her breath.

Though he felt frustrated at the lack of guidance, Gulzar knew the only thing to do would be to reach out the next time he saw his little goddess. He hoped, for her sake and his own, that it wouldn't be long.

CHAPTER 4

OSHEN

*O*shen shot up as he came to, sending water sloshing around the basin he was curled up in. His heart hammered against the inside of his chest, gills feeling like they were on fire as an ungodly taste overwhelmed his senses.

The Grutex!

Blinking quickly, he took in his unfamiliar surroundings. He was partially submerged in a basin that was far too small for his bulk, causing water to spill over the lip and onto the floor. *Where am I?* The room was cast in shadow, the only source of light coming from the gap beneath the door.

"Female?" he called softly, leaning forward to peer over the edge.

His ears twitched as hurried words filtered in from somewhere outside the room.

"I just need you to get here, okay? Bring your med kit." There was a short pause. "It's not for me. I'm fine, I promise. I have someone here I need you to help. He's hurt, and I can't take him to a hospital." Oshen tilted his head to hear her conversation better. There was no reply, so he assumed she was using some sort of comm unit. "It's complicated. He's not exactly human." The female hissed in annoyance, "It's not a Grutex! I don't actually know what he is, but he saved me, and I need your help. Please. I can't do this alone. I'm a marine biologist, not a medical professional, damn it!"

Oshen stood as slowly as possible to keep from displacing the foul-tasting water and noticed that his uniform shirt had been removed. There was instead a long, white bandage wrapped carefully around his torso. It was soaked now, but he placed a gentle hand on his wound and grinned as the female continued her conversation.

"You know I wouldn't have woke you up unless it was an emergency." His foot struck a box sitting on the floor beside the basin, making him arch a brow ridge. "He looks aquatic, Jun. I wasn't sure what he needed." Her voice sounded stressed. "I put him in the tub with some leftover aquarium salt from before I gave you the tank and turned off all the lights. What if he's sensitive to light?" He crept to the door, gently turning the knob and easing it open. Water pooled under his feet, leaving behind large puddles on the wood as he made his way down the hall toward her voice.

The female stood with her back to him, her attention focused on her task as she clutched an outdated handheld comm between her ear and shoulder. She bounced from foot to foot, her disheveled hair tied back in a careless knot at the base of her neck. The bright light overhead clearly outlined her form and she stood with her hip cocked against a small table. From his understanding of the data they had received from the Grutex, this was where human families ate their meals. In this respect, they were much like the Venium.

Oshen padded toward her, curious to see what had her so

distracted. The wood beneath his feet creaked, and she spun around to face him, screeching as she jumped. This close, he could see that the female was even smaller than he had originally thought, with the top of her head barely reaching the middle of his chest. A glance down showed him that she had been carefully working a small needle through his torn uniform top. Wide, startled eyes the same blue as the okeanos on his homeworld stared back at him from a soft, round face.

"He's awake," she breathed, her throat working as she audibly gulped.

Oshen took a step forward, and the comm fell from her shoulder as she stumbled away from him. A shrill voice howled from the device at her feet. "Amanda! Amanda, are you okay? I'm coming right now! That thing better not lay a hand on you!"

Oshen and the female both looked down at the comm, neither knowing what to say as her companion continued to rant. A frown marred his face as he took another small step forward. She had told another human about his location. He wasn't supposed to be on this planet, and he most definitely should not be interacting with the inhabitants in their own dwellings. He lifted his foot and slammed it back down on the fragile device, immediately cutting off the angry words as its screen shattered.

Threat eliminated.

"What the *fuck*!?" she screamed, jumping away from him.

"Using an unencrypted comm device is not advisable. You don't know who could be listening." He grinned down at the angry female. "No need to thank me."

"Since when have you ever worried about what is advisable?" his AI butted in from his wrist comm.

Oshen ignored the device and allowed his gaze to roam over the tiny dots that were sprinkled over the skin on her face and parts of her upper body. The voice on the comm had called her Amanda. He mulled the name over in his mind as she glanced around the room in confusion. Just a moment ago, she had looked so fiery, practically spitting flames at him, and he had found it incredibly interesting and surprisingly endearing. His bothersome AI, on the other hand, was going to find herself deleted if she didn't mind her own programming.

Amanda's eyes darted around the room in confusion. "Where did that come from?"

"It's the artificial intelligence connected to my internal *encrypted* comm unit." He gestured to his wrist where the device had been implanted many years ago. The slight movement caused the wet bandage to tug at his wound, and her face scrunched in concern as a small amount of his lifeblood seeped through the cloth.

"Oh jeez, look, what you did! It took me so long to get this thing wrapped around you. Bandaging an unconscious person— err, alien, wasn't as easy as I had hoped." She clicked her tongue as she fussed.

Running his hand over the wound, Oshen assessed the damage. The sudden slap from her tiny hand had his eyes darting up to her face.

"Don't touch it! I don't know where your hands have been, but I'm pretty sure they're dirty. Go sit down while I get some supplies. Shoo!" Irritation laced her voice.

He couldn't help the incredulous chuckle that fell from his lips. "This is nothing, Amanda."

Her eyes narrowed with suspicion as she shifted. "How do you know my name?"

"The manic voice from your comm used it when addressing you. I assumed it was your name." Oshen sank down into the cushioned couch just inside the doorway of the connecting room. "Was I wrong?"

"No." The way her blunt teeth tugged at her lower lip sent heat surging through him. "I'll be right back."

Oshen watched her dart down the hallway. One look around the space told him this was a place for people to gather. Across from the light-colored seat he sat on, there was a dark, worn chair. He wasn't sure if this was considered nice for humans, but it seemed warm and tidy. There were wooden shelves with small figures and frames holding pictures of many different humans scattered about on every surface and cluttering the walls. A frown pulled at his features when he saw that his blue lifeblood had stained the fabric of the furniture.

"Was it really necessary to trail water all the way down the hall?" Amanda asked as she dodged one of the puddles.

"I wasn't particularly concerned with that when I came out here to find out who had dumped me into a container of foul-tasting water."

"Was the salt too much? I wasn't sure what you would need and I sort of panicked a little."

"A little?" Oshen's lip quirked as she crouched down next to his leg and began to unwrap him.

"Maybe more than a little." She chuckled. "I noticed your blood was blue. Is it hemocyanin that causes it to be that color? I've seen it in horseshoe crabs, but I have no idea if a species from another planet would have the same thing. Couldn't help but notice you were aquatic. Do you all live in deeper waters? Do you also have piezolytes like a hadal snailfish that stop the molecules in your body from crushing you when you are so far down? What about—"

"Female," he interrupted, an amused smile tugging at the corners of his mouth, "I do not know what any of these *horse crabs* or *snails* are as they do not exist on my homeworld. As for the scientific portion of your questions, I'm far from capable of answering any of them."

"I'm sorry." Amanda's cheeks flushed red. "I have a habit of getting carried away. My parents used to say it was my nervous trait." Oshen watched as she spread her towels out, taking advantage of the calm to study her. She looked softer and more vulnerable than any of his kind with no noticeable natural defenses. Blunt teeth and barely any nails to speak of.

A rumbling, angry growl interrupted his assessment and he jerked his head up, ears flattening against his head when his eyes found the source. A small creature with flashing yellow eyes peered at him from the doorway. It was shaped like the cub of one of the deadliest creatures on his homeworld. A tigeara was capable of swallowing a Venium pup whole and was one of many reasons his people chose to remain in the water and limit any time on land.

Were humans so fearless that they kept miniature tigearas in their homes? What if she was unaware of the danger? What if this creature had snuck into her dwelling while she was caring for him?

"Female," he whispered, slowly moving his hand to her wrist. "I do not wish to alarm you, but there is a very angry creature in your home." The beast stepped closer to Amanda, hissing and flashing small, needle sharp teeth. Its striped tail swished behind it menacingly. "I'm not sure if you have anything similar to tigearas on Earth, but I would rather not take any chances."

"A what?"

Amanda frowned up at him as he stood, placing himself between them. If it decided to attack, it would have to go through him first. He had just saved her from the Grutex, and now he was going to have to fight off whatever this was? Was death really so keen to have her? The little beast puffed up its silver and black-striped fur, pacing near the wall as it watched him predatorily. A warning yowl rolled through the room and Oshen bared his teeth, his tail curling protectively around Amanda's leg.

The sound of her laughter caught him off guard and he

frowned, twisting to look back at her while keeping the creature in his sight. "This is amusing?"

"I'm sorry," A loud snort escaped her and she flung a hand over her mouth. "I have no idea what a tigeara is. That's just Hades. He's my cat." Another snort had her doubling over with laughter.

"Cat," Mouni repeated. "A domesticated carnivorous mammal. Many breeds exist, and they are widely kept as pets in human households." For once, she was being useful.

"This," he waved his hand at the creature, who hissed again, "is your pet?"

"Mmhmm. Hades is his name." He watched as she wiped tears from her eyes and smiled up at him. "What did you say your name was?"

"I didn't." Without taking his focus off of the cat, Oshen stepped back toward Amanda, loosening the hold he had on her with his tail. "It is Oshen."

A loud bang rang through the room as the front door was thrown open, and another even smaller female rushed into the dwelling. Her black hair was tangled wildly around her round face and her dark, nearly black eyes blazed angrily. In her hands was a primitive-looking plasma shooter aimed directly at his chest.

"Amanda!" she ground out, turning her gaze to the female at his side. "Did he hurt you?" Her eyes whipped back to him and he could practically feel the heat of her glare on his skin. "I'll kill you, *putang ina*."

Motherfucker, his translator supplied helpfully. "That is an awful thing to call someone." Oshen's lips curled in disgust. "I do not fuck my dam!"

The little tigeara—*cat*, he corrected himself—bristled, its ears flattening to its head before it turned tail and bolted back down the hall. Oshen stared at its retreating form. It was scared of the tiny female but not him? *Coward.* Were his claws not big enough? His teeth too blunt? He was far more intimidating than the small human. Wasn't he? He looked back toward the door.

"Hades!" Amanda called after him. "Come back! She's not here for you!"

"Tiny female, I am not a threat to you or Amanda." Oshen raised his hands to show her he was unarmed. "Why don't you just lower the weapon?" His tail tightened reflexively around Amanda's leg as he tried to keep the fragile calm.

The female raised the weapon from his chest to his head. Her lips pulled back over her teeth in a snarl as she locked eyes with him. This human was threatening a Venium warrior. She clearly had no sense of self preservation. "Let her go." She jerked her head toward his tail. "Now."

Oshen reluctantly withdrew the appendage, curling it at his feet. The loss of contact made him feel exposed, almost empty. A grimace stretched across his face as the angry female waved the weapon at him, indicating she wanted him to put distance between them.

"You can breathe outside of the water, yes?"

"Well, yes," Oshen responded with a frown.

"Good. Go lie down on the bed with your arms and legs spread."

"Jun, this really isn't necessary. I've got this under control." Amanda tried to interject but stopped short when angry eyes flashed her way. "Right. To the bed."

Ah, Jun. Finally, a name for the furious voice from the comm. Oshen walked backward down the hallway after Amanda, not willing to give the armed female a chance to catch him off guard. He could have easily overpowered both of them, but this was technically first contact, and as a Venium ambassador, it was his duty to behave with dignity.

With another glance at Amanda, he stepped through the

doorway she had stopped in front of and looked around. It was decorated in the same way the other room had been, with pictures and objects placed randomly around the space. There was a bed sitting in the center and he stared at it for a moment before turning to Jun as she stepped inside. "You want me to lie on this bed?"

"Are you having a problem comprehending?" came her snide remark.

He wasn't so sure he liked this human. She was rude and demanding, but he couldn't blame her entirely. If her only experience with aliens was the Grutex, he was sure she had good reason not to trust him. With his hands still raised in the air, Oshen sat down on the bed and turned his body so that he was lying in the middle of the small mattress. His legs hung over the end and his arms bumped the wall behind the frame as he waited.

From somewhere behind her, Jun pulled out a few small metal confines, handing them to Amanda as she jerked her head toward him. "Cuff him to the frame."

"Why do you own handcuffs?" Amanda asked with a raised brow as she stepped toward him.

"Why not? You never know when you'll need them."

As she enclosed one of his ankles in the metal, Amanda grimaced. "I don't like this, Jun. He saved me, tore apart a Grutex who almost abducted me."

"Do you hear yourself? He tore apart a Grutex? Imagine what he could do to us."

Amanda closed the last one over his wrist with a sigh, letting her fingers trail over his skin before she stepped back.

"Take this." Jun pressed the weapon into Amanda's hand. "Keep it on him."

"Wait, I don't want to take this—"

"You want me to stitch him up?" Amanda nodded. "Then I

have to run to the car for my bag. Just stay here and *do not* lower the gun."

Jun glared at him one last time before she darted from the room. The weapon trembled in Amanda's hands as she frowned down at it. It was pretty obvious his female didn't have much experience, but he would remedy that as soon as he was free.

My female? He grimaced, trying to shake the possessive feeling that rushed through him. They had known one another less than a few hours, and already his subconscious was trying to claim her? The female wasn't Venium, but perhaps that didn't matter. Something or someone had called him down here, and perhaps he was looking right at her.

"I'm really sorry about this," Amanda whispered.

"Stop being sorry," Jun hissed as she rushed back into the room with a large bag hanging from her shoulder. "This is for our safety." Amanda tried to hand the weapon back, but the little female refused. "I need my hands free to work. Just hold it on him until I'm finished." She pulled a small stool close to the bed and sat down. "I can't risk giving you anything for the pain since I have no idea how it will affect you, so you're going to have to suck it up for me." She looked back at Amanda who was chewing on her lip nervously. "Some people can't control their response to pain. I've had patients lash out at me and I'm not risking it with an alien this size."

"Or," Oshen grinned up at them, "you could just put the weapon away. I've already told you that I'm not a threat, and I've had far worse wounds than this. I'm not going to attack you for helping me."

"Shh!" Jun hissed. "No talking. Take a few deep breaths and let me know if you need to bite down on something." She rummaged around in the bag at her feet, pulling out the things she thought she would need. "Stay still so I can get this done."

It was the only warning he got before something sharp poked his side. "What are you doing?"

"I'm stitching you up. Stop moving."

Another sharp jab to the wound had him growling. "That hurts worse than the actual wound."

The female merely shrugged, "You have tough skin. Stop whining."

Just then, his wrist comm began to blink, alerting him to an incoming call. He struggled against the metal holding him to the bed and received another painful stab.

"I'm trying to stitch you up. If you move one more time, this is going to turn into a vivisection."

"Ooh!" Amanda's eyes lit up with a playful interest. "I bet we could learn so much about your species. I wonder if you can collapse your lungs the same way a Cuviar Beaked Whale can."

Jun stopped her stabbing for a moment to stare at Amanda. "There is something wrong with you, really."

His female stuck her tongue out and laughed softly. "It's for science."

The flash on his wrist caught his attention again. "Mouni, answer the call."

"Ahh! Do not answer that call!" Jun commanded.

"She is *my* AI and she will do as I say." He growled. "Answer the call, Mouni." The AI did as she was told, but nothing came through aside from the sound of interference. "Brin?" No response. "Brutok!" A sharp jerk on his wound as the flesh came together made him hiss as the call dropped. *Why is this female so violent?* "I'm beginning to doubt you have any med training at all," he grumbled.

For the first time since meeting her, he heard a laugh burst from Jun's lips. "I worked hard for this training." Although the stitching continued to be painful, he did notice that her touch became gentler. "How do you know English, Fishboy?"

"My name is Oshen, not Fishboy." He winced as the needle passed through his skin again. "I have an implanted translator that allows me to understand and speak any of the known languages in our database. Since the Grutex have been studying your people, we have a limited number of your languages available to us."

"Lucky you. I had to learn English all on my own," Jun mumbled.

"Humans are quite primitive. Even the comm you spoke on earlier, though similar to mine, is far behind anything you would find on Venora."

"Primitive? That phone you smashed was the latest model on the market, and it took me months to afford it!" Amanda's little snarl sounded almost Venium.

He felt a prickle of guilt at the fact that he had destroyed something valuable to her, but he wasn't actually sorry for eliminating a potential threat to both of them.

Brushing her hair away from her face with her forearm, Jun sighed. "I don't know much about your anatomy, Fishboy, but I think that should do for now. Like I said earlier, I would give you something for pain, but I have no idea how you might react. I'd hate for you to die from a bad reaction after all my hard work." She double-checked the adhesive strip she had placed along the new bandage and stood.

"My thanks." Oshen watched as Jun gathered her things, shoving them into her bag before she left the room. He glanced up at his silent comm and frowned. Something was wrong. They had never had issues getting in touch before, even from great distances. "Mouni, try pinging Brin."

"Pinging the most handsome man in the verse," she responded cheerfully. "No signal, Meatface. Would you like me to try again?"

"Yes."

He waited anxiously as his AI sent the call, but sagged in

56

disappointment, letting his head fall back on the bedding, when it was immediately dropped. A small, warm hand rested on his shoulder, and he opened his eyes to see Amanda with the weapon hanging at her side in her other hand.

"I'm sorry for all that."

"How many more will I have to deal with?"

Her brow furrowed. "How many more what?"

"Family members. How many more should I expect to stab and insult me?" He tried and failed to keep the irritation from seeping into his voice. The soft light that glowed off of her skin told him that his fushori was reflecting his uncontrolled emotions, and he took a deep breath to try to calm himself.

"I actually live here alone." Amanda frowned, rolling her eyes toward the ceiling with a sigh. "That's probably not something I should be telling strangers."

"Alone? Without your sister or parents?"

"My parents passed away a few years ago in a boating accident, but even then I didn't live with them and I'm an only child so I don't have siblings." She shrugged her shoulders as her fingers danced along his skin, tracing the glowing lines of his fushori.

The soft touch sent a shiver racing down his spine. "And Jun? Is she not your family?"

A warm smile spread across her face. "Jun is my best friend, but we aren't related by blood. I guess she's the only family I have left though."

"My apologies. I am very sorry for your losses," he said sincerely. Although his family was large and drove him crazy, he couldn't imagine losing any of them.

"What about you? Do you have a family back home waiting for you?"

"The Venium, my species, live together in family units to help care for the young. Many pups do not leave the dwelling even after they have mated and started their own families. My dam birthed a total of fourteen pups, of which I'm the second oldest."

"Holy hell! Fourteen kids? That's a pretty big family."

"It is," he grinned, "but my dam has a big heart. I think she would like you."

Before she could respond, Jun called for her from outside the room. "I'll be right back."

Disappointment at the loss of her company rolled through him, but he nodded as she smiled sweetly before rushing through the open door.

CHAPTER 5

AMANDA

"*L*et me get this straight, you thought you were just going to sneak out with your gear, steal the company's boat, and what? Dive at night with no one there to look out for you? Are you crazy?"

Amanda winced. "Okay, so it was really, really stupid. I didn't think it through. I was upset about the project getting bumped."

"I know you love what you do and I wish you could do it without the threat of abduction, but it's honestly for the best that it got postponed." Jun rubbed a tired hand over her face. "More and more people are coming into the ER every night because of the Grutex. I don't want to see you end up like them."

"I'm sorry," Amanda mumbled, shuffling her feet awkwardly. Anytime she got a lecture from Jun, it felt like she was a kid again.

"I have to go. My supervisor has been calling me since I got here. Something must have happened at work." Jun frowned and pulled Amanda in for a hug. "Be careful, okay? I know you don't think Fishboy is a threat, but try to keep him locked up until I can get back here. If he has to use the bathroom, use the gun."

"Sure, Mom."

"I'm serious." Jun laughed, shoving her away.

"I hear you. Thanks again for coming. You're the best."

"Damn straight I am."

With a wave, Amanda watched her friend back out of her driveway and sighed. The sun was already beginning to peek over the roofs of the neighboring houses, and she hadn't gotten a wink of sleep. It wasn't until she turned to open the door that she realized the gun was still clutched in her hand, but no key was left with her. *Damn it, Jun.*

Although she knew her friend had purposely left the gun for her protection, something deep inside of her told her that she wasn't going to need it. At least not for Oshen, though she needed the key. Walking to the kitchen, Amanda opened one of the drawers and carefully placed the gun inside, making sure the safety was on before closing it. Hopefully the alien wouldn't need to use the restroom until Jun got back.

The sun peeked in through the window above her sink, and she stood there for a moment, letting the rays play over her face. Hades jumped up on the counter, meowing frantically. She was sure he was giving her hell about Jun barging in and Oshen hissing at him, but she couldn't help but smile as she scratched behind his ears.

"Did that big alien think you were some vicious creature?" The memory made her giggle as Hades bumped his head against her chest. "You're just a big ol' baby, huh?"

Speaking of big babies, she should probably check on her house guest. The alien intrigued her more than she wanted to admit, but she couldn't help wanting to know more about him. It wasn't just that he was something new and she wanted to know more about his species, his biology, his culture; she wanted to know *him*. She dumped a cup of dry food into Hades' bowl and hurried down to her bedroom.

"Hey," she said awkwardly as she popped her head inside. "How are you?" Oshen's irritated gaze met her own and she winced, stepping hesitantly into the room.

"Are you going to release me anytime soon?"

He looked ridiculous, legs hanging over the end of her small mattress, his body stretched out across it as he stared at her. His muscles bunched and flexed with every intake of breath, rippling beneath his dark gray skin, and she felt tingles run from her toes up the insides of her thighs, warmth settling deep in her belly. Arousal clouded her thoughts as she looked him over.

Wow, Amanda, pull yourself together. He's still hurt and you're over here salivating and ready to jump his bones. She glanced at her nightstand where her favorite toy was hidden and groaned, knowing she wasn't even going to get in any self-play while he was in her house.

A growl brought her back to reality and she felt the blush creep into her cheeks. "Sorry. I was… distracted."

"Oh?" One of his brows arched in question, and she was sure he was playing with her.

He knew exactly what she had been thinking. It was written all over his face.

"I shouldn't be surprised that you can smell better than humans since fish can too. The deeper or darker the water is, the more dependent they are on their sense of smell…" She trailed off nervously as he watched her. "Look, I would let you out, honestly, but I'm pretty sure Jun took the key and I have no idea how to pick the lock on those." Moving to the far wall, Amanda closed the blackout curtains, casting her room into comfortable shadow. "I'll shower and change real quick and then come out to clean you up."

Grabbing something comfortable from her dresser, Amanda

headed into the bathroom. After taking the world's fastest shower, she threw on the shorts and an oversized T-shirt before grabbing the pretty basin her mom had given her years ago from beneath her sink, filling it with warm water. As she walked out, she snagged a washcloth and a soft towel from the shelf near the door.

"Still here?"

"Where else would I go?" Oshen drawled. The golden lines on his skin pulsed softly, and she smiled at his tone.

Setting the basin down on the nightstand, Amanda pulled over the small step stool to sit on as she dipped the washcloth in the water and rang it out. "Would you tell me about your home? Where do you live?" She smoothed the cloth over his skin, wiping away the dried blue blood.

"My planet is called Venora."

"Is it far from Earth?"

"It depends on the vessel you are in, but no, not terribly far."

She could feel his eyes on her face as she worked and willed herself not to blush any more than she already had. "Do you live underwater?"

"We do." He nodded. "In ancient times, we lived in deep trenches, but now we reside within dome cities."

"Why is that?"

"As we became more advanced, we began interacting with different species. In order for them to visit our officials, we needed to be able to accommodate them. The Venium, while most comfortable in water, are also capable of surviving on land. The dome cities now provide dwellings and safety to the majority of our species."

Amanda dipped the cloth, ringing it out again, before she turned back, wiping his lower stomach.

"I was working on a project here that would implement something like that for Earth, but I'm not sure when I'll be able to get back out there." Distracted, her hand swiped along the waistband of his black pants. "We could do that here, you know? The ocean is so big."

A soft growl rumbled within his chest. "*Quite* big, actually."

The tone of his voice had her eyes jerking up to his face as she quirked a curious brow. When his hips jerked beneath her hand, she followed his gaze down to the large bulge that pressed up against the fabric of his pants.

"Oh... *Oh!*" Averting her eyes, Amanda felt her cheeks blaze red with embarrassment. "That's not what I meant!" Water sloshed in the basin as she tossed the cloth into it before patting his wet skin dry with the towel.

"Wait!" he said as she stood. "I don't understand what I said. I thought you were—"

"Thought I was talking about your dick?" When he opened his mouth to speak, she continued over him. "I was talking about *the* ocean. The salt water that I assume you crawled out of before you saved me?"

Oshen was quiet for a moment before clearing his throat. "On Venora, we call it the okeanos. I apologize if I offended you in any way."

"It's fine. I just got flustered." Her head was starting to pound, and she knew she needed to get some rest. "I'll get you a blanket." Grabbing a couple of her spare comforters, Amanda headed to the couch to make herself a bed only to see that it was smeared with Oshen's blood. She sighed and turned back toward her room.

I guess we're sharing tonight.

When she walked back in, she saw that Hades had jumped up on the end of the bed and was staring daggers at her alien. "What is it doing?" Oshen whispered.

"Probably trying to figure out why you're in his spot." She laughed. "Make some room, big guy. We're having a sleepover." When he shifted as far as he could to one side of the bed, Amanda tossed a blanket over his body before settling down and curling into her own.

When she tried to angle herself away from Oshen, Hades yowled and pushed himself into her front so that she was forced to lean against the firm, muscled body behind her. *Jerk.* Arousal was still gnawing at her, but she squeezed her eyes shut and firmly ignored the ache. She was *not* going to fantasize about the attractive alien handcuffed to her bed.

~

Something had a hold of her. She could feel its claws digging into her arms as she struggled. *The Grutex.* The fear of being taken by him made her fight harder, thrashing from side to side as she kicked out against him. Warm breath fanned the skin of her neck, sending a shiver down her spine.

"Leave me alone!" she screamed, but the only response she got was a series of growls and clicks near her ear.

Her stomach clenched with dread as the massive arms circled around her body.

"Wake up! Amanda!" a voice called out to her, but she couldn't focus.

The grumbled language played again at her ear and she heard what sounded like her name among the unfamiliar words.

"Gynaika, please!"

When she was finally able to jerk her head back, she stared up into a face that had at one point been a comforting part of her childhood. *Zar.* Four violet eyes peered down at her from a face so similar to the ones she had seen abducting people that it had become hard to look at over the last few years without sending a jolt of panic racing through her.

"My heart!"

Heart pounding wildly in her chest, Amanda watched as her

64

not so imaginary friend from childhood began to speak, his hand coming up to brush the side of her face. *No, please. Don't touch me.*

Amanda's eyes shot open as a scream was torn from her throat.

CHAPTER 6

GULZAR

*G*ulzar woke with a strangled gasp, his whole body jerking as the room swam around him. A dark figure hovered above him and he felt himself flinch, instinctually shielding his body from the sharp sting of the elder's whip. They had roused him so many times in this manner that it had become more common than not for him to wake, even from the rare good dreams, in a panic.

"Hush now," a gentle, familiar voice whispered as slender hands slid softly over his xines. The soothing vibrations of a rattle filled the air, and he felt his tension immediately dissipate. "I am right here."

"Mitera," Gulzar mumbled, reaching out toward the figure as everything came into focus. The moment he saw the light blue pulsing of the fushori instead of the violet, he knew this wasn't his dam.

"No, Gulzar. It is only me."

Kyra's sad rattle swarmed around him and he sat up, shaking

his head to dispel the last remnants of the nightmare. "There was never anything 'only' about you, Kyra." Despite his words, Gulzar couldn't bring himself to look the woman who had raised him in the eye.

For someone who had never actually met her, Gulzar missed his dam more than he could ever properly explain. The only things he knew about her were from the stories Kyra had shared with him over the years, but it tore him apart to know that he would never get to experience all those things for himself. So many nights he had spent sprawled across his bed imagining what it would have been like to know her, to hear her laugh with his own ears, to know the softness of her touch on his cheek, to see the look in her eyes when he wrapped his arms around her.

When he was young, he could vaguely recall her face from the first and only time she had held him in her arms, but now the memory was little more than a shade. He liked to imagine she looked a little bit like Kyra, tall and slender, with cheerful eyes and a quick, genuine smile, but that was all just fantasy. Kyra had taken him in after the tragedy of his dam's death, nursing him and Kythea, who was born a few days before him. He knew the subject of her death was just as hard on her as it was on him.

Silence stretched between them, and he wondered for the millionth time if she knew about what the elders had done to him under the guise of reeducation. The sad looks she had given him as she helped him bandage his wounds each time he came home from one of their sessions told him that she had at least suspected it, but she had never asked and he would never offer the information. If the elders had gotten wind that he had told anyone about the beatings he received, he was sure his punishment would have been far greater. Even worse than the threat of harm to himself was the threat to Kyra and her family. No, he would never speak of it to them. The only person responsible for his status in life was himself. Hadn't that been beaten into him enough times to stick?

Her death is your *burden. Their deaths are* your *burden.* The aged voice of the elder echoed within his mind, but he shook his head again, silencing the memory.

"So?"

Gulzar's eyes jerked up to Kyra's face. She was watching him expectantly, the ridge of her brow raised in a question that he had obviously missed. "I apologize. I did not hear you."

Kyra shook her head. "Did reaching out to the goddess work?"

"No," He blew a frustrated breath through his crest, causing it to rattle loudly. "I believe I only made things worse."

"How is that?"

"She was so… terrified."

"Of who, Gulzar?" He felt Kyra's gentle hand on his shoulder.

"Of me." The look on her face when she pulled back from him would forever be etched into his mind. It had torn at his heart. "I tried to ask her what had happened, what was wrong, but she only fought me harder. It seemed like she did not even recognize me, like she thought I was someone else." Doubt and fear swirled within him and he whispered, "Or perhaps she did and finally realized I was cursed, that I am unworthy to even look upon her."

"Stop that!"

A loud crack echoed through the room just as he felt Kyra's hand come into contact with the back of his head. "Hey!" Gulzar exclaimed, rubbing a hand over the spot. She might not look very strong, but her swats sure did sting. "What was that for?"

"You act like such a youngling sometimes!"

"I do not!" Gulzar said, dodging her next swat. "Stop!"

"I do not know what those males told you when you went to the temple all those times, but they were wrong. You are not damned or cursed, or what it is you believe yourself to be."

"I am—" He began to growl, but Kyra's angry rattle drowned him out.

"For the sake of the goddess, Gulzar! You are not any of those things!"

"If I am not cursed, if I am safe to be around, then why did you lose every single one of the young you carried after you took me in and nursed me?" The regret he felt at his words was instant, and he wished he could take them back. "Kyra..." He reached for her hand in an attempt to soothe her, to lessen the hurt he saw in her eyes, but she stepped away from him.

"I do not know how to make you see that my losses were not your fault. Unfortunate and upsetting things happen to all of us. It is simply how life is, Gulzar." She turned her back to him but stopped in the doorway, looking over her shoulder last time. "You may not believe me, but none of the things that happened were your fault. *None* of them. You are not damned, and you do not deserve the curse other people have put on you."

He sat in silence as he stared at the spot she had vacated, letting her words sink in.

CHAPTER 7

OSHEN

*T*he bed shook beneath him just before the shadow of the big cat arched beside him, hissing in displeasure. Amanda thrashed, her arms and legs flailing as if she were fighting off some unseen assailant. Oshen growled, his fushori beginning to glow as it flared to life with his concern. "Leave me alone!" came her panicked scream. With a strange garble, Hades fled from the bed, his feet sliding against the wooden floor as he dashed into the hallway.

"Wake up! Amanda!" Oshen pulled at the cuffs around his wrists and heard the wood groan. *Brax!* He was going to have to tear this apart just to get free. When she screamed again, he didn't even stop to think about it. Wood splintered around them as he yanked himself free, sitting up to check on his female. *Mine.* "Gynaika, please!"

"Zar…" She gasped, her hands clutching at his arms as he took hold of her shoulders.

"My heart!" he pleaded, shaking her gently before stroking her face.

"No, please! Don't touch me!" she cried. A scream burst free from her throat as her eyes shot open.

The terror he saw reflected in the blue depths broke his heart and he pulled her into his arms, crooning softly into her hair as he pressed his face close. "You're all right. It's over now." His tail lashed anxiously against the bed beside him.

Amanda sagged against his body, her forehead falling down to rest on his chest as her hands clutched at his arms like she was trying to anchor herself. After a moment, she lifted her head and her tear-filled eyes locked with his. It was almost like he was seeing her for the first time, really, truly seeing her, and he was stunned by the rush of emotions that flooded him.

Breath seizing in his chest, heart pounding, Oshen struggled to form words, but she closed the meager space between them, pressing her lips to his gently. His hands stilled where they had come to rest on her hips and she moaned quietly as his fingers flexed against the fabric of her clothing.

"Please," she moaned when he made no move to return her affection, "I don't want to remember. Help me forget."

When she crawled into his lap, her legs straddling his hips, Oshen had to squeeze his eyes shut and fight the urge to do as she asked. The scent of her arousal permeated the air, and for the first time in his life, he felt his mating glands at the base of his kokoras swell.

This was a moment all Venium males waited for. He had been dreaming of this since the moment he was old enough to understand its meaning and yet he couldn't pull her more against his body, couldn't press his lips to hers, or claim her the way his entire being screamed at him to do. Even with her arousal coating his senses, Oshen could detect the underlying scent of her fear and pain. She was vulnerable right now, and he would never take advantage of that.

Instead, Oshen rested his forehead against Amanda's and drew in a deep, calming breath as he moved his hands up to her waist. When he slid her from his thighs back onto the bed she whimpered softly. A tear rolled down her cheek, and he felt his throat tighten.

"Amanda," he cooed to her, cupping her face in his hands and running his thumbs along her cheeks. "I cannot, gynaika. Not like this."

Oshen watched as her bottom lip began to tremble and more tears spilled from her eyes. "I'm sorry!" She sobbed, covering her face with shaking hands.

With a soft tsk, he pulled her back into his arms, resting his cheek on the top of her head and whispering, "Please don't cry." Her small body shook against his and he ran a hand up and down her back in an attempt to calm her. "No more tears, my heart." The name she screamed echoed in his mind, and he couldn't help the pang of jealousy that passed through him. "Who is Zar?"

Amanda stilled, going completely quiet before finally looking up into his face. "Did I say his name?"

With his hand, Oshen gently dried her tear-streaked cheeks and nodded. "In your sleep you did. Is he your mate?"

This drew a soft chuckle from her, and she shook her head. "No. Humans don't have mates. He was a friend of mine when I was little, but now I'm not sure what he is. I'm not even sure if he actually exists outside of my head."

"He frightened you?"

Amanda sighed, frowning down at her hands where they fidgeted in her lap. "Not him exactly. He just has the misfortune of looking eerily similar to the Grutex—those are the aliens that are trying to invade Earth. When this all started a few years ago, Jun and I saw one of them take a woman in broad daylight, and ever since then it's been hard to see Zar without remembering the way that one looked at me."

"How did he look at you?"

"Like I was next," she whispered, running her hands through her hair.

Never, he promised silently. She was his and he would protect her with his life if he needed to. "You see this alien, Zar, in your dreams?"

"Not always. Sometimes I see him when I'm doing things, like a daydream, and other times I just get this feeling, almost like I'm experiencing his emotions." A giggle burst from between her lips. "I know it sounds crazy."

Whether it was in fact crazy or not, Oshen found her description to be similar to something he had read as a child. It had come from a book of old lore, something that had only existed in ancient times among the Venium. Perhaps this was just coincidence, though.

"Let's just forget it, okay?" He watched as her eyes skimmed over the bedding that was littered with splintered pieces of the wooden frame she had bound him to.

"I apologize for the mess." An awkward prickle danced across his skin and he felt like a pup waiting to be scolded, but instead of the anger he was expecting, Amanda threw her head back and laughed.

"You could have broken out this entire time?" Shaking her head when he shrugged, Amanda wiped at the lingering tears. "Why didn't you?"

"I was hoping you would find the key so I wouldn't have to destroy your furniture." The light from his fushori dimmed as he relaxed.

Hades yowled from the floor, jumping up onto the bed and butting his head against Amanda's arm in a bid for her attention before wedging his large, fluffy body between them. The beast turned to rub his face along Oshen's hand in what he assumed was a show of friendship. When Oshen turned to run his finger along Hades's head, the creature had the audacity to bite him. It seemed like everyone he met here was out to hurt him.

"You are an ornery little creature."

Amanda laughed, pulling the cat close to her chest and pressing her lips to his head. "He's a bit of a grouch, but I love him."

The cat emitted a rumbling purr as it rubbed its head against Amanda. The little beast's tail curled around her arm before it gave one more pathetic grumble and jumped from the bed, looking back at him as it slipped out of the room once again as if it had won some battle. Oshen would keep an eye on that one.

"Do you think you can break out of the other pair?" Amanda asked, drawing his attention.

Oshen barely managed to stifle the self-assured snort before he reached down and snapped the links between the cuffs, doing the same for the ones still attached to his wrists so he could move more freely.

"If I hadn't been the one to put those on you, I'd think they were fake. I've never seen someone just bust out of them like that." She watched him from the corner of her eye as he stretched his stiff muscles.

Maybe he flexed a little more than he needed to when he saw the tip of her pink tongue swipe across her bottom lip, but who would blame him? She was his mate, after all. Every inch of his body tingled in excitement as he took a deep breath, drawing her scent into his lungs.

Mine.

His entire being vibrated with the knowledge that he had found her, that his instincts hadn't been wrong. The fact that she was not Venium didn't bother him, but it did perplex him. As far as he knew, the Venium had never mated outside of their species before. The council might find this interesting considering their current predicament. His mating may be an important step in saving his people.

"Son of a biscuit!" The strange curse was followed by a series of "Ouch, ouch, ouch!" as his female hopped on one foot, grabbing the other one in her hands as she struggled to balance.

"What happened?" Oshen jumped up from the bed and swept her up into his arms. "You're hurt?"

Her eyes went wide as he hurried from the room. "No—I mean, yeah, a little, but it's fine."

"It's not fine." He set her down on the couch, frowning at the blue stains on the fabric. "Let me see your injury."

"I'm pretty sure there's nothing there."

He lifted her foot, marveling at how small it seemed in his hands. Where he expected to find a cut or a puncture, there was only a tiny red indentation on her skin. "There is nothing." The disbelief in his voice seemed to amuse her.

"I told you as much." Oshen looked up at her, taking a moment to watch a grin crawl across her face as she wiggled her toes. "I just stepped on a piece of the bed."

Guilt assailed him and he rubbed the spot in the middle of her foot, frowning up at her. "I apologize for destroying your bed… and your couch," he added, eyeing the stain.

"And my phone?" Amanda asked, groaning as he squeezed her heel slightly.

Oshen smiled, laughter bubbling up from his chest. "I am not sorry for that one." A growl rumbled from her and he cocked his head to the side.

"I'm sorry." She laughed, her hand flying to her stomach. "I'm hungry."

"You growl when you're hungry?"

"My stomach does." He released her foot when she tugged it back and moved to the side as she stood. "I couldn't tell you the last time I ate. I can make us a little something if you want."

The data from the Grutex hadn't contained much about human diets so he had no idea what passed as food on this planet, but his empty stomach was becoming hard to ignore. At this point, he was willing to try whatever she had. If they were compatible enough to be mates, surely he could consume the same things she did.

"I would appreciate anything you are able to offer."

When she slipped into the other room, Oshen made his way back into the one they had slept in, gathering up as many pieces of the broken frame as he could and piling them on top of the blanket. He could hear Amanda singing as she worked, her voice low and smooth. The temptation to become lost in her, to ignore everything around them was strong, but Oshen knew he needed to try reaching Brin again.

"Mouni, ping Brin." The AI projected across his arm, the screen flashing momentarily as if the call had been received and disconnected. With a frustrated growl, Oshen repeated the command and waited.

"Bruto—" Brin's voice cut off, followed by a loud and unpleasant crackling.

"Brin?" Oshen called. Only static answered him. The signal was lost a moment later, and he mumbled a curse under his breath, dropping his arm to his side.

"Alien technology was discovered floating in the waters off the coast of a Tampa beach yesterday," an unfamiliar female voice stated.

"Oshen?"

"Authorities haven't released many details, but witnesses on the scene described the mangled wreckage as looking like nothing they had ever seen before." The other female continued as he rushed from the room, following Amanda's shout. He found her standing in front of a small screen, her eyes tracking the blurred image of something he recognized as a panel of the hull from the shuttle he and Brin had taken. "Many are wondering if this new tech could mean the Grutex have brought in allies to aid them in the fight for Earth, and what exactly this may mean for humanity."

Oshen growled low in his throat. "Allies with the Grutex? Ridiculous!"

"Is that your ship?" Amanda asked quietly.

"It was," he answered. "The Grutex destroyed it after they discovered us in Earth's atmosphere."

"Local government officials are asking anyone with more information concerning the wreckage to come forward and to report any suspicious activity."

Brax it all.

"Thanks, Diana," A man appeared on screen as Oshen stepped closer. "As we approach the official six-year anniversary of the start of the war against the Grutex, humanity is left asking itself what has changed? The One World Council reports that teams of scientists and engineers from all over the globe are working tirelessly in the pursuit of answers and solutions to end what feels like a waking nightmare, but what exactly is being done? Hundreds of thousands of men and women worldwide have gone missing over the course of this conflict, and many claim these numbers are inaccurate. They accuse politicians and government leaders of keeping the true count of those missing secret in an attempt to maintain order."

Amanda shifted beside him, her arms crossing over her chest as she frowned. "Informants within TOWC have expressed concern over the amount of funds redirected from research projects meant to help find ways to aid humanity's survival to projects specializing in what they believe to be dangerous chemical weaponry."

"Idiots," Amanda hissed, shaking her head. "We've already used chemicals against them, and humans were the only ones hurt by it."

If what the human male on the screen said was correct, the Grutex had been here far longer than they had told the Venium. Although the fact that they had lied to them wasn't surprising, it was worrying.

Oshen glanced sideways at Amanda and fear spiked within him as something new occurred to him. The Grutex must know about the compatibility of the Venium and humans. Why else would they dangle the promise of a solution in front of them if they didn't? His gynaika was not safe here. No human was safe here as long as the Grutex remained.

"Why exactly are you here, Oshen?" His female turned her face toward him, her blue eyes more cautious than before as she studied him. "What do your people want with us?"

He wasn't exactly sure how to respond. When the council back home found out humans were compatible, there was going to be mixed emotions. Some would insist on protecting the species that could be the answer to the dwindling population, but there would be those who found the idea of breeding with outsiders to be repulsive.

"I don't know." He sighed, his jaw clenching as he watched pictures of battles flash across the screen. In many of them, Grutex males held terrified humans in their grasps, their faces contorted with their fear. What was happening here was far worse than they had thought.

"What is that supposed to mean?"

"It means I have no idea what will happen now."

"Are you working with them?" she asked, her voice low and guarded as she stared up at him.

He could smell her fear and it made him sick. "No, my heart."

"So it's just a coincidence that you guys show up now?"

Amanda stepped away from him, arms still crossed over her chest.

"We came because the Grutex sent word to our council that they had found a possible solution to a problem our species is facing. That *many* species are facing."

"Not sure if you noticed, but we happen to be facing a problem too." Her eyes rolled toward the ceiling as she gestured at the screen.

"We had no idea this was going on, or that the Grutex had been here so long already." Oshen frowned as he eyed the screen. "The Grutex are not a species we can trust, and it was important to gain an understanding of what was happening here." Oshen turned to Amanda. "Were humans made aware of Galactic Law when the Grutex made first contact?"

His female huffed, her eyes rolling upward. "First contact consisted of them abducting people. There were no peaceful talks, no negotiations, only violence and intimidation."

That was no surprise. "We were given an order to refrain from interfering until Galactic Law was broken or until humans reached out to us for help. Brin and I disobeyed."

The pink tip of her tongue swiping across her lips distracted him, but he heard her question. "Why did you disobey?"

"Because of you."

Amanda's brows drew together and she frowned up at him. "Me?" When he nodded, she snorted softly, shifting from one foot to the other. "We didn't meet until after you crash landed. How am I the reason you left the ship?"

He took a cautious step toward her, his fushori pulsing as he reached out to slide a finger beneath her chin, tilting her face up to his. "I felt you."

"I'm not following."

"My sire described the pull to me when I came of age, but I had no idea it would be like this," he whispered, more to himself

79

than to Amanda. "It's so strong that it is impossible to ignore. You *have* to follow it." Oshen's other hand came up to caress her cheek and his body went tight when her eyes turned glossy, fluttering closed for a moment before she focused on him again. "I'm not sure what I expected to find, but it wasn't a human mate."

"Mate?" Her breath warmed his skin as he stepped closer, his fingers moving up to tangle in her dark hair. "I told you humans don't have mates."

"There is not a single doubt in my mind that you are my mate, my bonded." The faintest groan fell from her lips as his fingers worked through the strands. "You are my gynaika, my entire world."

"How can you be sure?" came her soft whisper.

"Earlier, after you woke from your dream, my mating glands swelled for you."

"You say that like I'm going to understand what that means." Amanda pressed her hand against his abdomen, the tips of her fingers brushing his skin as she leaned back. She opened her mouth for a second before closing it again as if she were considering her words. "You were right to slow things down earlier. I think we both need some time to figure out what this is." She gestured between them with her free hand.

Oshen sighed and then nodded, his hands slipping from her hair. "I've had an entire lifetime to prepare for you. Take all the time you need."

CHAPTER 8

AMANDA

"You believe him?"

Amanda eyed Jun sleepily over the rim of her favorite coffee cup before setting it down on the table in front of her. Jun might be used to waking up at ungodly hours of the morning, but she wasn't. Her fingers slid lightly over the ceramic tentacle that served as the handle as she considered the question.

Did she believe that this alien from another planet, from some place lightyears away from her, was somehow destined to be hers? Did she believe that they had been created for one another? That the gods had specifically brought them together?

"Maybe?" Amanda shrugged. "Who wouldn't want to believe that?"

"Me?" Her best friend snorted, leaning back in her chair with her arms folded over her chest.

With a laugh, Amanda stood, washing her cup out before

setting it on the drying mat next to the sink. "It just... I know it's crazy, but I feel *something*."

"Horny?"

"You are so very funny," she drawled, propping herself up against the counter. "I just mean that I haven't felt this sort of connection to someone since..." *Zar*. Amanda frowned. Was she really about to confess her love for her imaginary friend out loud?

"Since...?" Jun's brow arched as she leaned forward, resting her arms on the table.

Amanda shook her head. "You'll just think I'm crazy."

"I already do. That hasn't stopped me from being your friend so far." When Amanda stuck her tongue out, Jun laughed and waved her over. "Come on, tell me."

Blowing out a deep breath, Amanda took her seat at the table, staring down at the dark wood. "I had this friend when I was a kid. His name was Zar and we spent a lot of time together." An image of him danced through her mind and she shivered as his eyes sparkled back at her. The joy he felt had radiated through her that day. It was the first time she had said his name, or at least enough of it that he was able to recognize it. She could still hear his rough, gritty voice as he attempted her name, but he never seemed to be able to get it right.

"You've never mentioned him before. What happened to him?"

"He wasn't real," she whispered, rubbing at a mark on the table with her finger. "Or at least I didn't think he was."

"So this was an imaginary friend?" Jun's face pinched in confusion.

"I thought he was until I saw the Grutex."

"He's Grutex?" Jun's mouth dropped open. "What is it with you and aliens?"

"I'm not sure he's actually Grutex." Amanda ignored the last question. "He doesn't look exactly like them doesn't behave like them either. He's sweet and gentle. He's never tried to hurt me."

Jun shook her head as she frowned. "I don't get it. You're saying this like you still see him."

"I do," Amanda whispered. "Not as often as I used to, but I do still see him, hear him, feel him."

"So, what? You feel the same way about both of these aliens? Are they both made for you?"

Jun's tone wasn't harsh or sarcastic, but Amanda felt herself bristle all the same. "I don't know."

Her friend sighed loudly as she turned to look out the window. "What the hell?"

Amanda flinched when Jun jumped up and pried the cheap plastic blinds apart with her fingers, searching the small expanse of yard outside the window. "What?"

"You didn't see that light?"

"A light?"

Jun rushed to one of the other windows. "It was so blue. I swear it looked just like ..." She trailed off, pulling back with a frown before mumbling, "Must have just been headlights." But as Jun sat back down, Amanda could tell something was distracting her. "Look, I don't care if you want to believe that one alien or both are meant for you. I just want you to be safe, okay? We don't know much about the Grutex, and if this guy, assuming he isn't just inside your head, has been talking to you for so long, they might have abilities we never thought were possible."

They sat in silence, both seeming to be caught up in their own thoughts before Jun raked a hand through her hair.

"I need to run home and grab some clothes if I'm going to stay longer."

Amanda watched as Jun pushed back and stood. "Right now?"

"I've been wearing the same clothes for the last couple of

days while I stayed with you guys. I'll just grab the essentials and be back in a little while."

"You're leaving?" The deep voice sent a tingle of pleasure skittering over her skin.

Amanda watched from the corner of her eye as Oshen propped himself against the frame of the door, the muscles in his arms and shoulders bunching as he crossed them over his broad chest. The clenching of her stomach and thighs had her face flushing, and with the way he turned to look at her, Amanda knew he could smell the way her body reacted to him.

"You wish, Fishboy." Rolling her eyes, Jun walked into the kitchen, rummaging around in one of the drawers before coming out with the handgun she had left with Amanda a couple days earlier. "Keep this on you."

"How did you know it was in there?" Amanda frowned as Jun laid the gun down on the table in front of her. "And don't you need protection?"

"You hide everything in the junk drawer, and don't worry about me." She winked, tapping her hip softly. As she walked by Oshen, Jun jabbed her finger into his chest. "Keep your hands and tail to yourself. Got it?"

A slow smile crept across Oshen's face as he looked down at her friend. "I will do my very best."

His eyes swept over Amanda, and the heat returned to her cheeks, her neck—hell, her whole body was on fire. "Don't be long," she said, forcing her gaze back to Jun. "I'll be waiting."

❧

*A*nxiety curled in her stomach as she checked the clock again. It shouldn't have taken this long to pack a bag of essentials. Hours? Yes. Days? No. *Maybe she got called into work*, Amanda tried to rationalize. It wasn't like Jun could call and let her know what was going on, and she couldn't call Jun unless she ventured next door.

"I'm giving you until tomorrow," she mumbled under her breath.

"Giving who until tomorrow?" Oshen's voice glided along her skin, raising goosebumps in its invisible wake.

"Jun." She turned to see him watching her, his bright yellow gaze tracking her movements.

"I can't imagine anyone would be foolish enough to threaten her. She is a force." He rubbed his hand absently over the scar on his side, which had healed phenomenally fast. Even Jun had been amazed that the deep gash she had stitched was now only a slightly discolored, raised line. "Maybe cooking something will help take your mind off of Jun?"

A grin tugged at her lips and she rolled her eyes. This guy ate more than anyone she had ever met. "As it turns out, I already made something." The excitement she saw flash across his features made her laugh. "Hopefully you like it."

"I'm positive it can't be worse than the slop you tried to kill me with the other morning."

"It wasn't slop!" She laughed, shoving him away as he followed her into the kitchen. "Grits are delicious."

"It felt and tasted like sand from the deepest trenches on Venora." He cringed like the memory alone was enough to make him sick.

"Not my fault you have horrible taste." With a hand over her chest, she gave him a look of mock offense and rolled her eyes. Scooping up a single pancake, Amanda turned slowly toward him. "I present to you: a pancake."

"A pancake?" Eyes narrowed, Oshen poked at the food with a clawed finger. "Where is your pancake?"

"I'm waiting to see if you like this one." She wasn't going to make the same mistake twice and make a bunch of food he hated.

"I knew it. You're trying to kill me."

"Gods, you're impossible." She swiped a healthy amount of butter over the smooth top and raised a brow. "Come and sit." He followed her to the dining table, taking a seat before she set the plate down in front of him. "Oh, wait!" Amanda rushed back into the kitchen, snagging the warmed-up bottle. "Can't have a pancake without syrup." She nearly laughed at the over the hesitation in his eyes as he watched her pouring the syrup . "Enjoy."

With a deep breath, Oshen cut into the fluffy cake, frowning as the syrup dripped down onto the plate. He popped the moist lump into his mouth and chewed quietly for a moment before setting the fork down and turning to look at her. "You will teach me how to make these?"

"Uh, yeah, sure."

"Good," He grabbed the fork and scooped the entire pancake into his mouth. "We need more."

"So you like it?"

"Can we make them now?" He ignored her question, pushing his chair back as he grabbed the plate and headed into the kitchen.

"No patience." She grumbled, grabbing a bowl from where it had been drying on the counter as she followed behind him. The ingredients were still set out, and she tapped her finger against her lip as she considered where to start. "Flour first. Can you hand me that white bag?" When Oshen moved to follow her instructions, she grabbed a whisk and turned back just in time to see his sharp claws cut into the bag. The contents plummeted to the ground before a cloud of fine white flour shot up, covering both of them.

With his eyes and lips closed, Oshen forced air through the small slits that passed for nostrils, making it look like he was breathing smoke. She let loose a howl of laughter when he shook his whole body, sending flour back into the air as he tried to dodge the drifting particles.

Oshen's golden gaze caught hers and sent heat flaring through her, curling like a fist in the pit of her stomach. The laugh died in her throat as he leaned forward, wiping his hand along her cheeks and nose. A smile curled his dark lips as he stared at her.

"You've been hiding from me, little one."

"I haven't," she countered, her chin jutting out in challenge.

"No?" His breath whispered over her lips as he closed the distance between them.

Heart racing frantically within her chest, Amanda wondered how he was able to affect her so quickly.

"Some days I wish I had the defenses of a giant squid. I'd have ink made up of melanin, and whenever I needed it, I could release it and escape through the cloud." His lips only curved more, pulling back slightly over the sharp fangs in his mouth. "But then you wouldn't be covered in white because you'd be surrounded in the blue-black cloud." Her cheeks heated when she realized she was rambling again, and she ducked her head when he leaned forward to kiss her.

Feeling like a coward, Amanda fled down the hall into the bathroom. She locked herself in and pressed her forehead to the door, waiting to hear his footsteps, but he let her be and she wasn't sure if she was thankful or upset over it. She could feel all of her defenses breaking down, insisting she follow her heart, but how could she when she had barely known him a full week? They needed to get out of this house, even just for a moment, or she was going to give into everything her heart desired.

~

She'd managed to slip out to Mrs. Rogers' house for a few minutes. The older woman had been more than willing to let her use her house phone to give Jun a call, but it went to voicemail straight away. This wasn't anything new. There were times when they went days without speaking because Jun was so busy at the hospital. The war kept her and the rest of the staff on their toes, and if her phone was turned off, then there was most likely a good reason for it.

"This isn't anything new, Amanda," she told herself. *But it is the first time you've been left alone with an alien.*

Was it possible for aliens to have some type of pheromone that made you want to sleep with them and say screw the consequences? *Maybe you're just a hussy?* Frowning at her own thoughts, Amanda sighed as she flipped through the book in her hands. *Maybe you just need to get laid?* Sure, it had been a little while, but had it really been so long that she was looking at her alien houseguest like he was a slab of meat?

Amanda sat the book back on her shelf, peered around the corner, and watched as Oshen jerked the laser pointer to the right, his face scrunching in amusement as Hades chased it. She shook her head as he moved it to the wall, a laugh rumbling up from his chest as Hades ran headfirst into it.

Oh gods, she was falling for him. It didn't seem to matter what she did to keep him at arm's length because he was wiggling his way into her heart anyway. She couldn't afford to become attached to him.

A knock on the door startled her. "Shit." She rushed into the living room. "Get in the bedroom." He opened his mouth to protest, but she shoved him as hard as she could. "If someone sees you here, we're both in deep shit." The look he gave her said he didn't like the idea, but that he also didn't want to cause either of them problems. Another knock had her jumping and yelling, "I'm coming!" before she shooed him toward the hallway.

She waited for him to get in place and then rushed to the door, anxiety coiling within her. Turning the knob, Amanda took a deep breath and swung the door open.

"Jack?" She stared up at the familiar, handsome face. "I, uh, wasn't expecting you."

"I tried to call but your phone was off." An easy smile played on his lips. "I got worried when I hadn't heard from you so I wanted to stop by and see how you were. Especially after what happened at work."

"Oh, yeah." She laughed nervously. "My phone took a bit of a dip into the tub so it's out of commission for a while." The lie felt heavy on her tongue. She should have known Jack would come looking for her. They'd gotten to know each other at work, had even been on a date or two, but nothing too serious. Even though things hadn't worked out for them, she suspected that he still very much wanted her. Jack was a nice guy, easy to talk to, charming, smart, but he just wasn't... hers.

Not your mate, huh? She groaned inwardly, feeling herself blush at the thought.

"Well, accidents happen." Jack smirked, his green eyes sparkling humorously. "Can I come in for a minute?" His hand moved to the door as he stepped forward.

"Uh..." *Fuck, the couch is covered in blue alien blood.* "No!" Jack pulled back slightly when she slammed her hand against the back of the door. "It's just... I'm not really up for company today. My house is a mess and I'm a little upset over the project getting shut down."

"Let me help you clean."

He attempted to push past her again and she pressed her hand to his chest. "That's really sweet of you, but how about a raincheck?" She forced a smile, but from the look in his eyes, she could tell it wasn't convincing. "I think I'll replace my phone and give you a call later, okay?"

"Later? It's already well into the evening. Is there something wrong?" He looked over her head. "Are you hiding something?"

She could tell him, end this whole thing right now, but everything inside of her rebelled at the idea. "Nope."

When she opened her mouth to excuse herself, he closed the

distance between them, cupping her face in his hands and placing a soft, delicate kiss on her lips. The growl that echoed from somewhere behind her had him breaking the kiss and pulling back in confusion.

"Did you get a dog?"

"Probably just Hades. You know how he gets." Before he could respond, Amanda shoved him out the door, an apologetic smile firmly in place. "I'm really sorry. I appreciate you stopping by to check on me but, I uh, have my period, so I need to go." She slammed the door closed and covered her face with her hands. "On my period?"

"Who was that?" Oshen snarled quietly at her back.

"Just a friend from work. No big deal," she muttered, looking through the peephole to make sure Jack was leaving.

"He touched *my* mate. That is a big deal to *me*."

"I haven't agreed to that." She reminded him as she turned away from the door. "I've known Jack for a long time."

"He is not your mate. You are *mine!*"

Her breath caught in her lungs, fear spiking through her as his body seemed to grow even larger. Stumbling backward, Amanda gripped the doorknob tightly in her hand, ready to run if she needed to, but regret instantly flashed across his face, the yellow lines on his body he called his fushori lighting up as he took deep breaths.

"I need to go," he whispered before turning away.

"Go? You can't leave." The protest flew from her mouth before she could even think. "They're already looking for you."

"It's dark out." Oshen refused to even look her way. "I need space."

"If you go out the kitchen door, you can at least sit on the—" The words had barely left her mouth and he was moving, slipping out onto the back porch silently. She wondered if he'd be back as the door closed with a soft click.

CHAPTER 9

OSHEN

One uur and then another passed as he paced her backyard. Frustration, confusion, and pain churned within him, pulling his mind in every direction. The human male had kissed her, and Amanda had acted as if this wasn't something to be upset about. She was *his* mate. If he were home, this wouldn't even be a discussion because it would not have happened. On Venora, the mate bond was sacred. The moment a pair felt the pull, all other partnerships were dissolved. It was the way things were.

Your mate isn't Venium, and you are not on Venora.

Oshen sighed, rubbing his hands over his face in exasperation. Coming to Earth had been about protecting his people, making sure they weren't being led on by the Grutex. Never in his wildest dreams had he imagined he would find his mate, and yet here he was, struggling to give her the time she asked for as he fell deeper and deeper into the pull of the bond.

It didn't matter that they had only known each other a handful of days. She belonged to him as fully as he belonged to her. His entire being thrilled when she walked into the room, when she laughed, when she touched him, but humans were different.

Amanda had told him that they didn't mate in this way, that they could sever a bond just as easily as it was made, and the thought that she could decide to do this with him was terrifying. She wanted time to get to know each other, but this was so foreign to him. Venium who found themselves bonded learned about their mate from being with them, from interacting and living together. While they were essentially doing this within her home, Amanda had placed an emotional barrier between them that he didn't know what to do about.

It was understandable that the thought of leaving everything and everyone she knew was terrifying, and he knew asking this of her was only going to strengthen that barrier, but what choice did he have? If he stayed on Earth to bond with her, he would be condemned to a life within a cage and caught in the middle of a war. On Venora, his mate would be safe, but could he actually convince her that this was best? The only way to find out was to try.

Guilt over the way he had reacted inside slithered up and down his spine, settling heavily in his stomach. He had frightened her, and that knowledge shamed him more than anything he had ever done in his life. He didn't want her to look at him like he was some sort of monster, like he was no better than the Grutex, but he had seen and smelled her fear. As much as he had wanted to gather her up and reassure her that he would never do anything to hurt her, Oshen realized that sometimes distance was the answer.

Turning toward the house, Oshen smiled when he saw her shadow dart away from the window she had been watching him from. As he took a step forward, a noise from the tree line that

ECSTASY FROM THE DEEP

bordered the back of the yard caught his attention. He turned, scanning the shadows for any movement. Behind him, Oshen heard the door crack open, followed by the soft patter of Amanda's feet.

"Hey. I wanted to say that I'm sorry—"

Oshen cut her off, placing his hand across her mouth and nodding toward the woods. Something or someone was out there.

A small group of bushes rustled, and a flash of deep purple darted through the shadows. Grutex. He had expected human authorities, but a Grutex? Why would one be sneaking through the underbrush? A growl worked its way up his chest as he pulled his mate behind him. "In the house," he whispered, his fushori flaring to life.

Six red eyes glowed back at them. The Grutex tilted his head when Amanda gasped, watching as she stumbled backward. "Oshen..." Her face paled and she looked as if she was seeing a ghost.

With a snarl, Oshen rounded on Amanda, sweeping her up into his arms and rushing into the house. As soon as her feet touched the floor, Amanda was at the door, her hands fumbling with the locks.

"Mouni, commence perimeter sweep and then ping Brin." Oshen sent up a silent plea to the goddess. *Let this one through.*

"Sweep completed. No other life forms detected." There was a pause as his AI flashed through the information. "Pinging the most handsome man in the verse." The signal was weak, but it was there.

The screen on his forearm blinked in and out, crackling loudly before a fuzzy picture of Brin appeared. The other male looked exhausted, his normally bright blue eyes dull. "Where have you been?" Oshen hissed, parting the window coverings to scan the yard. "You look awful."

93

"Don't start with me, old man. I've been working day and night to get this braxing signal through. Fine timing, by the way." As Brin turned, Oshen caught glimpses of the background and narrowed his eyes. Was his brutok in a human dwelling?

A small portion of his screen still showed the life forms within the perimeter he had set up, each one represented by a small green dot. "I suppose I shouldn't have ever doubted your exemplary skills, Havacker." Amanda paced beside him, her bottom lip caught between her teeth. "What was causing it?"

"What else? The Grutex obviously don't want us knowing what they have going on here. They've put up shields that scramble everything. The humans wouldn't be able to reach out for help even if they knew we were here." A noise behind Brin had the male turning, and Oshen saw the blue glow of his fushori. For someone who exerted an immense amount of control over his emotions, Brin seemed to be having a difficult time. *Interesting.* "What is your status?"

"My mate is in trouble. One Grutex—"

"Mate?" Brin interrupted, his eyes going wide.

"I'll explain later." Oshen tapped out a message before pulling Amanda away from the window she had crept over to. "I've sent our location. Brin?"

"Yes, brutok?"

"Don't get us into any trouble."

Brin gasped dramatically. "Me? I'll remind you that this little excursion was *your* idea."

"Noted. Be ready for a confrontation. I have no idea how many are out there."

"You know I'm alway—" Brin's words were cut off, but Oshen sighed in relief when he saw that his message had gotten out in time.

"Signal lost. Should I try to ping him again, Meatface?"

"No, resume the perimeter sweep." With gentle hands, Oshen scooped Amanda up, carrying her into the living room before placing her on the couch. When he moved to pull away, she reached out and grabbed his hand like she was afraid he was going to leave. "I'm not going anywhere, gynaika."

"What does he want? Why would he come here?" Her lip trembled as she curled in on herself. "There are so many humans on this planet and he stalks me?" They sat in silence as he mulled over her words.

He was so used to her nervous rambling, the way she went on and on about the creatures of Earth's okeanos, none of which he was familiar with, that it was strange to see her so quiet. "You know this Grutex?"

Tears welled up in her eyes as she nodded. "I didn't realize it at first, but I *know* he's the one from the lab. The same one I told you Jun and I saw take that woman years ago."

"You're sure?" Oshen hadn't taken the time to really look at the male before attacking him on the dock. He wouldn't have been able to identify the Grutex even if he had gotten a better look at him in the shadows.

"I know it is." The way she looked at him told Oshen she absolutely believed it to be true.

"He won't get to you. I'm going to make sure the windows and doors are locked. Stay here."

The locks on her windows were far more primitive than he liked. The Grutex could easily take them if they were so inclined, and there was little Oshen would be able to do to prevent it. Hades followed on his heels, meowing out commands as if he doubted Oshen's competency. "Yes, Commander," he mumbled with a sarcastic salute. Big innocent eyes stared up at him, but he wasn't going to be fooled. On Venora, the more innocent the creature looked, the more dangerous it was. *Nice try.*

He stepped back into the living room and watched Amanda as she moved around the space, frantically rearranging everything in her path, down to the tiniest figurine on her shelves. His dam had done the same when she was close to whelping, and although he knew that wasn't the case here, he couldn't help the surge of excitement at the thought that one day they would be waiting on their own pups. *Hopefully.*

Amanda stopped, her hand braced against the wall as she shook, taking deep, gulping breaths. He moved without thought, coming up behind her and wrapping his arms across her torso, just beneath her breast. She stiffened for the briefest moment before relaxing into his embrace, her small hands coming to rest on his arms as he hummed one of the lullabies from his childhood.

It reminded him of his youngest sister, Ina. His dam's last pup was perhaps the hardest to deal with, and when all other options had been exhausted, this song had restored peace. Sadness thrummed through him at the memory and he nuzzled his face into Amanda's hair, drawing in the intoxicating scent. He missed his family so much and wanted more than anything to get home to them with his mate.

"I'm right here with you. Everything will be okay, I promise. Be calm," Oshen whispered into her dark strands as they brushed his face. He pressed his lips to the skin on her neck and felt her shudder.

"I don't know how to be calm right now." Her voice sounded strangled and it tore at him to know she was hurting. "He hasn't even tried to attack. What if he's waiting for backup?"

Although Oshen hadn't wanted to involve anyone other than Brin in this, he was starting to see that perhaps he had been arrogant. This wasn't something he could or should do on his own. It was time to admit that he needed Vog. "Do you trust me, gynaika?"

His mate turned in his arms, her eyes roaming over his face as she considered his question. "I don't know if I should." She sighed. "But I do."

Relief swarmed through him and he dropped his forehead to hers, taking a moment to thank the goddess for this small victory.

"Mouni, ping Commander Vog."

CHAPTER 10

AMANDA

*W*ith Oshen's arm wrapped tightly around her, Amanda relaxed into his embrace, letting her head fall forward against his chest. She had been trying to keep the flashes of her nightmares at bay since they had run in from the yard, but nothing helped until he had pulled her in and hummed the little tune near her ear. His tail was curled comfortingly around her waist, and he began to sway with her, his hand brushing over her hair and down her back. She had listened quietly when he called his commander, who hadn't looked the least bit pleased to see him and who was even less pleased with the things Oshen had told him.

"You... think I should leave Earth?" she asked.

Oshen stiffened beneath her, his hand slowing. "Yes."

She wasn't completely stupid; she knew Earth was in trouble, knew she and every other human on the planet was in danger as long as the Grutex were still able to pick them off, but this was her home. "You had already made the decision to take me before this, hadn't you?"

"I wasn't just going to abduct you if that's what you're asking."

Pressing her hand against his chest, Amanda leaned back so that she could look up into his face. "But you were going to try to get me to go back with you?"

"Yes."

"So, what? You thought you would just come in here and sweep me away from everything I love, everything I know, because you believe calling me your 'mate' gives you some sort of say in what I do?"

Oshen tilted his head, frowning as he considered his words. "Well, yes, but—"

"Excuse me?" She felt his grip on her tighten like he thought she might run. How astute. "You have no say over what I do or don't do."

"I am only looking out for what is in your best interests," he ground out, his jaw clenching.

"It *is* in my best interests for me to decide, Oshen!"

"I will not leave my mate here! I will not allow my pup to be born into danger! So, yes, you are coming with me."

Amanda felt the blood drain from her face, and she knew her mouth must be hanging open. "Your what?" Her hand flew to her stomach as she shoved out of his embrace. "We didn't even have sex. How the hell…" She hadn't thought to ask how his species reproduced, but she had assumed that it was similar to humans if he was claiming they were compatible. Oh gods, she felt sick. Shit. Shit. Shit.

"Amanda? You look unwell."

"Of course I look unwell! You just told me I'm pregnant with an alien baby via immaculate conception!"

"What the hell have I missed?"

Both Amanda and Oshen spun around to face Jun, who was standing just inside the front door. She had both hands wrapped tightly around the weapon like she had been expecting to walk into a fight.

"Jun! Where the hell have you—" But her words died mid-sentence when she saw the Venium male step out of the darkness and move up silently behind her friend. Where Oshen was lean, his muscles compact, this male was bulkier. Like a slimmed down bodybuilder with massive shoulders covered in nearly black skin, this guy was intimidating. Bright blue eyes stared back at her as he took a deep breath, the same way Oshen did when he was scenting. A shiver ran through her as she took a step backward, bumping into Oshen's chest. She hadn't even seen him move. "Who the hell is that?"

A soft growl vibrated against her back as Oshen ran his hands up her arms. "This is Brin." His hands came to rest on her shoulders and he slowly turned her back toward him. "And I never said you were pregnant. Yet."

"Your friend, Brin?"

"His brutok," the male chimed in helpfully.

"Okay, fantastic. The gang's all here!" She could feel her grip on reality slipping. "There's a Grutex stalking me, your commander is on his way, and my best friend just showed up with your best friend—"

"Brutok."

"—and I'm just supposed to leave with you and go gods know where."

"It seems like I missed something." Jun had lowered her weapon, tucking it back into the holster at her side.

"You missed something?" Amanda asked incredulously. "You left here to get an overnight bag, disappear for days, and then show up with another Venium. I think *I* missed something."

Jun narrowed her eyes on Oshen's tail as it wound its way up

Amanda's leg. "I told you to keep your hands and tail to yourself."

"Oh, little shayfia, leave him be."

"Shayfia?" Oshen asked, a hint of amusement in his tone.

"The most adorable one I've ever met." A grin spread across the male's face as he wrapped his tail around Jun's leg.

Her friend brought her foot down heavily on Brin's, making the big male wince, but his smile never faltered. "Catch me up," she said as she grasped Amanda's hand and led her toward the couch.

With a deep breath, Amanda launched into what had happened in her backyard and the argument they had walked in on. "I know that Grutex is looking for me and I'm terrified of what will happen if he gets me, but I don't want to leave. This is where my home is, where you are."

"I think you should go," Jun whispered.

"It's crazy to think—" Her eyes snapped up to Jun's face. "What did you say?"

"This guy is dangerous, Amanda. I've seen what these fuckers do to people, and I don't even want to imagine you being taken by one of them." She laid her hand on Amanda's thigh and squeezed. "You said you had a feeling about Oshen, that you wanted to believe him. I think you should trust your instincts and go with him."

"But what about you? What about my job?"

"What job? The project was put on hold, Amanda. And don't worry about me. I'll be fine. I'm needed here. We barely have enough medical staff as it is."

When Amanda opened her mouth to argue, Brin stepped into the room. "I will stay behind to protect her."

"No offense, but I don't know you."

"My, how the tables have turned." Jun laughed before scooting closer. "Brin is an idiot, but he's not bad." There was something in the way her best friend turned to look at the other male that had Amanda's brows rising. "I'm not getting into this," she said quickly, throwing her hand up in the air to silence Amanda's questions. "You're the only family I have here, and I want you to be safe. If that means shipping you off to an alien world, then so be it."

She felt someone crouch down next to her knee and turned to see Brin's blue eyes level with her own. "I promise you, little female, that I would give my life for Jun's. She will be well cared for in your absence."

"I can care for myself," Jun mumbled irritably, but Amanda saw the blush that colored her cheeks.

"What about Hades?" Amanda asked, glancing up at Oshen.

"Hades? Who is that?" Brin frowned, his blue fushori pulsing softly.

"*That* is Hades." Oshen jerked his chin toward the dark hallway where her cat sat watching the entire scene with a disapproving expression.

"The *brax*!" Hades hissed as Brin jerked away from her, falling back onto the wooden floor with a heavy thud.

With an agitated flick of his tail, Hades turned and disappeared into the darkness, leaving a bewildered Brin to stare after him.

"A ship is approaching," Mouni informed the room. "There is an incoming location transmission from Commander Vog."

Amanda felt a tingle of anxiety and panic skitter through her as Oshen held his hand out.

"Time to say your goodbyes, gynaika."

"Now?" She looked around her home, her gaze sweeping over all of her belongings. "I'm not even ready. I haven't packed anything." With a sniffle, she turned to Jun. "I'm not ready to say goodbye."

"You never will be." Jun rolled her eyes as she stood, pulling her into a tight hug. "You've got this," she whispered before turning toward Oshen. "Take good care of her or I will hunt you down."

"Bloodthirsty as always," Amanda said with a smirk.

"You should already know the lengths I'm willing to go to if it's for your safety."

"I'm honestly terrified on his behalf."

Jun laughed, squeezing her hand a final time before letting go. "Don't worry about anything here. I can get it all packed up, and we'll figure out how to get it to you once you're settled."

"I need to grab some clothes and food for Hades."

"Just the clothes," Oshen called after her. "The replicator can make something suitable for Hades."

He obviously didn't know her picky cat very well. As fast as she could, Amanda grabbed a few changes of clothes and a couple pairs of shoes before ducking into the kitchen for a few cans of cat food. Tossing her bag over her shoulder, she crouched down to scoop up her "little beast," as Oshen liked to call him, hugging him tight as she looked around her room one last time. "Off we go, big guy."

"I'll contact you once you get on the ship and let you know if I find anything," Brin was telling Oshen as she stepped back into the living room.

"Do you think he's still out there?" she asked, clutching Hades to her when he began to squirm.

"I don't want to stay long enough to find out." Oshen turned to Brin, and Amanda watched as the males pressed their foreheads together, their tails intertwining. She wondered if this was something all Venium did, something cultural she might be expected to do as well, or if this was a special sort of farewell between the two of them. "Until the Sun meets the Moons, brutok," Oshen whispered as the two stepped away. "Best not to keep the commander waiting."

He held his hand out toward her, smiling gently when she placed her own within it. With one last backward glance, Amanda allowed Oshen to tug her out of the house. As they hurried down the dark street, she looked down at their interlocked fingers, remembering the day she had explained the human custom to him. A soft hiss was the only warning that they had arrived at the ship, and she felt her mouth drop open in awe as the spartan like interior of the entrance appeared from thin air. Oshen nudged her forward, stepping in behind her just as the door closed with a woosh.

Excitement and anxiety warred within her, tying her stomach in knots as the ship started to lift off. A new love, a new home, a brand new adventure awaited her, but she couldn't quite shake the feeling that something important was missing.

CHAPTER 11

XUVRI

The warm night air blew softly against his exoskeleton as he watched her from the shadows of the trees. Xuvri wanted her, wanted to possess her in every way possible, but the Venium still stood in his way. His xines shook with rage. The wounds the male had inflicted on him were so deep that he hadn't fully healed yet. As much as he wanted to rip him to pieces, his mind was still clear enough to know this wasn't the time for a confrontation.

He willed his body to heal faster, to repair the damage done to him quicker, because if he didn't have her soon, he was going to descend into madness. Her scent was so ingrained within his mind that there was no room for any other. Not even *she* had been enough. The thought of the other female made him shudder and snarl.

The first time he had laid eyes on this little human, she was all that had existed, all that had mattered. He had struggled for solars with the memory of her face, of her scent, of the delicious terror in her eyes when she had looked at him. He *needed* her.

Xuvri peered through the trees once more, watching her as she sat with another female within the dwelling. She had been outside, within his reach, just as beautiful and enticing as she had been six solars ago, but the Venium had been there. His vision transitioned to infrared so he could get a proper head count of all those within. Two Venium males and two human females. A growl rumbled through his chest as he watched them move. Something was happening.

Destroy them all. Take what is yours! The madness roiled within his mind, moving and clawing, acting as if it were something entirely separate from him.

It didn't matter to him that the council had forbade him from taking action or that this would undoubtedly cause a rift in the fragile political relationship between his species and the Venium. She called to him like no other female had. With others, he had been able to scent their emotions, but his little female *projected* them. He had been able to *feel* them.

Take her. Possess her.

Xuvri shook his head, making his xines slap against his neck and shoulders. All six of his eyes tracked the female, and he growled low in his throat in disgust as the Venium took her hand. He rushed through the trees, keeping pace with them as they continued down the street.

Kill him! Take the female!

When they stopped, he inched closer, looking for an opportunity to snatch her away, but a door suddenly opened in front of them and he watched in a panic as she was placed inside.

No! No! This wasn't possible. He wasn't going to lose her again. Crashing through the trees, Xuvri raced across the uneven terrain, but he was too late.

"I will find you," he panted as he felt the telltale heat of a ship lifting off of the ground. "And when I do, I will make you watch me tear that Venium limb from limb." The comm on his arm buzzed and he looked down. "Tachin scum," he sneered before answering the call. "What is it?"

"If you have any hope of catching up to them, you need to leave now." The male sounded irritated, but Xuvri couldn't care any less.

"I will be there soon. Have the ship ready." He didn't give the Tachin any time to respond, ending the transmission with the swipe of one clawed finger. He tipped his head back, inhaling the last of her fading scent and shivered with anticipation. "I am coming for you."

Find her.
Possess her.
Kill the Venium.

CHAPTER 12

OSHEN

They had been able to lift off from the planet without an issue and made it to the safety of the main ship, where they were greeted by a less than amused Vog. Moving through the mothership after spending so many days inside his female's tiny dwelling felt strangely comforting. A few of his shipmates stopped dead in their tracks to stare as they passed, but Oshen only smiled, his eyes sliding down to the large feline in Amanda's arms. Hades watched everything with a curious tilt of his head, his tail swishing back and forth.

"Was it necessary to bring that along?" Vog asked with something close to a sneer.

"Of course it was. I couldn't just leave him on his own." Amanda pressed her face into the cat's thick fur, making kissing sounds. "You won't even know he's here."

Vog took a step back as Amanda held Hades out. "I doubt I will forget as I am going to have to spend an entire week alone with it." His dark tail lashed along the ground in agitation.

Oshen gently took the cat from his mate, rubbing the little beast behind his ears before setting him down on the floor of the ship. "Oh, I'm sure the two of you will get along just fine." As soon as the words left his mouth, Hades pounced on Vog's twitching tail, sinking his tiny fangs into the tough skin.

A menacing growl filled the room as Vog reached down, grabbing the cat by the scruff. "For the love of goddess! Take this to your lodgings." He placed Hades into Amanda's outstretched arms and sneered.

"Well, he's never done that to me. He must really like you." Oshen leaned forward, a grin tugging at his lips as he whispered, "Off to a great start, Commander."

"I need to meet with the council and begin preparations for our departure. I'll send you the time and location you are to report to afterward. Make sure you are dressed comfortably for the cryosleep. Take your mate and the little monster. You are dismissed."

"Commander." Oshen nodded, leading Amanda out into the hall. His heart warmed when he heard her soft giggle, and he looked down to see her burying her smile within Hades' fur. As he watched her, she went quiet, her eyes lifting to meet his as the smile fell from her face.

She took a deep breath, shuddering as it was released. Oshen admired her bravery, admired the courage that it had taken to pack up her life and come with him. His mate wasn't just leaving her home; she was leaving her planet and everything she had ever known. Even though this was exactly what he had wanted to keep her safe, he knew she mourned for all that she was losing.

"Amanda ..." He slid a knuckle over her cheek. "I swear to you that I will do my best to make you the happiest you can be." Her chin tilted up as she stepped into him, and he tucked a stray hair behind her ear before his lips dropped lightly onto hers. A soft moan slipped from between her lips as she opened for him, her tongue moving to brush against his as it delved within. He could hear her heart pounding against her chest as arousal swirled around him. She kissed him back with a fever that he hadn't expected from her, and this time the kiss felt... right. Pulling back slowly, he smiled down at her.

A loud, drawn out yowl rose up between them and Amanda jerked back, clutching the unhappy beast against her chest as Hades glared. Oshen swept the pair of them up into his arms and hurried to his quarters, ignoring the curious looks as warriors darted out of his path. The fact that these were some of the fiercest warriors among his people and they were scattering like pups made him grin. He pressed his hand to the wall outside his door, waiting as the panel was lifted into the ceiling, allowing him to slip inside.

Hades jumped out of Amanda's arms as soon as the door shut behind them, running into the attached room that served as his small office. For a moment, Oshen simply held her against him, trying to absorb the fact that she was even here, on the ship, in his quarters. When she squirmed in his arms, he slid her down his body until her feet touched the floor. As she looked around the space, he realized for the first time just how sparse and impersonal the room was. The only things that gave any hint that he actually lived here were the picture of his family from their last gathering that his dam had given him before leaving and the clothing hanging in the small closet.

He shifted awkwardly as she moved away from him, running her hand over the soft blanket that covered the bed. "I am sorry there isn't much here. Most of my personal items are left at home when I go on a mission."

"Don't worry about it." She grinned, stopping to look at the picture frame that rested on one of the shelves built into the walls. "Is this your family?"

"*Your* family as well now." He loved the way color crept into her cheeks when she was embarrassed. "These are my parents and all of my siblings." It was the most recent one they had, and he took a moment to point out and name each one of them.

"I'm never going to remember everyone."

"It is easy enough once you get to know them."

"I hope they like me." The whispered words might have been missed if he wasn't standing so close to her.

"Why wouldn't they?"

Amanda shrugged a shoulder, turning away to explore the rectangular window. Outside, the stars twinkled against the darkness of space. "They aren't going to be disappointed when they see me and realize I'm not even Venium?"

"Of course not."

"And you? Were you disappointed?" There was uncertainty and vulnerability in her eyes as she turned to him.

Was he disappointed?

He took in a deep breath and slowly released it. "I told you before that I'd been waiting my whole life for you. I must admit that when I tried to picture what my mate would look like, I never imagined anything quite like you." He framed her face with his hands, tilting it so that he could make sure she saw the truth in his eyes. "Was I surprised by you? Absolutely. Surprised, but never, ever disappointed. How could I be?" He dropped a line of gentle kisses across her forehead and then along each cheek. "You've proven yourself to be courageous, caring, loyal, intelligent, and above all of that, you have always been true to yourself." His lips brushed over hers and he felt her whole body shiver.

Her hands slid up his chest to fist the fabric of his shirt as she deepened the kiss, her tongue gliding out to meet his like it had when they had stood in the hallway. He felt her pulse hammering against his fingers as he slid one hand down her throat, stroking the sensitive flesh until she was shivering and moaning against him.

Without warning, Amanda shoved away from him, her hands tugging frantically at the hem of her shirt before she slipped it over her head, dropping it carelessly at her feet. The air left his lungs in a rush as he let his gaze roam over her exposed skin. He must have stared longer than he thought because she brought her hands up to cover herself as if she were uncertain.

"What are you doing?"

"Umm…" Amanda looked down at herself before raising a brow at him. "I sort of thought that was obvious?"

Oshen felt his lips twitch and tilted his head. "Why did you stop?"

"Well, you were just staring, so I thought—"

"Did it seem like I was uninterested?"

Her tongue darted out to wet her lips and she shook her head, loosening the messy knot at the back of her head that held her dark hair back from her face. His hands itched to fist it, to yank her head back and run his tongue up the side of her neck. His kokoras jumped within its sheath, pressing forward painfully.

"Keep going," he commanded softly.

His eyes tracked her hands as they tugged the stretchy pants over her hips, thighs, and ankles before they eventually joined the shirt on the floor. The smell of her arousal swirled around him, filling his lungs, taking over his senses until he couldn't resist the urge to touch her. She still wore her under garments, but he wanted to take those off himself. With gentle hands, Oshen moved his hands over her shoulders, across her soft skin, before feathering his fingers through her hair. It was then that he smelled it. *Fear.*

"If you don't wish to do this—"

"No!" The word burst from her mouth and she grabbed his hand before he could retreat any farther. "I just… I'm not very good at this." Her other hand moved up to fidget with the silky material that covered her breasts. "I don't know how to be beautiful or enticing. Sex appeal has never been one of my strong points."

"My heart." Oshen shook his head. "You don't need to know how to be beautiful. You're already the most beautiful being I've ever laid eyes on." He brought her hand to his lips, pressing a kiss to each knuckle. "The most enticing female I've ever had the pleasure of knowing." She caught her lower lip between her teeth when he slid his tail up her leg, wrapping it possessively around her thigh. "Just know though, if you have any doubts, this doesn't need to happen now. I would wait solars if that was what you wished."

"I have no clue how long a solar is, but I know any wait is too long." His little female leaned forward and whispered kisses along his covered chest. He had never been more frustrated by his clothing than he was at that moment. "I want this—I want you. I chose to come out here, to leave Earth and make a life with you, to be your mate. Show me what it means to be your mate, Oshen."

Goddess, give me strength, he prayed as her hand ran over his bulging kokoras where it pressed against the fabric of his pants, straining at the opening of his sheath and threatening to extrude. He nuzzled his face into her neck, breathing her in as he spun them around toward the bed. Amanda moaned when he pressed her back against the soft padding of the mattress, his hand at her throat, squeezing gently.

He was going to show her exactly what it meant to be his mate.

She arched up beneath him, sighing as he trailed the tip of his tongue from her navel to the decorative covering, nipping at the top of one breast.

Oshen's tongue slipped out to run along the side of her neck, the unique flavor she produced bursting over his taste buds and claiming permanent residence. The overwhelming demand for him to sample her very essence was staggering, but he needed to take his time.

Amanda's hand snaked around his head, pulling him closer to her body. Her breath hitched as his claws gripped her hips, and he ground himself against her. Oshen's world focused entirely on the female in his arms, each beat of his heart solely for her.

The growl that vibrated through his body was not a warning but a promise of pleasure. He kissed his way around her throat, stopping to nip at her chin. *His.* Every atom sang in joy as he allowed himself to accept that she would be the only female for him. His gynaika was finally welcoming his touch. As much as Oshen had hated to stop her after that first kiss, he couldn't regret it. This moment meant so much more to him.

"Oshen."

The whispered sound of his name urged him on as he picked her up, pressing her against the wall. He fisted his hand in her dark hair, tilting her head back so he could claim her lips. Passion seeped into each caress as she clung to him. Wrapping his hands around the backs of Amanda's thighs, his claws pressing gently into her skin, he pulled her up against his body. The change in position brought her core into direct contact with his pelvis. Her arousal permeated the air, and he fought for control over his excitement. The gyrations of her body against his and the soft sounds of her whimpers nearly had him releasing in his pants.

The taste of her mouth set off something primal inside him. She tugged his shirt up over his head before he even realized her intentions. Did she know how much he had wanted her since that first kiss? He had ached for her, but he hadn't wanted her to feel pressured into being physical. Amanda dropped the shirt to the ground and ran her hands up his chest until he took them in his own, pressing a kiss to the back of each one.

"Are you certain, gynaika?" He knew that she had already

agreed, but it was almost too good to be true and he needed to be sure.

A smile tugged at the corners of her mouth, and she rested her forehead against his. "Hell yes." She giggled before his lips descended on her own, nipping and tugging until she was breathless.

The moan that caressed his ears only drove him on. Oshen pulled back from the kiss, licking along the sensitive flesh of her neck as he took in her soft sounds of pleasure. His fangs ached with the need to bite her and leave a permanent mark, to make it known that she was his. He gave up everything to her as he allowed himself to become immersed in the pleasure they shared.

Everything had always been so hard for him; finding a gynaika was impossible, or it had been. He curled his tail between them, sliding the tip up the inside of her leg to rub along her cleft.

Mine.

His hand moved from her hair to cup her covered breast, testing the weight of one in his palm. He ran sharp fangs over her collarbone, working his way down her body. He wanted to taste her. Moisture coated the end of his tail as it soaked through the fabric that separated him from her cunt.

"Don't you dare stop!" she hissed between clenched teeth.

Amanda arched beneath his hands with a gasp, hips tilting down to allow Oshen better access. Her fingers dug into his shoulders like she was attempting to hold him in place, as if he could have pried himself from her. Watching the pleasure dominate her features as he wrung a scream from her throat sent a thrill down his spine. Her head fell back, chest rising and falling with her labored breathing.

"Brutok?" Amanda squealed in shock, her skin flushing as she buried her face into Oshen's shoulder timidly. Her hands moved between them, pushing his tail away in mortification.

Oshen's head snapped up at the sound of Brin's voice. *What the brax?* The holoscreen flashed a picture of the male's irritating face, and he thanked the goddess that they weren't within his line of sight.

"If the sounds coming from off screen are anything to go by, I'd like to say congratulations on the mating and *finish herrrr*!"

Oshen shoved away from the wall with a growl just as another voice, one Oshen was very familiar with, interrupted.

"Brin!" Jun yelled from somewhere in the background. "I swear to God, I am going to—"

"Don't have too much fun!" The feed cut off and Oshen sighed heavily. *Braxing pup.*

He turned back to apologize to Amanda, but she had her hands over her face and her body shook like she was sobbing quietly as she sat down on the bed.

"Gynaika, please don't cry."

I will murder Brin the next time I see him, he swore to himself as he rushed to the bed, but he came up short when a loud snort and uncontrollable giggles erupted from her.

"Are you laughing?" *Unbelievable.*

When she snorted again, Oshen didn't even try to hold back his smile; she was exquisite.

"I'm sorry." Her laughter turned into a surprised gasp when he bent down to taste her skin again. "Gods, Oshen. I think…"

"What do you think?" he asked, trailing his lips over her ribs, nipping playfully.

She grinned down at him, her eyes sparkling. "I think you should finish me."

CHAPTER 13

OSHEN

*A*manda squirmed beneath him as he stroked a finger up and down the inside of her thigh, nearly brushing the thin cloth that covered her center before he retreated. His mate was magnificent, all milky skin over ample curves that he wanted to run his hands and mouth over for days on end.

Careful to avoid nicking her soft flesh, Oshen slid his hands beneath her to unclasp the silky covering. A low growl rumbled up his chest as her breasts slipped free of the silk. Indulging his impulse, he closed his mouth over one stiff nipple, swirling his tongue around it before catching it gently between his teeth. Her gasp of surprise turned into a moan of pleasure, and he moved to the other breast, showing it the same delicious attention as she pressed herself closer.

When he released the peak, Amanda mumbled something unintelligible, clutching at him, but he slipped down her body. He trailed kisses over her quivering stomach, nipping at her skin before dipping his tongue into her navel as he looked up at her flushed face. Her hips lifted, begging him silently to keep going, but he only smiled.

Not yet.

He plucked at the material covering her core before slicing through the bands on the sides, pulling the ruined garment from her and tossing it behind him.

Wedging his shoulders between her thighs, Oshen allowed her scent to overwhelm his senses. He dropped more kisses along her legs and whispered against her skin, "I swear that you will want for nothing."

Her hands tugged at his braids as she arched her hips toward him. "Please," she moaned. "Oshen…"

"I swear to love you without reservation." He trailed his knuckle up her inner thigh before sliding it over the slick folds between her legs, his chin resting low on her belly as he watched her face contort.

Her hips jerked up at the contact, and she gasped. "Stop teasing me!"

A deep chuckle vibrated through his chest as he moved his knuckle over the tiny nub at the top, making her jerk upward again. *Interesting.* With one last nip at her skin, Oshen spread her sex and ran his tongue over the sweet slickness that coated her. A long, drawn-out hiss escaped her as he did it a second time, stopping to press with the tip of his tongue, swirling it around the little nub that seemed to be so sensitive. "You're starting to sound like Hades."

Amanda slapped her hand against the bed, fisting the blanket before she lifted her head to glare down at him. "You're starting to sound like someone who's got a death wish. Less talk, more of that thing you did with your tongue."

The way her entire body shuddered beneath him when he returned his attention to that little nub had him aching. His engorged length had already pushed past the sheath, and he felt it jump when she moaned. Her legs fell away from his shoulders as she bucked against his mouth, moving her hips in frenzied circles. Goddess help him, he almost spilled right then and there from the sight she made.

Beautiful. Sensual. His very own goddess.

"Mine." He growled, shooting to his feet to rip the clothes from his body. A sigh of relief nearly left his lips as his kokoras sprang free. He stroked his length once, growling when Amanda's eyes lit with desire. The heat of her gaze was nearly hot enough to sear his flesh. Need blazed through his veins, and he slapped his hand against the control panel on the wall, running his fingers over the commands until he had brought the platform just below the level of his hips, putting his mate exactly where he wanted her.

A shudder worked through her as she eyed him, her tongue sneaking out to wet her lips in the same manner that had been driving him crazy since the day he had woken up in her dwelling. He settled himself between her legs and leaned over her before brushing his lips over hers. Being with a female had never felt this intimate, and she coaxed him deeper and deeper still, entangling him in the web of desire and passion she was weaving. Her hands swept over bare skin, her touch feverish and frantic, as if she thought he was going to pull away.

Amanda caught his lower lip between her teeth, sucking it into her mouth and then releasing it on a moan. His hips thrust forward, and he felt his kokoras slide against her heated sex. She moved her hand down between them, her fingers wrapping around his shaft as she stroked it from the head down to the base, where she ran her fingers over his sheath. He hissed through his teeth in pleasure, his muscles clenching as he tried to allow her time to explore.

"What are these?" she asked as her fingers played over the ridges that circled the base.

"Mating glands," he managed to grind out between clenched teeth. "Meant to seal us together and ensure procreation." The engorged member jerked in her grip as the largest ridge began to pulse. He was going to spill in her braxing hand like a pup. "Amanda." He leaned down, raking his fangs over the skin on her shoulder. "I need to be inside you."

With a muffled laugh, he felt her guide him to her entrance, running the head through her wet folds, drawing another moan from her lips. He pressed into her, working her slick along his length, slowing his movements for fear that he might hurt her. Her hands flew to his forearms, her blunt nails pressing into his skin as she tilted her hips in invitation. A moan of pure, uncontrolled ecstasy burst from her lips when he finally seated himself completely within her. The searing heat of her body pulsed around him, her muscles clenching at him as he pulled out a little only to push back inside. He felt drugged by her pleasure, dazed by the way she drew him in.

A satisfied groan rumbled through him as the ridges began to expand, dragging against her walls as they tightened around him. His fushori pulsed, casting Amanda in a golden glow that nearly took his breath away. This was where she belonged. Her scent changed slightly, growing stronger, more potent as her pleasure spiraled out of control. Every thrust of his hips against hers brought him closer to the edge, every whispered caress threatening to make him spill.

He twisted the dark strands of her hair in one hand, pulling her head back and exposing the side of her neck. The sounds of their panting, grunting, and whimpering filled the air, accompanied by the rhythmic slap of his flesh against hers. Her body pulsed around him, tightening like a fist as she cried out. For a moment, he could do nothing but watch her as she came undone beneath him. She was gasping, writhing against the bedding with her eyes closed as she let go.

"You're mine." He growled just before he leaned in and sank his fangs into the exposed side of her neck, piercing the soft flesh. He rocked against her almost desperately, driving into her as she spasmed around him.

The metallic taste of her blood flowed over his tongue, undoing all of his carefully kept control. The mating glands around his kokoras expanded, locking them together so that every stroke was a delicate balance between pain and pleasure. His tail curled around one of her thighs, spreading her wider as his hands flew to her hips. The tips of his claws dug into her soft skin as he initiated the mating hold, but instead of crying out in pain, his little mate moaned in pleasure. His release struck him then, taking him by surprise. He came with a loud, rumbling growl as his seed pulsed into her body, bathing her walls.

The length of his tongue slid over the wound on her neck, helping to heal the flesh and stop the bleeding. She sighed beneath him when he rested his forehead against hers, running her fingers over the sides of his face and over his ears as she caught her breath.

His female. His mate. Oshen felt his throat tighten with emotion as he closed his eyes, seeing their future take shape the way he had always hoped. They would be bringing pups into the world and raising a family together. Living without Amanda would never be an option. He was wholly and unconditionally hers until the day he drew his last breath.

~

"*A*re you ready to go, gynaika?" Oshen asked as he walked out of his office carrying a small bag that contained the few personal items he had brought with him from Venora. Amanda turned from the window with a smile, her bag slung over her shoulder, and reached down to scoop Hades up into her arms.

"Shuttle time, big guy," she said as she followed Oshen out into the hall.

The shuttle bay wasn't as busy as it had been the night before, but even so members of the flight crew moved back and forth between the small fighter crafts in the center and the larger shuttles that lined the outer edges. He narrowed his eyes, scanning the names and numbers on the crafts before he found the one he was looking for. *Starmaze* was painted on the side in blocky letters. It was tinier than all the other crafts surrounding it, but according to Vog, it was the fastest and most reliable.

"This way," Oshen told her, placing a hand on her lower back to guide her down the stairs that led toward the walkway. The lights on the outside of the shuttle were blinking white and red and the hum of the engines told him that the crew had already begun the systems check. Oshen felt her steps slow as they approached the entrance and he ran his hand up her spine, settling his palm on the back of her neck. "A bit farther now, gynaika," he whispered before dropping a kiss on the top of her head.

Amanda drew in a deep breath, blowing it out as she stepped through the open door. They followed the short, narrow corridor until it opened up into the center of the shuttle. Directly ahead was the cockpit, large enough for one Venium to man the controls. He watched as his mate stepped forward, her eyes touching on every one of the blinking lights and buttons that were spread across the panel.

"Do you know how to operate this?" she asked, setting Hades down in the pilot's chair.

"I know the basics, but I don't believe you would want me to be the one in charge of getting us home safely," Oshen said, nudging the cat from the seat. Vog would have a fit if he saw Hades there. The little beast glared as he jumped down, wandering off to inspect beneath the control panel. "Come. We will get the chambers set before the commander arrives."

"This is sort of terrifying."

Oshen grinned as he keyed in the code on the cryochamber, releasing the lid so that it popped open with a soft hiss. "It's completely safe."

She frowned as she looked inside, running her hands over the padding. "Why are we getting in these again?"

This was at least the fifth time she had asked. "Tiny ship with two full-grown Venium, a human female, and a little beast." He gestured around the cabin that contained the upright chambers as well as a very small, uncomfortable cot attached to the wall. "We would drive one another crazy over the course of travel. You and I will go into the cryochambers while Vog remains out here to keep an eye on the ship's systems and Hades."

"Have you done it before?"

"A few times." Oshen pulled her into his arms, dropping a kiss onto her head. "There is nothing to worry about, gynaika. I would never put you in there if I thought for even a moment it could harm you."

"I know." She pulled back with a sigh, smiling up at him as she traced a path down his chest with her fingers.

The bite on her neck was still a little pink, and the sight of it sent a jolt of lust and need through his body. He had felt a pinch of sadness at the fact that she couldn't mark him, that he would never carry her mark on his skin in the same way she did his, but this morning when he had woken up with her wrapped around him, it didn't matter all that much.

"The beast is on my bed."

Oshen lifted his head to see Vog staring over at the cot where Hades had just made himself comfortable.

"Where's he supposed to sleep?" Amanda asked.

Vog motioned toward his feet. "There is a perfectly good floor right beneath us."

His little mate snorted, her eyes rolling up. "Good luck getting your bed back, bud."

The commander mumbled something under his breath, glaring at the cat as he stepped into the room. "It's time."

Amanda peppered kisses on Hades' head and nose before she turned to Oshen, tilting her face up for a soft brush of his lips on hers.

"All will be well," he whispered, stroking her cheek.

Oshen helped her inside, squeezing her hand before latching the door. He watched as sleep slowly took her before stepping into his own chamber.

"Safe journey." He nodded to Vog before the darkness closed in.

CHAPTER 14

VOG

"*J* would appreciate it very much if you did *not* do that!" Vog growled as he scooped the animal off of his control panel. If the beast kept stepping all over everything, he was going to end up sending Oshen and the human into space.

"You are a braxing menace," he grumbled.

Hades, as the human had called it, looked up at him like *he* was the one being an absolute inconvenience. Just this morning, the beast had almost initiated the self-destruct sequence and taken solars off of Vog's life.

This had to be what it was like to have a pup. His poor dam.

"If you touch these controls again, I am going to have you for dinner." He sneered, displaying all of his sharp fangs, but Hades only tilted his head and meowed.

Vog pushed himself up and out of the command seat, looking around the black interior of the ship for something to distract the cat. His tail was littered with tiny punctures from where Hades had pounced on it. He ran his fingers through the loose strands of his dark hair, thankful that he could forgo the classic braids that had become the military standard. Here, on this tiny ship with this mischievous little creature, he was actually more relaxed than he had been in solars, safe from the demands of the royalty and the council.

It was dark and comfortable within the ship, but the walls were beginning to feel as if they were closing in on him already. Being cooped up in the mothership for so long hadn't helped, but at least he could move around there. He looked back at the cryochambers, his eyes falling on the human's face where she slept peacefully. If they could safely reproduce with humans, this would be a breakthrough for his species. It could save them. Perhaps this news would loosen the council's chokehold on him.

"Commander Vog," the ship's AI broke through his thoughts. "There is a discrepancy within the perimeter."

"Project onto the main gazer," he commanded, stepping back toward the panel. The screen lit up before him and he focused on the little flashing dot on the left-hand side. "Can you identify the object?"

"Not at this time, Commander."

"Keep working on it." He watched closely, frowning as the AI went quiet. If it was a ship, the AI should have been able to discern that. It didn't move like space debris. This thing, whatever it was, moved with purpose. Uur after uur passed like this, Vog watching while the AI tried to sort out what was going on. The object had stuck with them, getting closer and closer as time went on. "Send out a ping. Let's see if we get a response."

"Sending ping." There was silence and then a soft crackle as the communication was accepted. "Transferring video to main gazer."

The face that appeared on the screen was not one he had been expecting. "Who am I speaking with?" the Tachin male asked.

Vog shuddered as the alien's large black compound eyes

stared at him. This species reminded him of some of Earth's insects from the database they had been given, with their narrow, needle-like snouts, green iridescent bodies, and transparent wings. "I am Commander Vog of the *Starmaze*."

The buzz of his voice filled the room. "Greetings, Commander. You seem to be carrying something of ours aboard your ship."

Vog had to stop the shiver of disgust that worked through him as the Tachin's tongue slithered out of its mouth to wet its face and a hooked hand scraped over its head. Watching the creature made him feel like there was a layer of slime sliding over his body. "I can assure you that I have nothing aboard my ship that would interest the Tachin."

"That is where you are wrong. If it is not handed over, we will wipe you out of the solar system."

"What exactly do you believe I have?"

"The human female."

Vog shook his head, arms crossing over his chest. "She does not belong to you."

A loud snarl came from somewhere off screen just before a large scarred Grutex shoved the Tachin aside. Despite the male's visible rage, Vog stared back unflinchingly.

"You will hand over my female!"

"She is not your female. She is the mate of the Venium male also on this ship."

"She. Is. *Mine!*" The Grutex slammed his hand down on the control panel in front of him and Vog felt his ship lurch. "I will have her."

Something flashed in front of them, and Vog stared into the center of what could only be a black hole.

"Commander, I am detecting a spatial anomaly."

"I see it." Vog gritted his teeth, trying to override the system and take control. The ship began to turn, but they were too close.

127

"What are you doing?" he heard the Tachin male hiss in frustration.

"What I must." The Grutex growled before the communication was severed.

"Brax!" Vog strapped himself in as the ship began to shake and the pressure increased. He squeezed his eyes shut, listening to the alarms that rang out, and hoped the Grutex wanted the female enough to know not to send them some place that was going to kill them all. He felt his entire body stretch and compress as they passed through the void and were deposited on the other side.

An uncertain yowl drew his attention to Hades, and he grinned when he saw the cat sprawled out on the floor beneath the cot. "You've survived. Wonderful." He looked around at the unfamiliar depths of space and sighed. "This is going to take us a bit longer than expected."

～

ive weeks later...
Vog wanted to sigh with relief when Venora appeared on the main gazer. He was home. Hades looked up from his position in Vog's lap and meowed.

"You doubted me, but I told you I could get us here."

The cat made a chirping sound and Vog huffed.

"I don't appreciate your attitude."

"A ship has been detected," the AI informed him.

When he switched the viewer, he shouted a curse, startling Hades.

"Braxing Grutex." They were so close to the planet that he swore he could smell the salty waters. He couldn't risk increasing their speed for fear that they would burn up upon reentry, but the hostile ship was gaining on them.

"Hold on tight," Vog whispered to Hades as the cabin began

to shake. He hadn't survived six weeks inside this ship with this little beast to die in orbit above his planet. Flames licked up the sides as the exterior heated and alarms echoed in the cabin.

Then the shaking calmed, and they dropped from the cover of the clouds. The okeanos spread out before them, blue and glistening in the light of the sun. Something shot past them moments before the ship lurched to one side.

"We have taken fire, Commander," the AI informed him.

Vog snarled, shifting his grip on the controls. "Brax it all."

CHAPTER 15

GULZAR

The little goddess had been eluding him since their last shared dream, and he was more determined than ever to find her. There had to be some way to open the connection they shared. He was sure they had done so as young ones, but the memory escaped him. Perhaps he could find one of the flying metallic domes the wayward offspring of Ven used. Surely he would be able to reach her then.

He gathered a few supplies, tucking them into the small pouch at his hip. The house was quiet this early in the morning. Kyra had yet to rise to prepare the morning meal, and Ky should have already left to begin her duties at the temple. Gulzar crept out of the house, carefully closing the creaky door that had gotten him caught more times than he could count.

"Gulzar?"

He winced when he heard the younger female's voice from across the open courtyard. "Yes."

"What are you doing sneaking out so early?"

"I am not sneaking anywhere." He grumbled. "I could not sleep."

"What kept you up?" She probed, shuffling after him when he turned toward the gates.

"The little goddess needs—"

Her xines rustled with impatience as her fushori flashed. "Did you strike your head when you fell in the woods? I thought you were past this. You told me yourself that you have not seen her in days."

"I have not," he agreed, but he didn't care to explain to her yet again why this was important to him. "I was going to take a walk, clear my mind."

"I could walk with you," she offered cheerfully. "My duties at the temple will not take very long."

"It is kind of you to offer, Ky. I know you mean well, but I would like to be alone for this."

A gentle smile tipped her lips and she nodded. "I understand."

He swung the gate open for her, closing it softly behind them before turning in the opposite direction of the temple.

"Gulzar?" She called before he had taken more than a couple steps. "You are the closest thing to a brother I have ever known, and I care about you, but..." Ky seemed to struggle with her words. "Mitera still holds out hope for the two of us, but I wanted to let you know that there is a male that I—"

"Kyra is holding onto the last pieces of my dam and sire that she still has. She will have to face the truth eventually."

"Maybe so." She sighed, plucking the basket from the hook on the outer wall.

"I wish you all the love of a happy bonding, Ky."

"Thank you." She pressed a kiss to the palm of her hand and held it out to him. "Be safe, brother."

"Always." Gulzar watched as she turned her back on him and headed toward the other end of the village where the temple

131

resided. There was something so final about their conversation, and it sent a shudder down his spine. Around his shoulders, his xines wriggled restlessly, and he shook his head as he turned away from the only home he had ever known.

He picked his way along one of the lesser known paths, cutting through the dense foliage as he put as much distance as he could between himself and the village. There was no way to know if he would ever return, but he couldn't allow himself to think about what he was leaving behind; his little goddess needed him, and he was going to do everything in his power to make sure she was safe.

Having spent many days within the forest over the course of his life, Gulzar was familiar with the paths that the wayward offspring of Ven took when they flew their domes overhead. Once, when he was very young, he had let his curiosity get the better of him and followed one such dome out to the shores. He had watched from the trees as it descended from the sky, but fear propelled him back home before he could see exactly where they went.

The hours passed silently, and he stopped a few times to drink or gather small plants he thought might be useful. He was close enough to smell the salty air of the shore when a loud bang rang out from above. Through the cover of the trees, Gulzar could just make out an object plummeting toward the ground as it fell free of the main dome.

His entire body tingled in a way he had never experienced before, and a compulsion came over him that was so strong that he had taken several steps before he even realized what he was doing. Another dome followed the first, red blasts flying from the front and slamming into the back of the other as they careened through the sky.

Anxiety gnawed at his gut as he raced through the forest, scattering small prey animals as he crashed through the underbrush.

The air switched direction and blew downward, causing the boughs of the trees to actually bend, their leaves fluttering against the violent gale.

Above him, red lights flashed, and he winced at the whine of metal sliding over metal. Pressure grew around him, like a powerful storm about to erupt. And, then, a booming blast rippled through the forest. In the shock wave, he lost his balance, falling to his knees. For a moment, the earth continued to tremble beneath his feet. Then, all lay still.

Rising to his feet, the pull dragged at his consciousness. He had to follow it, had to know where it would lead. He wasn't sure what or who was pulling him just yet, but the prospect of finding out almost made his feet glide over the ground in his haste.

When he reached the edge of the trees, he skidded to a stop, panting heavily as he watched a tiny figure stumble out of the wreckage. His whole body stiffened in shock when he caught sight of the creature's face.

His little goddess. She was real... She was *here*.

His instincts screamed at him to run to her, scoop her up and carry her to safety, but the memory of their last encounter filled his mind and he hesitated. The goddess had been scared of him and pushed him away. They had no way to communicate, no way for him to assure her that he was doing this for her own good.

He would watch and wait, he decided. If she had need of him, he would be there.

CHAPTER 16

AMANDA

*H*er head was pounding and her whole body ached. Amanda pushed up against the broken lid of the cryochamber, sliding it all the way off before sitting up slowly and glancing around. Sun, sand, and water. If it weren't for the green sky and the odd trees in the distance, she would swear they were on a beach somewhere on Earth. Waves crashed against the sand as she pulled herself up, taking a few deep breaths.

She stepped out of the wreckage of the chamber, scanning the area for any sign of danger. She wished so badly to have Jun there. Her best friend always seemed to know what to do during a crisis; she took charge, organized everyone, got things done.

I'm not equipped to handle this clusterfuck, she thought as her feet sank down into the soft sand. The heat here was far more intense than any place she had ever been. Nausea rolled over her as she struggled to make it to the shade of the trees that lined the top part of the beach. Bile filled the back of her throat, and she fell to her knees, gagging as it forced its way up and out. Her whole body shook as her stomach emptied and she gasped for air.

The heat had never had this effect on her before. Maybe it was a concussion or a side-effect of the cryosleep that was making her feel so sick. Amanda breathed deep, trying to clear her head. She had been in the chamber on a ship, but there was no sign of one anywhere on the beach. Why had she been on a ship? She pinched her eyes shut, digging her fingers into her hair to rub her scalp.

"All will be well."

The voice echoed in her mind and the picture of a foggy figure appeared. She knew this person... didn't she? Her head pounded as she tried to sort through her memories.

"Oshen!" She gasped, her eyes flying open. "Hades?" How could she have forgotten about them? She tried to get to her feet, but a wave of dizziness overtook her and she fell back onto her bottom in the sand.

Tears welled up in her eyes as she sucked in lungfuls of air. Her poor cat was probably scared out of his mind, assuming he even survived whatever had happened. Amanda wiped at the tears that streaked down her cheeks. Hades would be okay; Vog would see to that.

Both of the Venium males were more than capable of taking care of themselves, but now she needed to find them. Oshen had told her about the underwater dome cities, but he hadn't mentioned anything about them residing on land. The beach was most likely her best bet, but the heat was beginning to get to her again. Already, she could feel the nausea bubbling within her stomach and turned to crawl up toward the trees and the few scattered bushes.

Just as she reached them, her stomach roiled and she spent the next minute dry heaving into the closest shrub. A small, almost bird-like creature fled as she wiped her mouth, startling her. She watched as it fluttered up into the trees above, chirping and whistling, no doubt telling her off for disturbing it.

"Sorry," Amanda said, pushing herself up and brushing the sand from her hands. "Didn't mean to puke in your bush." The ground within the shade of the trees was littered with tiny plants that looked very similar to coral. Elkhorn, pilar, and tube types all shot up around the base of the trees, colored in brilliant mixtures of reds, blues, and greens. She had never seen anything like this on land, and she smiled as she ran a gentle finger over one close to her. This place was amazing.

A sound like the bleat of a sheep caught her attention, and she squinted as she scanned the woods for the source. Just on the other side of the bush to her left she found a small creature curled up into an awkward position. It looked like a fawn, staring up at her with the biggest most innocent eyes she had ever seen. Maybe it was hurt.

Oshen had mentioned that there were predators on Venora, like the one he had mistaken Hades for, but this couldn't be one. The creature before her looked nothing like a cat. Three fleshy ribbons arched up from the top of its head, curling around the long, slender neck and resting against its back. The skin on the front of the throat looked as if it were laced up like a corset.

Amanda swallowed back another wave of nausea as she inched closer on her hands and knees, cooing at the creature. "It's all right, baby. I'm not going to hurt you." She got up on her wobbly legs, stepping around the bush as she glanced around. She couldn't just leave the little one out here alone, could she? What if one of those predators came along and gobbled it up? The soft cry it emitted squeezed at her heart.

"Did your mama leave you here on purpose or are you lost?" She mused out loud, stepping closer. Amanda extended her hand, trying to coax the baby out of its hiding spot.

As it struggled to stand, Amanda smiled, encouraging it softly, but the smile slowly faded as the creature raised its head and the seam along its neck peeled apart, revealing long, jagged teeth set inside of a gaping maw. Too late, Amanda realized that she should have kept some distance between her and the creature. She stumbled back as it stretched to its full height.

The coral plants crunched beneath her feet, tripping her as she tried to get away. Amanda looked around frantically for anything she could use as a weapon—a tree branch, a rock, anything—but the creature lurched forward and she fell backward into the sandy soil. Gods, this couldn't be how she died. She flung handfuls of sand at it, but it didn't seem to deter the neck-mouth fawn at all.

"Get out of here! Shoo!"

She scrambled back as it stalked toward her. It screeched, crouching like it was ready to pounce, and Amanda closed her eyes tight shielded her head with her arms. Instead of the impact of the body against her own, Amanda heard a snarl and a loud thud before an inhuman shriek reached her ears.

Her eyes flew open, and she stared in stunned horror as she met the violet gaze of the Grutex. All four of its eyes watched her as a tidal wave of fear crashed down upon her trembling body. His blood-splattered mauve chest heaved and the vine-like tendrils attached to his head snaked around his shoulders. He looked like a barbarian. The nostrils at the end of his sloping head flared wide as he took in a deep, rasping breath.

When he spoke to her, it wasn't in English like the one from the lab, but a growling, rumbling language. She relaxed a little as his claws retracted into the tips of his fingers but recoiled when he reached a hand out to her.

"No, no!" She shook her head, dragging herself away from him. He slowed his speech in an obvious attempt to communicate, the black-tipped protrusions around his head twitching as he looked down at her.

The last time she was this close to a Grutex male, it hadn't gone so well, and Oshen wasn't here to rescue her this time. The memory of that night clouded her mind and she shuddered. He crouched down in front of her, his hands up in the universal sign of *'I'm not going to hurt you.'* His gaze shifted down to her stomach and she laid a hand over it, frowning up at him. "What?"

The male reached out toward her, placing his palm gently over the hand that rested on her stomach, looking at her almost ... reverently. *Maybe he's got a thing for big girls?* He spoke to her again, tilting his head as he met her gaze.

"I don't understand you." Something about this male seemed familiar, but the Grutex were so hard to tell apart and her head was still throbbing.

A soft rumble rose up from his throat as he held out his other hand to her, beckoning with a curl of one finger. The time that had passed since the attack at the lab hadn't done anything to ease her anxiety over the Grutex as a species. If anything, it had only made her more cautious of them. There was something about this one that made her want to trust him. He wasn't anything like the ones on Earth. Where those males had been harsh and brutal, this one was gentle. He touched her like she was precious and delicate, like she would break if he were too rough.

Instead of hurting her, he had saved her from the nightmare fawn. Amanda looked him up and down, waiting for him to change his mind and pounce, but he only looked on with his hand held out silently. Whoever he was, he was certainly impressive. Oshen towered over her, but she was sure this male was even taller than her mate. If she had to guess, she would have put him around eight feet tall, giving him a good foot over Oshen. His shoulders were broad and led down to strong, toned arms. He was built like a warrior, muscular and lean, but she could see the kind spirit in his eyes.

As if determining she wasn't going to get up of her own accord, the Grutex reached down and curled his arms around her torso, plucking her off the ground. She clutched at his arms as he shifted her into a more comfortable position. The mangled body of the nightmare fawn was skewered on the dagger-like tip of his tail and trailed behind them as the male stepped away from the bloody sand. She squealed in surprise when he lowered his head to her belly and nuzzled against it, his voice quiet as he spoke. The ridges near his face rubbed along her body, bunching up the thin shirt she had worn for cryosleep.

A soft buzzing noise rose up from him and she blinked in astonishment. Was he purring? Her entire body vibrated softly against him, and she felt the nausea that had started to build up within her dissipate as quickly as it had come. *That's nifty.*

His long white tongue slithered out to run along the exposed skin of her abdomen and she shivered. Amanda pressed her hand to his face, not sure if she should push him away or let him continue, but he hissed, lifting his head to look into her face. Her fingers glided down over his neck to his chest, and to her surprise, the plates of his exoskeleton were warm beneath her skin. The male turned his head, looking around before he seemed to decide on a direction.

"Hold on." Amanda twisted in his arms in an effort to keep the beach in her sights. He was taking her into the woods. "Wait, big guy, I need to go to the water." *Shit, what had Oshen called it?* "Okeanos! I need to go to the okeanos."

The male tilted his head but continued on through the trees, purring and patting her hip as if he were trying to console her. Amanda sighed and settled into his embrace, knowing there wasn't much use in arguing with an eight-foot giant who couldn't understand anything she said. She would have to wait for an opportunity to escape.

CHAPTER 17

OSHEN

*B*right light filtered through his eyelids, making his vision a hazy red. His skin felt hot, like he was underneath one of the heat lamps that the Hisar, a reptilian species, used when they visited the dome cities on Venora. Oshen opened one eye and then the other as he stared up at the cloudy green sky above him.

Green?

Oshen frowned, feeling the grittiness of the sand beneath his body as he struggled to collect his thoughts. The only planet with a green sky he knew of was Venora, but why was he out of the ship? He was supposed to be in cryosleep with—

"Amanda!"

He shot up from the ground, his head whipping around in every direction as he searched for his mate among the wreckage. Pieces of the black admentine that made up the ship floated in the surf or stuck up from the sand where they were lodged. Lying on his side between two large sections of the outer hull was Vog's battered, unconscious body.

"Brax." Oshen cursed as he rolled onto his hands and knees to crawl across the sand and rubble. "Commander," he rasped, reaching out to gently shake the male's shoulder. There were deep cuts to his face and limbs, but those would heal in time. "Vog, can you hear me?"

Vog turned his head to squint at Oshen, groaning as he ran a hand through his tangled hair. "That was exhilarating," he said.

"What happened?" Oshen asked.

"We were attacked by a Grutex working with Tachin scum." Vog sat up, sighing as he looked around.

"The Tachin don't work with others." Oshen frowned as he pushed himself to his feet, his legs feeling unsteady beneath him.

"This one was. I suspect the Grutex is the one your female was running from."

"How did he find us?"

"It was days into the journey when they made themselves known." Oshen watched as Vog picked up a scrap of admentine before tossing it aside. "I have no knowledge of the tech they used, but they were able to create an anomaly that displaced the entire ship. We were set off course for a further five weeks."

"Five weeks?" He gaped. "Why didn't you wake us then?"

"Wake you for what reason? So you could drive me even more insane than the creature I was cooped up with?" The male pressed a hand to one of the deeper wounds and grimaced.

"Where is my mate, Vog?" Oshen paced across the sand, his tail lashing behind him. It felt as if something were trying to get out just at the prospect of his mate being gone, trying to break free. But he pushed back on the feeling. Now was not the time to lose his temper. He was an ambassador.

The commander hesitated for a moment. "We encountered them again when we reached Venora's orbit. They engaged us once we were in the atmosphere and one of the shots must have hit something that triggered the ejection sequence."

"The ejection—" Oshen felt the lifeblood drain from his face. "She was *ejected*?"

"Within her chamber, yes."

Oshen's knees nearly gave out at the thought that she could be injured somewhere with no protection and no knowledge of anything about this planet. "I have to find her."

"The chamber has a tracker within it for emergency situations like this." Vog ripped the bottom of his shirt before securing it around the top of his arm. "You retrieve her, and I will go for help."

"Are you certain you can make it?" He looked pointedly at the wounds.

"I steered the ship as close to the tunnel as I could. It isn't very far from here."

Oshen's gaze fell to the mangled remains of his own cryochamber and he shuddered, praying that Amanda's had fared better. His head jerked up when he felt a hand land on his shoulder.

"She will be fine, Oshen. Your mate is a fierce and determined female." He hoped the commander was right because he didn't know what he would do if something had happened to her. "The same goes for her little beast."

By the goddess, he had completely forgotten about Hades. There was no sign of him here on the beach, and Oshen hoped that meant that the cat had escaped unharmed. "I sincerely hope nothing on this planet is stupid enough to mess with him."

"I was able to teleport him to the surface at the last moment, but I have no idea where he was placed or how his body handled it."

As worried as he was for the little beast, Oshen needed to find his mate and reassure himself that she was safe. "I'll search for him once Amanda is within the dome."

"Safe journey, Ambassador. I hope to see you both soon." Vog nodded and then turned away, headed in the direction of the surface-to-dome tunnel.

Oshen stood in silence, watching as the other male disappeared behind an outcropping of rocks where the opening to the tunnel was hidden, before turning his arm over to speak to his AI. "Mouni, bring up the tracking beacon for the cryochamber labeled 'human female.'"

"What's the magic word?"

Oshen growled low in his throat. "I should have shut you down and never let you listen to all those human movies."

"This is why I like your female more than I like you." There was a pause before the notification chime. "Cryochamber has been located. Would you like me to provide a route?"

"No." He looked up to the top of the beach where the tree line started and grimaced, knowing that the ones who had followed them before could still be near, listening. "Show the location on the screen." The tiny blip on his screen showed him which direction he needed to go, and that was good enough. As he headed into the shelter of the trees, Oshen stayed alert, scanning the area for not only the Grutex that might be out there but also the predators native to Venora that wouldn't hesitate to take him on.

After he had gotten halfway to the location his AI had provided, Oshen stopped next to one of the freshwater streams that fed into the okeanos, dipping his hand into the cool water and bringing it up to his mouth for a drink. A noise to his left had his head snapping up, swearing he caught a glimpse of something before it disappeared behind a tree. Minutes passed as he scanned the area, waiting to see if whatever was out there would show itself, but it seemed he was alone.

He stood, his tail curling and uncurling in irritation as he set off again toward Amanda's location. As he walked, he sent up prayers to the goddess that she had stayed near the chamber and that nothing had come around to investigate the strange new scent. Shadows followed him as he weaved his way around the gnarled black trunks of trees and through the dense pockets of underbrush.

Every so often, he swore he heard raspy breathing or heavy footsteps, but nothing showed on the perimeter sweeps he performed. If Vog was right and the Grutex had teamed up with the Tachin, who knew what sort of tech they possessed? Oshen's gills flared in annoyance as he picked up his pace, ducking behind bushes full of red and orange leaves, racing over the fosalli plants that grew in the shade of the towering trees whose branches reached high above him.

Why don't they just attack already? Oshen wondered, but then it occurred to him. The Grutex knew Oshen would search for Amanda and would lead him directly to her. That wasn't going to happen if he could help it. Oshen changed course, hoping whoever stalked him didn't notice the detour. He needed to find a distraction, something that would keep them busy so he could double back and find the most important being in his world.

The thought of leaving her for longer than originally planned ate at him, but it was the only way to keep her safe. If there was one thing Oshen was thankful for in this situation, it was the chance to stop the male who threatened his mate, who thought he could take Amanda away from him. He would put an end to her terror.

CHAPTER 18

GULZAR

*H*eart pounding against his chest, Gulzar looked down at the fall of brown hair that flowed gently over his arm. He still couldn't believe she was here or that she had fallen from one of the flying domes the wayward offspring of Ven used. What had she been doing with them? He had watched her stumble toward the tree line before emptying her stomach and wanted to go to her when he felt her distress, but shock and the sense of shame over his station had rooted him to the spot.

All of these solars, he had thought her beautiful, but seeing her in the flesh had taken his breath away.

When she had ventured up near the small, hard growths of the fosalli plants, Gulzar was entranced by her smile and completely missed the presence of the young shayfia lying in wait. Watching her try to lure the juvenile out had stunned him, but she was a goddess. Surely she could protect herself. His ignorance had almost gotten her killed. He barely reached her in time, and the thought of what could have happened to her made him shudder even now. A shayfia of any age was a master of manipulation and used its innocent appearance to draw in prey before swallowing it up.

She was so small and defenseless that the beast could have eaten her in two or three bites. She shifted against him, resting her hands between her face and his chest. In the distance, a clan of tigearas called to one another, their low growls and chirps bouncing off the tree trunks as he carried her farther into the woods.

He wasn't going to allow anything to harm her or the budding life he sensed growing within her.

He wondered what had brought her here. What would compel her to risk not only her life, but that of her offspring? Was she meant to breathe new life into a species that seemed on the brink of death? Perhaps she was going to somehow cure whatever it was that had caused his people to decline. Was this the reason he had been connected to her for so long?

His people, the offspring of Nem, had prayed diligently for the return of the goddess. Though *his* goddess was not Una herself, maybe she would bless them in her own way. Unlike the tainted ones, Gulzar's people had continued to live as Una commanded for as long as they could and they, more than any others, deserved this blessing for their devotion. While they hadn't been able to create triads for generations, perhaps his little goddess was a sign of forgiveness. The thought that he might be the one to bring this blessing to his people brought him joy, making each step feel like a leap forward. The elders would have no choice but to finally acknowledge that Gulzar the Damned was indeed worthy.

"You will be safe with me, little one," he whispered.

She squinted up at him before rubbing her eyes. Her smile was radiant, lighting up her entire face, and it was aimed directly at him. Like she had done for as long as he had known her, his little goddess began speaking, filling the silence with a language he was familiar with but had never mastered. When they were young, he had attempted to teach her his native tongue, but gave up soon after when she could barely pronounce his name.

"Did you know about the Sanctus?" he asked, more to himself than to her. "They were taken from us, stolen away. Very few of us remain who possess the gifts they passed down."

Her big eyes stared up at him. The little female truly was beautiful; her light skin glowed like the sun in the light that filtered down through the trees as they passed beneath. There was a smattering of light brown flecks along her nose and cheeks that reminded him of stars against the dark sky. Her body was soft and rounded, not at all like the females among his tribe. While some were like Ky and Kyra, with lean, slender forms, there were many others who were more muscular with a firm exoskeleton like Gulzar. This female was ethereal, and a sigh fell from his mouth as he moved his ridges to take in her addicting scent once more. She smelled sweeter than the stagorkike root.

Up ahead, just visible in the dim light, was the outline of the standing caves, a grouping of large, porous rocks that provided shelter for many of the hunters who traveled out this far. They could sleep within the hollow center for the night and continue on in the morning. Gulzar set the little goddess on her feet and pointed to the floor.

"Stay here while I fetch you something to eat. Stay. Do not move." She just looked up at him and he sighed, crouching down in front of her so that he was looking up into her face. "Please, do not leave this cave."

Unable to resist, Gulzar nuzzled his face against her rounded stomach, minding his ridges as he rubbed against her soft skin. His tongue slipped out to trail a line from the one side to the other, absorbing her taste. Surprise lit his eyes when her scent shifted, changing from the sweetness he had come to know as distinctly her to a more musky, potent aroma. Was she actually responding to his touch or was this some sort of test? She was looking on with wide eyes, her chest rising and falling as she breathed in and out through her parted lips.

Damned. Shamed.

The voices of the elders floated through his mind, and he cast his eyes downward in humiliation at the memory of the last time he was in the temple with them. He had stood before Una's statue as they proclaimed him fit to live among them; they hadn't ever let him forget that this didn't mean he was forgiven. A small hand stroked his face and he looked up, staring at her quizzically as she mumbled something under her breath. Possessiveness welled up inside him and a growl escaped his throat before he could hold it back.

No. She was not his, and he would not be the death of another female.

"Forgive me," he whispered as he pulled away from her touch, his hands brushing her hips as he stood. "I forgot myself for a moment." He dropped the body of the dead shayfia on the ground at his feet, shaking it from the tip of his tail. "I will make you a fire before I leave."

Gulzar stepped back out into the darkness, searching the trees around him until he found what he was looking for. A large leilei leaf stretched away from the main trunk of the tree, its waxy skin reflecting the light of the moons. Within the cup-shaped top of the leaf, water had gathered, and he carefully funneled it into the waterskin at his side.

He had no idea what the little goddess could eat or drink, but he hoped that they were similar enough that nothing he could provide would harm her. It frustrated and annoyed him that after all this time, he still could not communicate with her.

As he walked back, he rummaged for a few broken branches

and twigs, grabbing some of the dried bark off of the chari tree to help feed the flames. "I brought water—"

He came to a stop in the entrance, his eyes darting around. She was gone.

"Gleck!" Gulzar dropped the materials he'd been holding and spun on his heel. Why would she have left? The woods were dangerous, especially at night. She hadn't even been on the planet for an entire day and this was already the second time she was putting herself in danger. Frustration rolled through him, causing his xines to slither over his shoulders in a frenzy.

Who would have known that one little female could cause so much trouble?

Once he had her back in his arms, he wasn't going to let her leave his sight again. Every terrifying situation she could encounter on her own flitted through his mind and he snarled, following her scent as it disappeared farther into the woods. Tracking her wasn't hard since she seemed to have touched everything she passed.

Not far ahead he caught the sound of frantic footsteps and took off. With the noise, she was making, she was bound to attract something big. A scream rang through the forest and his heart stopped when it went silent again.

"No!"

Gulzar rushed in the direction it had come from, crashing through a tangle of vines before he saw just what had gotten her.

A sionaea was tipped upward, its petals closing around the goddess's kicking legs. The massive carnivorous plant struggled to keep her contained, but she was putting up quite the fight. A growl tore from his throat as he lunged forward, wrapping his hands around the thick brown stem and pulling up, yanking the knotted roots from the ground. The flower released her immediately, letting loose a sharp screech as it twitched, its green lifeblood oozing over his hands and down his arms. When it went still, he tossed the wilted plant as far as he could and turned to the female as she sat crying and trembling on the floor of the woods.

"Do you have no sense of self-preservation?" He crouched down to check her for injuries.

There was a long cut near her ankle from where one of the plant's teeth must have nicked her, but aside from that and being covered from head to toe in the sticky golden nectar, she seemed to be fine.

"Are you testing me? Is that why you did something so incredibly reckless?"

She flinched when he reached for her and he sighed, sitting back on his haunches before closing his eyes.

"You have no idea what you mean to me," he whispered. "I would give my life for yours without question, and yet you ..." When Gulzar opened his eyes, he saw that she had stopped crying and was looking at him curiously.

He held his arms open and sent up a thankful prayer when the little goddess crawled over the ground, tucking herself into his embrace before mumbling something he didn't understand against his chest. Gulzar lifted her up and stood, turning back in the direction of the shelter where he had left her.

When he set her down inside the cave, his little goddess pressed her back against the wall and watched him with large, teary eyes as he gathered the wood he had dropped on the ground. She was quiet as he stacked the wood and nurtured the tiny spark he created from his flint, feeding it the dried bark so that it grew larger and hotter.

Her lower lip trembled like she was going to cry again, but he didn't think his heart could take anymore of her tears tonight. Thinking back on how Kyra used to console him as a young one, Gulzar sat down beside her and began to stroke her hair, running his fingers through the dark strands. She froze like prey beneath him, her eyes growing wider as her body tensed.

Well, that wasn't how he had expected it to go. Forcing air over the ridges inside of his crest, Gulzar did his best to imitate the rattling sound he had heard the crested males in his tribe use to soothe their mates or young.

He dropped his hand to the waterskin at his side, bringing it up between them before offering it to her. At first, she shook her head, refusing to take the skin from him. He brought the opening of it to his mouth and took a drink of the cool liquid to show her she had nothing to fear. The second time he held it out to her, she snatched it from his hands immediately and began to guzzle from it like she hadn't had anything to drink for days.

"Slowly," he chided when she started to cough. "You will drown yourself and I will have saved you for nothing." A soft pat on her back seemed to help calm the fit. "If you are this thirsty, you must also be hungry."

She watched him closely as he began to clean the carcass of the shayfia, laying out the hide and cutting out the best parts to cook for her. The process was just as natural to him as breathing at this point.

Gulzar hunted and lived in the woods far more than he did within the village, avoiding the painful glares and sharp tongues. Most of the females hurried away, shooing their young out of his path. Out here among the trees and animals, Gulzar was alone.

The strips of meat sizzled over the flames, cooking quickly, and he pulled them off, laying them on a section of dried bark before handing them to the goddess. He popped one into his own mouth, chewing the tender meat to show her once again that it would be safe. She needed little reassurance this time, stuffing two of the strips into her mouth and humming in pleasure. She ate zealously, even accepting the ones he had taken for himself when he placed them on her bark.

As her belly filled, the little goddess relaxed and her eyes began to close. He watched as she sank to the floor of the cave, her arm curling beneath her head as her breathing evened out.

A tickle of awareness brushed against his mind and he rattled quietly, placing his palm against her stomach, feeling the answering mental hum of the young within her. His heart ached at the knowledge that he would never have this experience for himself. The only females within his village who spoke to him were Kyra and Ky, and he wasn't going to be mating with either of them. Even if he were to find a female who didn't care about his status within the village, he would never feel comfortable risking her life to reproduce.

The little life within her thrilled when he pushed another rattle through his crest and a small vibration moved against his hand. Choking back the emotions that coursed through him, Gulzar pressed his face against her belly like he had earlier, but this time he felt the gentle ripple of movement.

Two small hands landed on his shoulders, stilling when the little one moved once more. His little goddess gasped, jolting upright. When he looked up into her face, he saw the shock that registered in her eyes as she stared down at him. Perhaps she hadn't been aware of the pregnancy.

No matter. He would protect them both for as long as he was able. Her fingers played over his xines in an almost affectionate manner, reaching to cup the back of his head and bring him closer with the next flutter. For a moment, he could almost imagine this was his life, that his little goddess was actually his, that they had created this life within her.

This will never belong to you. You are unworthy. You are damned.

Gulzar closed his eyes, banishing the voices as he let her touch soothe him. For this one night, he would allow himself to dream, to pretend that this was his, and he would cherish every second.

~

*G*ulzar caught the little goddess by the arm, saving her for what felt like the hundredth time since they had started off on their trek. The sun was still low in the sky, but they had already made many stops. She seemed to be completely oblivious to all of the dangers hidden within the woods around her, and he was certain he had already lost solars off of his life just trying to make sure she didn't get herself killed. Like Ky had the day she went out on the hunt with him, the little female made enough noise to alert anything within earshot that they were there.

"Sare, sare. Aye doont meen taoo bee ah bhurdin," she told him, brushing her hair away from her face.

He wished that he had been blessed by the goddess so that he could communicate and understand her, but that was a privilege he would never be allowed. Gulzar ran a clawed finger over her chin before scooping her up into his arms.

"We will travel much faster this way."

The female kept her eyes affixed to his face like she was mapping all of his features. It made him uncomfortable. No one but her had ever paid him so much attention in his entire life. With her safely clutched against his chest, Gulzar moved quickly over the uneven ground, dodging large rocks and fallen trees, avoiding problem areas where predators liked to converge. He glanced down at her to find her still watching him, but now her brows were drawn together in what seemed to be concentration. Perhaps there was something wrong with his face. Shifting her weight, he freed one hand, pressing it against his chest.

"I am called Gulzar." He indicated himself. "Gul-zar."

"Nkoul-zar," she tried, failing to produce the guttural sound at the beginning of his name just as she had all those solars before.

"Guul-zar," he repeated, drawing out the syllables as clearly as he could.

"Knoul-zar." A rumbling laugh vibrated through his chest. He continued on, watching as a female feondour and her young scurried out of his path. The long barbs that covered her back ran along the ground behind her as she led the younglings into the thick undergrowth and out of sight.

"Zar?"

The sound of the old name caused him to stumble. He had been sure she had forgotten about it, but he saw the recognition light her face.

"Yes, little goddess."

"Yew... yew arr Zar." Her mouth dropped open as she stared at him. "Holi fhuk."

He wasn't sure what "holi fhuk" meant, but he caught his name and nodded. "Yes. I am Zar and you are my little goddess."

Tears welled up in her eyes as her hands framed his face before she threw her arms around him. His entire life he had wished for this, to be able to actually hold her outside of a dream.

"Ahmaenduh." She pulled back and moved her hand to a spot just above her breasts.

"Ahmaenduh," Gulzar grinned with pride at his pronunciation, but her brows drew down and she shook her head, repeating herself.

Pursing his lips, he tried once more, watching her mouth as she spoke her name and mimicking as best as he could. After a few attempts, however, she giggled and shook her head in the same way she had done when they were young, waving her hand as if to say he should give up. Gulzar forced a rattle through his crest and pressed his hand to her chest as he said, "Mikri thea." It was an old term in a language they rarely used anymore that meant "little goddess," and it had become his name for her.

Her slender hand came up to cover his where it rested against her skin, and she gave him the sweetest smile. "Mikri thea."

Something brushed against the edges of his mind just as she

flinched, moving her hand down to rub over her abdomen. The youngling was awake and vying for attention. Gulzar rattled again, sending a mental caress along the link that had already formed between them.

It fascinated him, this bond that he felt with a being that he had no part in creating, who he had only just met. No one in his tribe, not even the ones he counted as his friends, had reached out to him in this way. To have someone so innocent and pure initiate a mental link this strong humbled him in a way nothing else ever would.

They didn't get very far before it was obvious that she was in distress. She wiggled free from his arms, stumbling over to a small tree before emptying her stomach. He rubbed her back as she bent over, his other hand holding her hair out of the way as she gagged. Maybe the meal hadn't agreed with her.

When she turned back to him, her complexion looked pale and waxy as she wiped at her mouth. Anxiety shot through him as her legs gave out and she fell to the ground. Something wasn't right. He gathered her up, ignoring her weak protests. She needed a healer, but he wasn't convinced she had it in her to make it the rest of the way to the village. His fingertips brushed along her cheek.

He would find shelter and allow her to rest. Tomorrow, they could try again.

CHAPTER 19

AMANDA

a gentle hand squeezed her shoulder, trying to wake her, but she grumbled against the massive body in front of her. This didn't feel like Oshen, but she felt the pull all the same and snuggled closer, burrowing back into her dream.

There, she felt little hands clutch at her fingers and heard the gurgles of the newborn in her arms. The dream flashed to the excitement of chasing little feet through a home full of love and laughter; of feeling like she would go crazy from the amount of chaos to feeling as if her heart would burst with affection.

The hand shook her again, and this time, she managed to pry her eyes open. The hard mauve plates of Zar's chest filled her vision and she frowned.

"Gynaika."

Amanda's head snapped back as the familiar voice whispered close to her ear and she turned to see the soft golden glow of her mate's eyes. "Oshen! You're all right!"

"Shh." He nodded toward Zar, who still slept next to her.

"Let's get you out of here before he wakes up." His hands slid beneath her, helping her to her feet. "Come."

Oshen took her hand, leading her to the entrance to the cave Zar had brought her to earlier. "Wait, I have to tell you something." Amanda tried to tug her hand from his grip, but he held fast. "He's not going to hurt me." She could see a sliver of one of the double moons when a terrifying growl filled the cavern.

She spun around, watching as Zar got to his feet, all four violet eyes focused on Oshen as he stepped in front of her, blocking her view. Zar's grumbly language rolled over her and she tried to duck around the massive Venium male. There was a softness in his eyes when he looked at her and he let loose one of those magical purrs that never failed to calm her racing heart. She had found it made her uneasy at first, but what could one expect from a noise that was half-alligator mating call, half-tyrannosaurus rex growl?

"Run, Amanda," Oshen told her, pushing her toward the entrance of the cave. "Stay away from my mate, Grutex." He growled, his fushori pulsing brightly.

Zar stepped closer, towering over both of them as Amanda tried to get around Oshen's tail. This was ridiculous. They were going to hurt each other over a simple misunderstanding because one of them couldn't understand her and the other wasn't listening to her.

Just as the males reached one another, she managed to slip in between them, her hands pressed to both of their chests as she tried her best to shove them apart. Unsurprisingly, neither one budged at all.

"This is insane! Stop it, right now!"

Oshen frowned at her hand on Zar's chest, and she turned to look up into the violet eyes of the other male. He was watching her hand too, and when she looked down, she gasped at what she saw. The plates were glowing, radiating a violet sheen beneath her palm that rippled over his mauve exoskeleton. This hadn't happened any of the other times they had touched.

"Zar? What is that?"

"Zar?" Oshen growled, narrowing his eyes on the male. His tail wrapped around her thigh as his arms snaked around her torso and he lifted her up against him. "This is the male who you dreamed of? The one who frightened you?"

"He saved me, Oshen." Amanda ran the tip of her finger over his cheek, touching a small cut on his skin before pressing a soft kiss to his chest. "He's been my friend for a long time. He isn't going to hurt me." A wave of nausea overcame her and she pushed frantically at his arms until he released her. She barely made it to one of the small bushes outside before the bile rose up her throat. Oshen's hands swept her hair up, and she felt Zar's hand soothe down her back. The sickness began to recede as Zar's purr rolled through her, and she scrubbed her hands over her face.

"My heart," Oshen murmured, stroking her arm with a clawed finger. "Tell me what's wrong."

"It's going to sound crazy, but I think I might be pregnant." Her voice caught and she let out a shuddering sigh, resting her head against Oshen's arm exhaustedly. Amanda didn't realize just how much she had missed him. Having Oshen and Zar with her made her feel strangely whole and secure. "It's only been a week so this shouldn't even be possible, and it's not like there was anyone before that. Not lately, anyway." Zar crouched down next to her and she smiled when he twisted a lock of her hair around his finger. "It's crazy, I know it is, but I've been sick. I thought it might be a concussion from the crash, but I…" Amanda frowned, placing her hand over the small bump that seemed to have grown even more within the last day.

"What is it?" Oshen nuzzled his face into her hair. "What happened?"

"I felt something move," she whispered, tears filling her eyes as she looked up at her mate. "What if I have a parasite?"

Oshen placed his hand over hers, caressing her belly as his fushori pulsed gently. "Pregnancy isn't impossible," he said, his tail curling around her calf. "We were in the cryochambers for five weeks longer than we had anticipated."

"Five weeks? I thought we were going to make it here in one. And where's Hades?"

"There were complications and Vog did what he needed to do in order to get us here safely." When Amanda raised her brow, he smiled. "Well, as safe as he could manage. He said he was able to get Hades to the surface, but we aren't sure where he went."

Her poor Hades, lost somewhere on the planet all alone. She hoped he wasn't nearly as inept as she apparently was. "What sort of complications?"

Before Oshen could answer, Zar growled, his eyes narrowing on a spot somewhere within the woods in front of them. She saw them then, the six red eyes watching them from a distance. He had followed her here.

"It is not safe here. My plan didn't work," Oshen said, and although she was sure Zar couldn't understand the words, he seemed to agree, taking her hand and tugging her back. "Does he have a village?" Oshen asked, nodding toward Zar as he took hold of her other hand.

She shrugged, looking up at Zar, who was busy scanning everything around them. "I'm not sure, but we were traveling somewhere yesterday when I got sick and he stopped here to let me rest. Wait, what plan?"

"It doesn't matter. Vog went for reinforcements, but I think it might be best to follow Zar for now. With both of us with you, I doubt our friend out there will be brave enough to try anything stupid."

Amanda turned back to where the eyes had peered out at her

and shuddered, clutching the hands of the males on either side of her tightly. "Okay."

They walked for what seemed like hours in silence, giving Amanda time to obsess over everything Oshen had said. Someone had followed the ship, had complicated things so much that they had spent an extra five weeks in space traveling here. After seeing the eyes in the darkness, there was no doubt in her mind that it was the Grutex from Earth. What was it about her that he could possibly want so badly? She wasn't special, wasn't what many would consider beautiful, but this Grutex had stalked her from one planet to another. And what about the fact that Oshen believed she was pregnant? Her hand drifted down to her stomach as she turned her head to watch him in the growing light of the morning sun.

"How did you find me anyways?"

"I used the tracker on your cryochamber and then followed your scent from there. It was only by luck that it did not rain." He pushed a branch out of her way so she could walk past it.

"Oshen?" His gaze found hers and her heart leapt. "What you said about the pregnancy earlier... do you really think it's possible?"

"I believe so."

"It's just that humans aren't able to feel their babies move this early." Even as she spoke the words, Amanda felt a small flutter beneath her hand and stopped in her tracks. "See? Feel!" She grabbed Oshen's hand, placing it on her stomach as the flutters became stronger.

"Gynaika..." he said, dropping to his knees in front of her, a grin stretching across his face as the movement continued.

"Oshen, this isn't normal!"

"Perhaps not, but for Venium females this is appropriate." When she arched a brow at the remark he laughed. "I've witnessed twelve of my dam's pregnancies and births. This is nothing new to me. An average pregnancy lasts four months, give or take a few days. I've never known any Venium to mate outside of our species so I couldn't tell you how this might differ, but assuming you progress like my dam, you are nearly halfway through."

Halfway through her pregnancy and she was just finding out. Amanda took a deep breath as her nerves made her queasy again, but before it could get worse, she heard the low rattle, felt it flow through her as her body settled. Her eyes met Zar's and he tilted his head to the side, watching the interaction intently. He must have known the whole time. All those moments when he had pressed his face against her belly or touched it, he had been telling her in his own way.

Amanda covered her face with her hands and groaned. "Zar must think I'm the worst soon-to-be-mother ever."

"What?" Oshen frowned, his gaze shifting between her and the other male. "Why would he think that?"

"I put myself in danger so many times here and he's had to come to my rescue more than once. He must think I'm horrible." Tears fell down her cheeks, and she felt Oshen stand and pull her into his chest.

"I'm sure he doesn't think you are horrible."

A soft brush against her hip had her turning to see Zar crouched down at her side, his eyes fixed on her tear-stained face. "Mikri thea." He used a knuckle to wipe away her tears. She didn't understand what he said after that, but the way he looked at her made her heart race.

A war raged within Amanda between her heart and her mind. One told her that being here with both of them was right, while the other told her she was only inviting trouble. Amanda rested her head on Oshen's chest as she let her fingers trail over Zar's face, watching the play of violet light shimmer in its wake.

She could hear Jun's voice in her head as she stood there

161

between them, feeling safe and secure even with a deranged alien stalking them.

"So, what? You feel the same way about both of these aliens? Are they both made for you?"

When they held her like this, it sure felt that way.

CHAPTER 20

AMANDA

*T*he rest of the journey through the woods had been uneventful so far, with no other sightings of her alien stalker. It seemed like the presence of both her males had given the Grutex second thoughts.

Both of my males? Why did her conscience sound so much like Jun?

She grimaced to herself and shifted in Zar's arms so she could look over her shoulder at Oshen as he walked beside them. Both males were on constant alert, scanning the trees that surrounded them. Her mate's face was drawn into a frown and had been ever since she decided to let Zar carry her.

"I'm more than capable of carrying my mate." He grumbled, narrowing his golden eyes on Zar.

"I never said you weren't." Amanda sighed, pinching the bridge of her nose. *"But you've been in an accident."*

"I was not injured," he protested.

"I don't want to argue with you about this, Oshen." She pulled his head down to hers, pressing her lips against his. *"Let Zar help."* Oshen's jaw clenched, the muscle ticking before he nodded.

"Are you upset with me?" she asked.

"Why would you think that?" He turned to her, his frown deepening. When Amanda nodded toward Zar, Oshen sighed. "I won't tell you I wouldn't feel better holding you myself, but I am not upset by your decision."

"Your face says otherwise."

She frowned dramatically, making him smile and shake his head. "I am thinking."

"Oshen? Thank you for coming after me." She extended her hand toward him and he reached out for it, pressing a kiss to her palm before releasing it.

"Gynaika, you are the most important thing in my life. Nothing in the universe could stop me from finding you."

The little one in her belly fluttered gently and she smiled. The sickness that had been plaguing her off and on had been absent since the three of them had started their journey and she was thankful to be feeling more like herself. She wasn't sure how Zar's vibrations were able to do it, but she wished she could bottle it up for all of the women on Earth who suffered through months of nausea. She looked at him from the corner of her eye and smiled when he glanced down at her stomach and vibrated.

The flutters within her increased, and she rubbed her hand over her bump. Sometimes it seemed like Zar was communicating with the baby, soothing him or her with the sounds he made. The baby responded the same when Oshen put his hand on her belly and the thought that the little one reacted to both of them in such a way made her heart clench with emotion. She wished Oshen had been there for the first movements, but she was happy to share these moments with him now.

A massive gate made of stacked stone came into view, beautiful and intimidating with its high walls. It was the first unnatural structure she had seen on Venora, and it left her speechless. The sounds of people conversing, yelling, and talking grew louder as they approached the entrance, and she felt Zar's arms tighten around her. He slowed to a stop and set her down on her feet before he turned to Oshen, speaking softly.

"Do you know what he's saying?" she asked.

Oshen shook his head. "I don't, but Mouni is working on it. Some of the words sound familiar, but I don't know if they have similar meanings."

A commotion up ahead caught her attention and she squinted to see what was going on. A call went up, and the sounds of heavy footsteps filled her ears as Oshen and Zar both tensed. "What's going on?"

"Stay calm," Oshen told her quietly, taking her hand.

"Oshen..." People began rushing forward. Some of them looked similar to the Grutex, like Zar, while others had what seemed like Venium features. "What the hell is going on here?"

"They're hybrids," Oshen murmured, looking just as shocked as she felt.

A male at the front of the crowd shouted something at Zar before spitting at his feet. Oshen growled low in his throat, but Zar only looked away. A shout came from the back, silencing the group that had gathered around them as three large males who favored the Grutex pushed their way through. The one in the lead had a rainbow hue to his exoskeleton that she hadn't seen before. It shimmered in the sunlight, almost looking like it was dancing across his body. He spoke in clipped tones that spoke of his displeasure with whatever situation they had found themselves in.

Beside her, Zar shook his head, replying quietly. From somewhere deep in the crowd, a rock was thrown, barely missing Zar's head.

"Hey!" Amanda yelled, stepping forward. No one was going to treat either of her guys that way. "That was rude!" Before she could think twice about her decision, rainbow guy grabbed her around the waist. She struggled in his grasp as he hauled her up against his chest. "Put me down!"

"Wait!" Oshen stepped forward, hands spread in an attempt to show he meant them no harm. "Be easy with her." He turned to Zar, who was watching the other male with deadly focus. "Tell them, Zar."

But there was no time to react. Both Oshen and Zar were attacked from behind and wrestled to the ground, their faces pushed into the dirt as Amanda screamed.

"No, no! Stop! Please, don't hurt them!" She struggled against his iron grip, kicking and twisting.

"Stop, gynaika," Oshen ground out. "Do not give them a reason to harm you."

Tears ran down her cheeks as she watched one of them press his foot against Zar's neck. "Please stop! They've done nothing." She turned her head to look up at the face of the male who held her. "What is wrong with you?"

"Mikri thea," Zar whispered, his labored breathing disturbing the dirt beneath his cheek.

There was an audible gasp from the mob when she twisted in the rainbow male's arms and slapped him across the face. When she raised her hand to do it again, he caught it, muttering something under his breath before he placed her on her feet. If she would have known all it took to be freed was a slap, she would have done it sooner.

When she tried to run to her males, the crowd began to shout. The ones guarding Zar and Oshen stepped into her path. "You can't do this to them!"

"We are all right, gynaika. Stay where you are."

"I don't know what to do, Oshen." She dropped to her knees in front of them, reaching to brush her fingers over her mate's cheek despite the murmurs of the guards at his side. When she extended her hand toward Zar, the reaction was far more explosive. The males around him growled, dragging his body farther away. Zar shook his head frantically in a silent warning when she tried to follow.

Amanda pressed her hand to her stomach as the baby within her stirred, rolling and kicking gently. The low, familiar rattle filled the air and the little one moved excitedly in response until it was abruptly cut off when one of the males slammed his foot down on Zar's head.

She swallowed a strangled cry. "Stop that!"

Murmurs rippled through the crowd as the sounds of distant screams and shouts drew closer. Amanda turned to see two more aliens racing toward them, their skirts clutched in one hand as they waved their other ones frantically. They looked a lot like the Venium females she had seen pictures of aboard the mothership but seemed broader at the shoulders, with the vine-like tendrils of the Grutex coming from their heads. Both had matching aqua-colored eyes and glowing fushoris that trailed over their nearly transparent white skin.

The rainbow male who had grabbed her tried to stop them, but they spoke to him in angry tones before dropping down in front of Zar, touching his wounds and fussing over him. When he spoke to them, the smaller female glanced over at her curiously, her head tilting as she responded to whatever Zar had said. Amanda felt an irrational surge of jealousy at their intimacy.

Was this female his mate? Was this why the others were so angry with him?

The other female turned back to the male who stood behind them, speaking quickly. Amanda wasn't sure what was being discussed, but she had a feeling it was about her with the way they all began gesturing in her direction, their voices raising until they were practically yelling. The smaller female, the one who had been watching her, came between them, speaking calmly, bringing some sense of order to the madness that had erupted.

She offered her hand to Amanda with a smile. When Zar nodded, Amanda sighed and stood but didn't accept the help. None of this was making any sense.

"What do you think they want?" she asked Oshen, taking a step back.

"It seems like Zar trusts her."

The female stepped closer, grabbing her hand and tugging her forward. "Wait, I don't want to leave you two!"

"Go, Amanda. We will be fine." Oshen smiled, his eyes softening as he watched her. "Be safe, my heart."

The two women pulled her away, sneering and scolding anyone in the crowd who came too close. She was hurried through streets that were lined with curious faces, but her breath caught when she saw the architecture of the buildings they were passing. High arching columns framed entrances into what looked like small courtyards, while statues of alien deities supported the roofs of some of the homes. It reminded her a little of the summer she had spent in Greece visiting the ancient ruins in Athens and Delphi.

Sitting in the middle of one of the open spaces in the town was a massive statue of three people. One of them was clearly a Venium male, and the other seemed to be a Grutex. Both were entwined around an alien female of a species she hadn't ever seen before. She looked ethereal and was humanoid in form, with what seemed to be feathers along the sides of her body and on her head. Two massive hooked horns with three ridges along the base arched above her head, with two small elven ears just below.

Amanda's steps faltered as she tried to take in the beauty

around her; everywhere she looked was something new and wonderful. High up on one of the hills was a building with large pillars and aged stone steps. It looked just like the photos in museums showing people what the ancient Greek buildings looked like in their prime. It was like she had traveled back in time with an alien twist.

Instead of heading up the hill, the females steered her toward a gated entrance to an incredibly modern-looking home. A small courtyard with a pretty little fountain in the center greeted her as she stepped through the modest archway. The home itself was constructed from light grey stone and the beautiful black wood from the twisting trees she had seen in the forest. It was large, stretching the length of the courtyard and beyond, with a second story that looked out over the entry.

She was shocked to see advanced technology throughout the structure. Zar hadn't had anything on him that would have hinted at this level of tech.

"Kythea," the younger female smiled, placing a hand on her chest before gesturing to the older woman. "Kyra." She then held her hand out to Amanda, pressing it against her chest with an expectant look. They wanted her name.

"Amanda."

Kythea's lips twitched as she moved further into the home, stopping outside of a small room with a large tub. Amanda gasped. *They have plumbing too!* She didn't need to be able to understand the language to know what they were offering. Traveling through the forest had left her feeling grimy and dirty.

There was no shower, at least not anything she recognized as one, but there was a giant tub, and she nearly danced in delight at the thought of sinking down into hot water. A giggle had her gaze swiveling in Kythea's direction. The female grabbed what looked like a glass bottle of soap from one of the wall nooks, handing it to her along with something that resembled a giant cotton ball. She had no idea what it was for, but she accepted it.

Kyra walked into the room with a dress that was absolutely stunning, similar in fashion to a chiton worn by the ancient Greeks. Gold clasps were attached to the straps that held the white fabric together, a belt of the same color hung over the material, and what looked like a long white himation with sky blue tips laid just under the belt.

Amanda reached out to run her fingers over the material, but the dirt on her hands had her pulling back. It would be a shame to dirty something so beautiful. "Umm, I think I should probably bathe first." She gestured toward the tub. "A bath?"

Kyra nodded, draping the dress over the back of a small wooden chair near the doorway before she guided Amanda across the room. The woman ran her hand along a knob on the wall, and a second later water was pouring out of a wide mouthed faucet, filling the bottom of the basin.

An excited gasp burst from Amanda's lips as she dropped the soap and fluff so she could tear at her soiled clothing. She hadn't ever really been the modest type and she wasn't about to worry what this woman thought of her now. Kyra laughed, bending to grab the discarded clothing.

"Oh, you don't have to worry about those. I can take care of them after I clean up if you just show me where they should go." But the older woman waved her off, bundling the clothing in her arms. "Thank you, really. I appreciate this." Amanda laughed to herself. "Not that you can understand a word I'm saying."

The moment her foot sank into the water, Amanda moaned, lowering her body into the warmth, feeling her muscles begin to relax as the tub filled around her. It had only been a couple of days since she had woken up, but in reality, she hadn't bathed in weeks.

When the water reached her chest, Amanda turned to ask

Kyra how to turn it off, but the woman had left the room at some point without her even realizing it. *Well, hell.* She ran her hand along the knob, but instead of slowing the stream, the water gushed faster out of the faucet.

"Shit!" Everything she touched only seemed to make it worse and soon the water was lapping at the edges and splashing onto the floor. "No! Stop coming out faster! I want you to *stop*! Turn off, damn it!"

With a final hard twist of the knob, the water cut off. Amanda sighed and dared a peek at the floor. *Oops.* She'd clean it up when she was finished. If she could figure out where anything was in this place.

By the time she was through washing her hair and body, it looked like she was sitting in a pool of gray liquid. *Eww.* She wrung her hair out and climbed out of the tub. The moment her feet touched the floor, the water began to disappear, both on the ground and inside the bathtub.

"Heh, nifty trick."

She picked up the fluff that Kythea had given her and stared at it, wondering how she was expected to dry off with whatever it was. As soon as it touched her skin though, it soaked up every bit of water.

"Holy hell," she whispered as she pulled the material all over her body, drying in mere moments. She wondered if the Venium used these as well.

When she was finished, Amanda picked up the pretty white dress, rubbing it between her fingers. The material seemed so delicate and was cool to the touch. They hadn't given her any undergarments. *Looks like we're going commando*, she thought with a shrug and pulled the dress over her head.

A soft knock on the door was the only warning she had before Kyra and Kythea stepped inside. The older woman smiled, running her hands over Amanda's shoulders. The younger one,

Kythea, took the gold belt from the chair and helped fasten it around her, just below her breasts. When she was dressed to their liking, the women sat her down in another chair in front of a long mirror and fussed over her hair, twirling it up on top of her head.

She hardly recognized the person she saw in the mirror, but gods, did she look pretty. She wished Oshen and Zar were here to see her. Before she could focus too much on the fact that she was missing both males, Kythea came back in with something clutched in her hand. Amanda wasn't sure what she said as she held up the thin gold chain, but she seemed excited. Hanging from the chain was a small glowing violet stone. It flashed in the light, and Amanda couldn't resist the urge to run a finger over it.

"How pretty."

Kythea nodded and fastened the chain into her hair so that the stone sat lightly against her forehead. She'd never been a fan of head jewelry, but the stone reminded her of Zar's expressive eyes. The women talked to each other, and although she still wasn't sure what they said, she swore she caught a word or two of English mixed in.

"This is all... so, so pretty. Thank you." She turned to Kyra. "Will Zar and Oshen be allowed to come here soon?"

Kyra and Kythea shared a look, one that made her feel like she wouldn't like whatever answer they had to offer. Instead of replying, the two of them turned and headed for the door, gesturing for her to join them. They brought her to a comfortably furnished bedroom, showing her a closet full of more gorgeous dresses and pretty footwear.

This ended up being the room she would call her own for the next couple of days. Each morning, Kyra or Kythea came to wake her and brought an assortment of food for her to try. Anytime she started asking about Zar or Oshen, the women did their best to distract her with something new and unfamiliar. Each day she was there, she noticed that she recognized more and more of their words and that Kyra and Kythea had an easier time communicating with her.

Still, the only thing she wanted was to know that her males were safe, but she wasn't sure she was going to get answers anytime soon.

CHAPTER 21

OSHEN

Zar, Amanda's childhood friend, was real.

Oshen couldn't say he was surprised, but he had never imagined that the male lived on his home planet along with an entire village of hybrids. He had watched the way they interacted, taking it all in and realizing he would never be able to replicate what they had built over the solars. They couldn't even communicate with one another yet Zar seemed to be attuned to Amanda's every need.

He watched as the females tugged his mate away from him, disappearing into the crowd. Their faces were a mix of Venium, Grutex, and Sanctus features. It couldn't be possible for these people to exist here without the Venium government knowing, but why would they keep this a secret, and who exactly was privy to the information?

Did his sire know? As one of the highest-ranking ambassadors on Venora, surely he must have known something. The male who had been holding him down yanked him to his feet, mumbling something to the male on his other side.

"Mouni, have you figured out what language they're speaking?"

"It is not currently within my language database." Heads turned toward him curiously as she spoke. "It will require more time for me to search the archives. Please check back later when you are prepared to offer more samples, Meatface."

The large male with the Sanctus-hued exoskeleton stepped forward, taking Oshen's arm and examining it with something akin to reverence on his face. He was sure this was a leader of some sort, perhaps a council head or even a chief.

"Have you seen an AI before?" Oshen asked as the male ran a finger over the skin of his wrist.

Zar hadn't used one during their travel, but he had no way of knowing if they were familiar with them or not. Before he knew what was happening, a cloth had been placed over his eyes and he was being led away. He heard Zar growl something, but it was swallowed up in the commotion.

Stay calm, he told himself. *Remember all of that training you went through. Solars of studying for moments just like this.*

When the cloth was ripped away, he found himself standing within a small, dimly lit cell. He turned just in time to watch the male slam the door in his face.

So much for diplomacy.

Oshen made himself comfortable on the floor, propping his back against the wall as he tipped his head to stare up at the ceiling. This wasn't at all how he had imagined it would go. At least it seemed like his mate would be safe here. His heart thudded within his chest when he thought of her and he squeezed his eyes shut. He was going to be a sire. The news barely had time to sink in before she was taken away from them, but he took a moment to digest it now, alone in the silence with his thoughts.

They were going to be parents. They were going to bring a tiny life into this world, and he was going to do all he could to make sure that world was safe.

CHAPTER 22

GULZAR

The sound of the whip snapping as it bit into his back made Gulzar flinch. His lifeblood began to drip down his back as a ringing filled his ears. He had done nothing wrong, but this wasn't the first time he was being punished because he had angered the elders. Another crack rang out before he felt the sting.

"You dared to touch the goddess!" one of the elders hissed.

"I did it to keep her safe," he ground out.

Another crack of the whip.

"You are damned! You are not permitted to touch her!"

An image of his little goddess filled his mind and he focused on her, blocking out the pain as the whip lashed at him again. She had felt so right curled up in his arms, her head resting against his chest as she trailed her fingers over his plates. He had broken tribe law, but every moment spent with her was worth it.

"I saved her life," he said again.

"You know your status! To touch her was a violation!"

another elder shouted.

"Did you believe you could turn her against us?" someone asked from his right.

"No." A grunt was pulled from him as the tip of the whip struck him again.

There was no doubt that he would be adding to his collection of scars today.

"And to bring a wayward offspring of Ven into our village ... did you think this would turn her away from us?"

Years of whippings had taught him to hold his tongue, but they always broke him eventually. Gulzar couldn't even communicate with his female. How did they think he was going to manipulate her feelings about them? If he could have spoken to her on his own, he may not have ever returned to the village at all. Not even for Una's blessing.

"You will keep your distance from Kyra's home or you will be placed in the cells with the son of Ven." Disgust laced the voice of the elder. "Guards will be posted there to ensure you do not attempt to make off with her."

He heard the shuffling of their feet as they walked away, leaving him bloodied and in pain. They had done this knowing he wouldn't be able to seek out Kyra, knowing that he would have to wait and heal on his own with nowhere to go. Gulzar laid his head on the large whipping stone and closed his eyes, letting the warmth of the sun heat his body.

"My friend, wake up."

Gulzar's eyes snapped open and he looked into the face of Trakseer, his chief. The male laid a familiar hand on his shoulder and smiled.

"You fell asleep."

The sun had already set, but the moons were still low in the sky.

"I was whipped for aiding the goddess," Gulzar sneered.

Trakseer pushed to his feet with a sigh. "I cannot change what the elders proclaimed at your birth. I myself wish you no harm, but the elders are beyond even my control. I am not your enemy, Gulzar."

"Gulzar the Damned," he snarled.

"Yes, but you must know I do not see you that way?"

"You ordered her taken from us. You had the guards detain us even though we had not threatened you."

"I only did that for your sake! Can you imagine what they would have done if I had not intervened?" Trakseer threw his hands up in exasperation, as if *he* were the one who should be pitied. "Do you know why she has come?"

Gulzar narrowed his eyes as he sat up. "Ask her yourself."

"I had a vision once of a goddess coming to our village. Do you remember?" Trakseer turned excited eyes his way. "This must be the reason you brought her here."

"She carries another male's young. The goddess is obviously not meant for you."

Trakseer waved his hand dismissively. "The goddess brings with her fertility. I will claim the goddess and her young and perhaps the sire will be our third. We will form a sacred triad."

"I believe you think too highly of yourself, *friend*," Gulzar hissed between clenched teeth.

He wasn't going to tell Trakseer that he had responded to her touch, that she and the male he presumed to be her mate already had a third.

The chief's smile faltered. "You are forgetting your place and who I am." He made a show of brushing off his clean tunic. "I am the chieftain, and if I want someone for my mate, I take them."

"You may be chief, but you do not have the power to proclaim yourself mated to anyone you please, much less a goddess. Only Una may decide, and since you did not light beneath her touch, you must seek her blessing."

179

"I have not lit *yet*." The way he smiled made Gulzar's plates crawl. "However, I plan to bring her to the temple to seek Una's blessing as soon as possible." When Gulzar growled, Trakseer snarled. "Perhaps you have forgotten that your status prohibits you from bonding to any female. That includes the goddess."

"I have not forgotten. I will never forget." Gulzar held back the rage that threatened to consume him. "But it seems you have forgotten the son of Ven who accompanied her. He is her mate."

"If that is true then the *wayward* offspring of Ven will complete our triad." The male stood proudly as if he had the answers to all of his problems. "We have him in confinement until I can secure my part of the mating."

"Keep deluding yourself," Gulzar said, but he didn't give the chief time to reply.

He pushed himself off of the stone, turning his burning back to his chief. Now that he knew where Oshen was, he needed to get to him and figure out a way to save Amanda. Kyra and Ky would look out for her, but he didn't trust Trakseer or any of the elders.

Before he did that, he needed to see her again.

The elders had told him that guards would be placed outside her home, but the ones he saw there didn't seem to be taking their posts very seriously. The two out front sat together, playing a tossing stone game and laughing, while the one on the side of the house had fallen asleep propped up against the outer wall. He found the old footholds he had carved into the wall as a young male and climbed up and over the wall, dropping quietly into the small garden. Kyra was going to kill him for crushing her plants.

Gulzar followed the instinctual pull to his mate, opening the door to the room she had been given and fighting the urge to laugh when he realized Kyra had put her in his. Perhaps she had finally let herself see that he and Ky were never going to mate. His little goddess was curled up in the middle of his bed, looking

180

much smaller and more defenseless than he remembered. Her face was shrouded in shadow and he stood there for a moment just watching her.

"Little goddess," he whispered as he crouched next to the bed.

"Zar?" she breathed in her sleep, turning her face toward him.

A soft rattle worked its way through his crest as the little youngling inside of her called out to him. "Hello, little one." He placed a hand on her stomach and smiled when he felt the gentle movements in response.

His little goddess looked exhausted, and he knew they had pushed her hard during the journey. Gulzar pressed a gentle kiss to her forehead, breathing her in for a moment, calming his nerves.

"Sleep well," he whispered before ducking out of the room.

Closing the door quietly, Gulzar turned and immediately came face-to-face with Viseer. The older male stood with his arms crossed over his broad chest and Gulzar knew he must have seen him come in.

"You just could not wait for things to settle down, could you?"

"No, I could not." Gulzar felt like a youngling again, getting caught sneaking out of the house, and he tried not to cower. Viseer had been the only sire he had ever known and even when he was stern he was loving. "I needed to see her."

"I know." Viseer nodded.

"Please, do not tell Kyra I came here."

"If you leave while the guards are distracted, I may even refrain from telling Kyra who crushed her favorite herb plants."

Gulzar winced. "I am sorry for that."

"Go now. Be safe."

"Thank you." Gulzar moved through the house, going back the way he had come. He needed to find Oshen and let him know what Trakseer was planning.

CHAPTER 23

OSHEN

The light of the twin moons filtered in through one of the small windows of the room he was being held in. They had come to move him from the cell the day after his arrival, but this wasn't much of an improvement. He was still locked in and they had refused to let him see his mate at all. Mouni seemed to be slowly learning their language, but what he could understand was rough at best.

"Mouni, any progress with the language transference?" Oshen asked as he paced the room. "I need to be able to communicate with them."

"They seem to be using something that combines elements of a human language and one that has been saved in the archive as 'the tongue of the gods.'"

Oshen frowned. "A human language? How would they even have access to that?"

"That is still unclear, Meatface. I am continuing to scan the data."

"Can you connect with the dome, Mouni?"

"Yes."

"I think it is time to see what the status is on our reinforcements." He had waited as long as he could in the hopes that he could convince someone to listen to him, but something told him that he was running out of time. He might not have been able to warn humanity, but he was going to do his best not just for his mate but for the people here who knew nothing of the outside world. "Ping Daya."

"Pinging Daya."

A few soft beeps followed his AI's words before he heard the crackle of the connection and his dam appeared on the screen.

"Oshen? Where have you been? We've all been worried sick." Her face was pinched, and she looked like she hadn't slept in days.

"I'm sorry, Daya. I had no intention of worrying you." Oshen glanced out the small window in the door to make sure no one was listening. "Did Vog make it back safely? He was supposed to send reinforcements as soon as he made it to the dome."

His dam's gaze shifted and she ducked down somewhere dark, speaking in a hushed voice. "We are being monitored, Oshen. The council is refusing to send anyone. We were forbidden from contacting you."

"For what reason?"

"They claimed they are not willing to risk lives for one alien female, nor will they risk the alliance with the Grutex."

"My mate is pregnant, Daya!"

"She's pregnant? Oh…" He saw her smile before her hand flew up to her mouth. "We cannot let them know that yet. They are already talking about an alliance with the Grutex and if they found out about your pup… humans would be taken against their will. Your sire has nearly pulled his hair out trying to talk sense into them."

"They cannot simply take humans. That is a breach of Galactic Law, of the laws *they* made!" Oshen growled, rubbing his hand over his face in frustration. "Una herself forbids this sort of madness."

"The commands of Una no longer seem to matter to them. They have lost faith with everything that has happened. The loss of the triads, the fall in birth rates and matings. Can you really blame them?"

"I have a triad." Oshen's gills flared with the confession. He had spent the last few days trying to come to terms with it himself.

"A triad? With who?"

"I suspect it's the Grutex male who saved Amanda."

"A Grutex male saved her?"

"There is an entire braxing village of hybrids here. Venium, Grutex, even Sanctus seem to have been interbreeding here for generations. I don't know much about them because I've been locked up—"

"Locked up?" A face incredibly similar to his dam's appeared on the screen. Her skin was nearly black and it made the gold of her fushori seem almost metallic in contrast. His older sister, Evafyn, was beautiful and deadlier than anyone he had ever met. "Oh, my poor baby brother!"

"You are only a few months older than me." They had been arguing this for the last thirty-four solars.

"Fear not! I will rescue you, Ambassador." Evafyn's wide grin filled the screen.

"That's enough now," he heard his sire say before he appeared on the screen. "Send us your location. We will gather Luz and Leif and leave immediately before anyone has time to delay us."

"Have they treated you well? Are you feeling all right?" Daya asked, her face pinching in concern.

"They have treated me well enough, I suppose." He looked

down at his hands with a frown. "I cannot seem to retract my claws though."

Daya snorted softly, a grin taking over her lips. "Your sire had the same problem when we were newly mated. He said he felt like a beast in those early days, but this will pass."

Oshen grunted. He could relate to that more than he cared to admit. Every day, he felt as if he was losing more and more of his control. "I will see you soon, Daya."

Oshen felt his shoulders sag in relief as Mouni sent his coordinates. It wouldn't be long now and he would have his mate back in his arms.

CHAPTER 24

AMANDA

"*I*s ready?" Kythea asked in her fractured English as she tilted her head into the doorway of Amanda's room. They were getting better at understanding one another, but she couldn't quite get every word. It seemed like many things just didn't translate well.

With a little nod of confirmation, Amanda picked up the silky wrap that hung over the back of the chair near the bed, pulling it over her shoulders "Your English is coming along really well. You all are far faster than I could ever hope to be."

"Blessing," Kythea said, gesturing at her arm. There was a small mark on the inside of her wrist that reminded Amanda of placement of Oshen's AI. "Listens. Learns."

She wasn't sure what the blessing was exactly, but she was grateful for it all the same. Not being able to communicate with Zar had been frustrating. "Where are we going again? Kyra wasn't really clear."

"Food." She cupped her hands and brought them to her mouth, pretending to chew.

They had been bringing food to her room, but she had struggled to keep anything down. The times she had gone looking for the kitchen to find a snack to settle her stomach, she'd been unable to locate it. She wasn't sure she had ever seen a house without one. Where did the food come from if they weren't making it here? She sighed. It seemed like she was about to find out.

Kyra popped her head in. "O Trakseer mas perminei, Kythea!"

"Yes, mitera." The younger female waved her off, rolling her eyes.

Amanda had figured out that 'mitera' was their word for mother and that Kythea was Kyra's only child. It was something she and Kythea had in common. The incessant tapping of Kyra's foot told Amanda she was in a hurry and that the two of them needed to get moving.

"I'm good! I'm good! All ready to go," Amanda told her, but before she could even make it to the door her stomach began to twist and she threw her hand over her mouth, darting for the bathroom. Both women followed, trailing after her like mother hens as they held her hair and rubbed her back in tandem, murmuring to her as she emptied her stomach.

The longer she was stuck here, the more she missed Oshen, the more she missed Jun, the more she worried about Hades. And the longer she was away from Zar, the sicker she seemed to be getting. She was filled with worries and fears that there might be something wrong with the pregnancy. Her baby was growing far faster than any human child, and she worried that it was putting strain on her already weakened body.

When she had finally finished and cleaned herself up, Amanda allowed Kyra to guide her from her room and into the courtyard, where the older woman's mate, Viseer, was waiting for them. His eyes lit up and he nodded to her before ushering their party through the gate and out into the street. As they walked, they were joined by other families who chatted excitedly with Kyra and Viseer.

The sun was low in the sky, and the dual moons were just starting to rise at the other end of the horizon by the time they made it into what she now knew was the center of the town. The giant statue of the alien deities seemed to glow in the fading light, casting long shadows across the ground in front of it where massive wooden tables had been set out.

Dishes piled high with steaming food lined the tables, and plates sat between pitchers of liquid and baskets of treats that looked similar to bread rolls. Kythea took Amanda's hand and led her to one of the chairs, encouraging her to sit. Everyone around her seemed to have been waiting just for this moment and began filling chairs all around the circular table, vying for spots as close to her as they could get.

Families of all sizes sat clustered together, some with many children while others had only a handful. She noticed that Kythea's parents were the only older couple who seemed to have only had one child. Maybe it was because Oshen's mother had birthed so many, but she found it strange that, in a culture that seemed to revere large families, these two had stopped early on.

"This probably isn't any of my business, but why didn't your parents ever have any more children?" she asked quietly when Kyra and Viseer were called aside.

Kythea's brows pinched together, and it seemed like she was struggling to find the words. "Child, death," she finally got out.

"Her children die?" Amanda puzzled over her words before it dawned on her what they meant. "She lost the other pregnancies?"

Kythea nodded her head. "Curse."

"Cursed?" Amanda shook her head. "Sometimes women just can't carry babies. It isn't anyone's fault." Many women on Earth dealt with miscarriages, her own mother being one of them. It was a horrible and heartbreaking reality, and Amanda felt awful for even bringing it up. "I'm so sorry she went through that."

Kythea waved her apology away. "Trakseer," she whispered, looking over Amanda's shoulder. "Chief."

She turned to see the rainbow male who she had slapped the first day in the village watching her. "That's your chief?" Kythea nodded and they both watched as he stood, weaving his way through those that had gathered. His gaze was predatory and set her on edge.

When he reached her seat, he kneeled on the ground at her side, smiling in a way that made her shudder.

"Come..." He tugged at her hand.

"Go where?" She turned to Kyra, who was watching her chief with pursed lips.

"Come." He took her hand, pulling her after him.

"Wait!" She struggled to keep up, but he didn't slow down. "Are we going to see my mate?" No answer. "Oshen? Zar?"

He glanced back at her with a frown and shook his head. Well, shit. She didn't trust this guy as far as she could throw him. When she dug in her heels, he scooped her up in his arms.

"I think you need to put me down right now!" But Trakseer ignored her and turned down the street that led to the temple steps.

CHAPTER 25

GULZAR

*T*hey had moved Oshen from the cells, and it took a few days of sneaking around for Gulzar to finally find where he was now being held. He was making his way there when a familiar voice called out to him.

Ky raced toward him, holding the skirt of her dress as she ran.

"You have to hurry!" She panted, grabbing frantically at his arms.

"What's wrong?"

"Trakseer! He has taken your mate to the temple. I do not know what he has planned, but I did not like the look in his eyes."

"My mate?" Gulzar hesitated. "How do you know that?"

She gave him an exasperated look. "I have known you my entire life, brother. The way you looked at her is the same way she looked at you and that other male."

He didn't want to have to hide it anymore. "Does Kyra know?"

"Who do you think sent me to look for you?" She clutched his

190

hand and pulled with far more strength than he would have expected from her. "We need to get you blessed."

Gulzar frowned as he followed. "You know that is forbidden for me."

"Will you stop talking and move faster? Mitera is delaying Trakseer so that we have time."

"You would do this for me? You would go against the word of the elders?"

"Just as you would for me." She gave him a crooked smile over her shoulder. "Mitera gave up her position when she took you in, and I will do the same if it means you are allowed the happiness you deserve."

"You truly are amazing."

"I know. Now come on!"

They ran, taking shortcuts they had discovered as children and praying they got there before Trakseer. Bounding up the stone steps and through the doors, Gulzar stared up at the statue before him with uncertainty.

"What if this does not work for me, Ky?"

"I have seen the ceremony done countless times. I know what I am doing." She moved him where she needed him, taking hold of his arm and placing it within a hollowed-out section at the very back of the statue. "Keep it here. Do *not* move it." She placed her hand on the base of the statue, her fushori pulsing to life as she spoke. "Warrior Gulzar, do you swear to follow the way of the goddess?"

"I do."

"Do you, Gulzar, swear to never use the gifts you are given by the goddess to inflict harm on the innocent?"

"I do."

"And do you, Gulzar, swear to do your duty to your people by continuing to protect them against the corruptions of outside technology?"

Although his mate seemed to have come from a society with such tech, Gulzar would never allow himself to become reliant on it.

"I do."

"With the light of the goddess, witnessed by her beloved mates, I proclaim that you are worthy." Ky's eyes seemed to glow brighter as she shifted her hand over the stone. Just as he thought to snatch his arm back, Gulzar felt the pain of a sharp sting radiate up his arm. '

"You are blessed," Ky murmured.

The sound of voices approaching had them both scrambling to find a place to hide as Trakseer rushed into the large hall. Zar peeked his head out, his xines moving almost furiously over his shoulders in agitation when he saw his mate in the male's arms.

The little goddess looked malnourished, as if they hadn't given her any sustenance in the days they had been apart. Dark circles hung under her eyes, and her body shook as if she were exhausted. He almost stepped out into the hall when he noticed how dull and lifeless her eyes had become.

He knew Kyra was doing her best to keep the little goddess comfortable, but something was wrong. Even though she was dressed in their finest clothing and wore a lovely headdress, she looked weak and pale. He reached out to the little one within her, trying to reassure himself. His head tilted curiously when he received two responses.

Two younglings?

Two tiny lives growing within her.

He stood in silence, shocked that he had somehow missed the second, quieter mind that was reaching out to him now. It was tucked just behind the first, a softer, gentler twin to the boisterous spirit that had called to him during the journey. Both were distressed and he desperately wanted to comfort them, to let them know he was nearby.

His little goddess glared at Trakseer as he sat her down on one of the stone benches.

"Rest for a moment while I greet the goddess so that we may converse more easily." He stepped away from her, placing his hand on Una's foot, causing a bright blue light to flood the temple. "Goddess, I ask that you use your wisdom to bridge the gap between languages so that we may speak freely."

"Provide a sample of the unknown language." The goddess' voice echoed through the room.

Trakseer reached over, nudging the female gently and a string of words fell from her lips. "Weel yew stap dewing thaat?" She huffed. "Where are Zar and Oshen? I'm getting tired of repeating myself."

Hearing her clearly, being able to understand her for the first time in his life, made his heart throb. She was looking for him. He had missed the sound of her voice, the way it danced through his mind when she babbled on and on, the way her breath fanned across his exoskeleton when she slept against him, the way she looked at him with warmth in her eyes when he communicated with her younglings.

"Are you able to understand me now?" The chief's eyes lit up with excitement.

"Oh! I can," she exclaimed, clapping her hand over her mouth. "Does this mean I finally get to see Oshen and Zar?"

"Gulzar the Damned is not permitted to see you." He sneered. "He would never be found worthy to be your bondmate. I would do much better for you, give you whatever it is you desire. As long as Una and her mates permit this." Trakseer nodded at the statue. "I am confident they will grant it."

"Bondmate?" Amanda rose from her seat, stepping away from the male, her face filled with confusion. "Sorry, but I'm not really looking for one of those." A nervous laugh fell from between her lips as she cradled her stomach.

"Did Gulzar defile you?"

"Excuse me?" Her eyes narrowed on the chief.

"Do not worry. I will raise the youngling as my own."

"Listen, I'm not really following whatever it is you think is happening here. I'm not in the market for a bondmate and I don't need your help raising my baby."

"Goddess—" Trakseer reached for her, but she recoiled, stumbling over her own feet in an attempt to get away.

Zar's heart lurched in his chest as he watched her fall to the ground. Beside him, Ky gasped, grabbing at his arm as he rushed by her to get to his little goddess. The quick movement pulled at the wounds on his back that were still healing, but it didn't matter. She needed him.

"Do not touch her!" He snarled at his chief as he bent to scoop her into his arms, his tail held up between them like a spear. "Are you hurt? Stand and let me look."

"I'm all right." She cupped his face in her hands and smiled. "You're glowing again."

Her hands trailed down his neck to his bare chest, and he watched the lights dance over his plates as the breath stilled in his lungs. Gulzar had considered that maybe he had just imagined the lights, that his mind had conjured them because he wanted so badly to belong with her, but here they were. His little goddess' fingers hovered over him, grinning as she left a trail of color in her wake.

"This is impossible," Trakseer said, his eyes wide as he looked on. "How? Why would the goddess bless one of the damned in such a way?"

She was his, and not even the elders or Trakseer could change that. He may still be Gulzar the Damned, but he had truly been blessed. His mate gasped as the little ones within her began to roll and kick.

"Oh man, it's like he knows you're here."

Gulzar forced air through his crest, rattling gently and calming the younglings. They brushed gently along his mind and he felt his heart ache.

"How do you do that?" she asked with a sigh, her whole body relaxing as the tension in her muscles fled.

"Do what, little goddess?" Being able to understand her was better than he ever could have imagined.

"Hey, you," She snapped her fingers at Trakseer, whose head jerked up. "Can you give us some privacy?"

The male's tail beat against his legs angrily as he turned toward the front of the temple. "I will get the elders."

Gulzar recognized the threat in his words, but he didn't care. "Little goddess—"

"First of all, my name is Amanda. I've been telling you that for years and I've always wondered why you called me that."

"Because you are little and a goddess."

She laughed, shaking her head. "I'm clearly not little." A frown tugged her brows down as she glanced at her diminished curves. "Well, I guess I was bigger before. This morning sickness diet has done a number on me, huh?"

"You have been ill."

"More than I care for." She grimaced as she smoothed her hand over her belly. It had grown in the couple days they had been apart. "Well, I might be little compared to you and Oshen, but I'm definitely no goddess."

Gulzar frowned at her as she lowered herself to the bench. Was this some sort of test? If you called a goddess a liar, surely that was blasphemy, but if he agreed that she wasn't a goddess, wasn't that also wrong? He looked up at the statue that towered over them and sighed. *Una, help me.*

"You are not a goddess?" He looked back at her in disbelief.

"Nope." Amanda shook her head as she leaned back on her hands to watch him.

"Are you not one of their descendants?" Gulzar asked, gesturing toward the murals his ancestors had painted on the walls of the temple. They depicted the gods intermingling with his kind, sharing meals, visiting homes, and blessing them. "These were created by those who were alive when the gods and goddesses walked among us."

He watched her stand and walk over to one of the walls, her fingers trailing over the painted faces.

"What in the world?" Her mouth dropped open. "How is this possible?"

"I can show you."

They both spun around at the sound of Ky's voice as she stepped out of the shadows. Moving her palm lightly over the foot of Una, she spoke directly to the goddess.

"Goddess, please show her the history of the fall."

The light of the goddess changed as she began to play the ghosts of the past. People walked on a land full of green, with technology that had been lost to them so long ago that there were none alive to remember it. Great paved streets stretched in every direction, and both his kind and hers intermingled freely.

"The link between this world and the great land, Atlantia, once ran strong, leading to a land of prosperity for the race of the gods and the offspring of Una." The scene changed, flashing to people fighting as the sounds of yelling filled the room.

"That's Earth," his little goddess whispered as she stepped closer to the projection.

"A great fight bred animosity between the people, causing them to lose the blessing of the gods and goddesses of Atlantia. During the Great Fall, the link that once held the two worlds together was destroyed by fire, consumed in the chaos. The gods were so angry that they turned their backs on the offspring of Una, deeming them unworthy to reside among them."

"Those aren't gods. Those are humans." Amanda shook her head as she watched.

All of the "humans," as she called them, disappeared one by one.

"And so the children of Una were lost. As if losing the land of the gods was not enough, the daughters of Una were stolen away." Rainbow females slowly faded away, leaving only the depictions of two others. "The wayward offspring of Ven were the first to turn away, taking on a new name, Venium. They hid themselves away in the okeanos." The aquatic species blinked out. "Then went the tainted offspring of Nem, taking on a new name of Grutex. They claimed they would find the lost females, leaving this world but never returning." The tainted ones that his mate had mistaken him for blinked out. "But the remaining offspring of Una stayed strong and kept their faith, following her commands as they took on her many blessings." Only his mixed people were left, kneeling at the feet of Una and her mates as they held their arms out in worship.

"Humans know about the Grutex. They attacked us."

"They attacked the gods of Atlantia?" Ky gaped in shock. "Have they really strayed so far?"

"We're not actually gods. We're just aliens to you." She looked up at the statue of the goddess. "Atlantia, I think, refers to an old legend on Earth. It's about an ancient island we called Atlantis. The people who lived there were thought to be techno-logically advanced, far beyond their time. It's thought that a volcano erupted and sank it to the bottom of the Mediterranean Sea. Which would explain why you guys have so much in common with ancient Greece, especially if you thought we were gods," she finished with a giggle.

"Then you do not bring fertility to our tribe?" Ky looked pointedly at her midsection.

"This," she grinned and ran her hand lovingly over her stomach, "is the result of my mating with Oshen. He's the Venium who came to rescue me from you." Her eyes fell on Gulzar's face and her lips trembled. "I haven't seen him since the day we came here."

Gulzar felt his xines rustle as he let out another rattle.

"Your mate." Amanda nodded. "This change that happens when you touch me…" he said as he took her hand and placed it on his chest, illuminating his plates once more. "It means you are also my bondmate."

"Your chief seemed to find that hard to believe."

Gulzar nodded, hanging his head. "Because I am damned."

"I don't understand what that means."

"It means he is unworthy, goddess," Drafir, one of the elders, spoke as he led the other older males into the temple. "He is a murderer."

Amanda's eyes snapped up to his face and she frowned. This was it; this was how he was going to lose her. He clutched her hand in his as his heart pounded against his chest. "Who did he murder?" she asked, her tone little more than a whisper.

"The female who gave him life."

CHAPTER 26

AMANDA

*S*he turned to the older male with a frown. "His mother? How?" Zar's jaw was clenched tight and he refused to meet her gaze.

"He took her life when she brought him into the world. As a result of her death, his sire soon followed." The elder spit on the ground in disgust. "Two lives were the cost of his own."

"I'm sorry, what?" Amanda couldn't believe what she was hearing.

"Not only did he take their lives, but he brought his curse down upon the female who nursed him."

"Hold on." She put her hand up to silence him. "You're telling me Zar's mother died giving birth to him and instead of taking care of her baby, you blamed him?" Her features twisted in disgust when they nodded. "What's wrong with you?"

The elder who had spoken snorted in indignation. "Gulzar is not worthy of the blessings of Una since he has killed her offspring."

"Are you really that ignorant? Death during childbirth isn't something new. Humans used to experience it often before we created technology to help us, but even that doesn't guarantee a safe delivery." Amanda shook her head. These people were fucking nuts. "You're all just a big ol' satchel of Richards!" It had been her father's favorite phrase, and it seemed more than appropriate for this occasion. "I want to see Oshen now. Can you take me to him?"

"If that is what you wish, little goddess." He placed her hand back at her side. "I suspected that once you heard the story of my birth that you would be ashamed."

"Ashamed of *you*?"

Zar nodded, turning his face away from her. "Yes."

Amanda took his face in her hands, tugging until he met her eyes. "If all of this is true and you really are my bondmate, do you think I'd leave you here with these assholes?"

That seemed to surprise him, and he glanced over at the group of older males. "I am not sure."

"The answer is no, I would not leave you here, and I'm definitely not staying somewhere run by people who punish children for the deaths of their parents."

The look on his face broke her heart. He had lived his whole life thinking he was unworthy of love, and she wanted to show him how wrong they had all been.

"You would bring me with you? Your mate would allow it?"

Amanda wasn't sure how Oshen would react to having another male thrust into their relationship, but she couldn't just abandon Zar. After all, she'd loved him her entire life. She hoped that Oshen would understand when he saw the proof of their bond. Leaning in close, she pressed her hand to Zar's chest, watching the violet glow emanate from beneath her palm.

"You're also my mate and I want you to come with us."

Amanda took his hand in hers and tugged him to the front of the temple, Kythea following close behind.

Just before they stepped outside, Zar stopped and turned back to the stunned group of elders and Trakseer, who must have come in on their heels. "It would seem you have failed the test."

Without anything further, Zar turned and swept Amanda off of her feet, pulling her tightly against him. He looked *way* too smug as he walked out of the temple, practically running by the time they reached the stairs that led out into the streets. She glanced back over his wide shoulders and almost felt guilty over not correcting him when she saw the crestfallen looks on their faces. *Almost.* A smirk tugged at her lips as she buried her face against his neck.

"Do you think we could convince Kyra and Viseer to come with us when we leave?" she asked as he descended the stairs. His answer was a string of grumbling growls, just like it had been in the forest before they'd come here.

The idea that the "goddess" had been translating for him and that she wouldn't be able to understand him once they left hadn't occurred to her. They both frowned and Gulzar huffed in agitation, running his finger down her cheek.

"He says that soon his blessing will learn."

"I can understand you so much better already."

"The goddess must have strengthened my blessing. Gulzar's blessing is still new to him. I am sure it will strengthen soon," Kythea reassured her.

Zar's determined strides ate up the ground and people rushed to get out of his way, staring after them as voices buzzed.

Kyra was standing in the middle of her courtyard with Viseer when they burst through the entrance. "Amanda!" Kyra's eyes went wide when she saw that she was wrapped in Gulzar's protective embrace. "Gulzar? What has happened?"

"We are leaving." Zar's voice startled her when it came

through the AI in Kyra's wrist. "We need to find the Venium who came back with us."

"Where will you go? What about the elders and Trakseer? Gulzar, they will punish you, and I cannot bear that again."

As he set Amanda down on her feet, her hand skimmed over his arms, leaving a violet trail. Kyra's hand flew to her mouth as she stepped closer, gaping at the telltale sign. "We will go with the Venium. The elders cannot interfere now."

The older woman smiled. "I suppose this means I can stop holding out hope that one day you would respond to Kythea." She gave him a sassy wink and laughed at the look of revulsion that screwed up his face.

"You know very well we never saw one another that way."

A laugh sounded from one of the doorways that led to the courtyard. Kythea had caught up to them and propped herself against the wall as she tried to catch her breath, a huge smile plastered across her face. "Who would ever want to mate you anyway?" Her eyes lit up playfully as she shoved away from the building and made her way to where they stood. "Only a goddess could endure the torture of being bonded to you."

The low rattle of Zar's T-rex purr danced along her senses, and she didn't resist when he pulled her into his side. "Come with us."

"Our whole lives are here. It would be impossible to leave on such short notice."

"At least let us take Ky away from here. You know they will not allow her to leave on her own since she is an unmated female."

Amanda looked between Kythea's parents with fondness. They had been nothing but kind and generous to her, and they had tried their hardest to help with her sickness. "I'm sure when we get Oshen and tell him what you've done for me that he'll want to repay your hospitality. Maybe we can help you as you've helped me."

"They are right, Kyra. Kythea may find her bonded among their people. She has not responded to anyone here," Viseer murmured to his mate.

"But it goes against the will of Una." Kyra looked helplessly torn as she gazed up at Zar.

"Kyra, your people cast out a baby for something that wasn't his fault. They're the ones not following the right path. In the little time I've known you, I could tell you were different. I'm no goddess. The temple has it all wrong. Don't you think it's possible that they've misinterpreted the will of Una?"

"Mitera," Kythea placed a hand on her mother's arm, "maybe it is time to follow our hearts. Surely Una and her mates would not fault us for going where we feel compelled."

"At least stay one more night," she pleaded. "You are so weak right now. Rest here and I will try to talk to the others about releasing your mate."

Amanda sighed, feeling the weariness already pulling at her. She didn't want to stay here one minute longer, but Kyra was right. "One night, but that's it."

"Stay here with Ky. I will go with Kyra to speak with the elders." Zar ran his hand over the side of her neck. "Rest."

She watched as he and Kyra left, and anxiety sank like a stone in her stomach. Something told her the universe was about to throw her another twist.

~

*Y*ou can't leave the house. You shouldn't *leave the house.*

Amanda paced the room as she waited impatiently for Zar to return with Oshen. They were taking far too long.

You don't even know where they're holding Oshen, she told herself.

She wasn't sure the elders would be terribly pleased with her right now, but if she could find Zar then he could help her find Oshen and they could get the hell out of here. With her mind made up, Amanda set off for the stairs, stepping as quietly as she could.

"Where are you going?"

She gasped and spun around to see Kythea looking down at her with a frown. "I, uh—I was going to go help Zar."

Kythea's lips pursed as she thought. "And do you know where Zar is?"

"The temple?"

"Just give him a little longer to speak with the elders." When Amanda sighed, Kythea smiled softly. "We could go out to the courtyard for some fresh air if you would like."

"Sure." Amanda nodded as the other female descended the steps before taking her arm.

"I know it can be frustrating to stay behind and wait while others do the talking for you. My mitera wished many times that she could storm the temple and clear Gulzar's name, but this is something he must do. He will not give up." Kythea took Amanda's hand, squeezing it. "You are an amazing gift to him, to all of us."

She wasn't really sure how to respond to that. "Uh, thank you."

Kythea led her through the archway and out into the courtyard. The night air was cool and she tipped her face up, drawing in a deep breath to settle her nerves. Many of the people within the village had been wonderful to her since she had arrived. Here, she had been lucky enough to find another support system.

Her stomach turned when she thought of all that Gulzar had been through in his life. What kind of people would cast out a child over something that was out of his control? She could still see the contempt on their faces as they had looked at him and it broke her heart to know how long he had endured that. Growing up, she never would have guessed that these things were happening to him.

"Oh, god—" Amanda lurched toward one of the pretty flower bushes along the wall and retched.

"You poor thing," Kythea said, rubbing her back as she cooed softly.

Amanda gasped, spitting to get the bitter taste out of her mouth. "I'm so sorry about the bush." She wanted this to all be over. She wanted to get to the domes, to have Zar and Oshen with her so that she stopped feeling so awful.

Kythea pressed her forehead to Amanda's. "You are almost there. Do not give up." She pulled back with a smile and glanced over at the open archway. "I will fetch you some water, yes?"

Anything to wash the taste from her mouth would do. Amanda nodded, running her hands over her face as Kythea rushed off. The nights here were strangely quiet. She almost missed the sounds of sirens, cars, planes, even the annoying crickets that liked to hang out beneath her window and sing the song of their people at three in the morning.

Somewhere from within the shadows at the corner of the courtyard came a rustling noise. She glanced over, sure it was her imagination or one of the small bird-like creatures she had sat and watched during the day, but something told her not to chance it. Amanda fled toward the safety of the house, hoping Kythea wouldn't be far.

Just as she reached the first corner of the house, a clawed hand shot out of the darkness and covered her mouth, preventing her from screaming. A second arm caught her around the waist, pulling her back against a hard chest.

"Where exactly are you running off to?"

The blood left her face as recognition dawned on her. She knew that voice, had woken up from nightmares with it echoing in her head. He growled low in her ear when she struggled, kicking her legs and clawing uselessly at his body.

"They thought they had won. They thought they could hide you away in this backwoods village and I wouldn't be able to get to you, but I've been here watching, posing as one of these fools." The Grutex's hot breath warmed her skin, making her shudder as he pressed his face closer. "Time to go."

He lifted her feet off the ground and spun around.

Stupid! So fucking stupid, she chastised herself as tears welled in her eyes. She should have just gone inside with Kythea, but she had assumed she was safe inside of Zar's home. Her complacency had put her and her baby in danger.

She was going to die, and no one would ever know what had happened.

CHAPTER 27

GULZAR

The twin moons were high enough that their light illuminated the statues of the moon gods, bathing them in an ethereal glow. Gulzar tried to calm himself even as his xines writhed in agitation.

"My mate is not a goddess. She has told you all this herself," he snarled.

"It is but another test!" Drafir shouted. "We will not risk all that we have. We have come too far!"

They were going in circles. No matter how many times he tried to make them understand, the elders were old males, set in their ways and not willing to change or accept that they could have been wrong.

"This is not a test, and it has nothing to do with anything except for the fact that you wish to maintain control." Gulzar sneered at Drafir as he stood to pace.

"How dare you speak to me that way!" The elder slammed his hand down on the table in front of him, shoving his chair back as he came to his feet. "You are damned! You should not be permitted to speak so freely!"

"The female you are so adamant is a goddess has accepted him as her mate. He is not damned and he never was," Kyra interjected, stomping toward Drafir. "I failed him for so long, but I will not let you continue to mistreat my son!"

Warmth filled his chest as she turned to him. It was an honor to be seen as one of her own.

Drafir snorted. "Your son? Have you not suffered enough for him? Are the losses of your own young not proof that he has brought this curse upon you?" He turned to the other elders, raising his hands in the air. "You were once a priestess, Kyra. You were respected among our people until you took him in. Gulzar should have been left to die that day as payment for his deeds."

He saw the flash of pain wash over her face, but it was replaced with sheer determination. "I never stopped being a priestess. That was granted to me by the goddess herself, not by you." Her hand dropped down, resting gently on her abdomen. "And the goddess has granted me another chance. A blessing."

"Impossible!" the elder shouted as he looked down at the hand she held to her stomach.

"My only curse was you and your poison."

Drafir's face went slack and his mouth dropped open. "How did you—"

"I saw you the last time you tried to poison my food. I came to ask you about Gulzar's dreams and I saw you." There was heat in her eyes, barely restrained rage. "The only thing I want to know is why you did it."

"He was supposed to die, but you … you just could not let that happen." The elder shook his head. "If you had been successful in breeding again, then the others may not have believed he was damned. It would have undermined our authority.

He may have gone on to procreate and risk the life of another female. We could not allow that."

"So to save one female, you murdered innocents?" Kyra spit on the table in front of the elders. "You all disgust me!"

"Gulzar!" The door of the temple slammed against the wall as Ky burst into the room, her breathing labored. "You have to come! Now!"

She tugged at his arms frantically. "What is it? Where is my mate?"

"We were in the courtyard when she became ill. I only left her for a moment to get water!" Ky rubbed a hand over her face as Kyra rushed forward. "I was just coming back outside when I saw someone take her."

"Who took her?" Kyra demanded.

"I did not recognize him. He was not from the village." Ky pulled at him again. "He wore strange clothing. I think he was one of the tainted."

Gulzar wanted to rage, to ask her why she hadn't tried to save Amanda, but Ky wasn't a warrior. She was a priestess, and she would not have stood a chance against a full-grown male.

"We need to find Oshen and then you will show me where they were." A growl worked its way up his chest as he moved toward the door. "I will deal with you later, Drafir," he warned.

"There will be no need for that." Trakseer was glaring at the elder. "I will see to his punishment myself."

Gulzar hurried out of the temple, Ky and Kyra practically running to keep up with him.

"I will get Viseer and meet you there!" Kyra called as she split away.

The house of the elders was not far from the temple, situated near the large city center. It was where the elders handed out punishments which meant he was all too familiar with it. They rushed past the guards, ignoring their calls for them to halt.

"Ah, visitors. How nice. Have you come to let me out?" the Venium male asked, irritation lacing his voice.

Gulzar smiled. It seemed as if the blessing he had received was finally working.

"Yes, actually." The male jerked his gaze up in surprise. "Hello, Oshen."

The Venium narrowed his eyes on Gulzar. "How do you know my name?"

"Our mate used it during the journey."

"*Our* mate?" His fushori lit up as he took a step forward. "She is my mate, Grutex."

"I am not Grutex, and she is mine also. My plates lit when she touched me. This is an indication that we share the same female."

"The old texts tell stories of the triads formed between our people. They were revered, seen as sacred matings. This is a blessing from Una. For it to happen now, after all this time is surely an omen that we must come together again for the future prosperity of our people."

"Ky," he grumbled. "While that is fascinating, it is not what we are here for." He turned back to Oshen. "We need your help."

"I refuse to assist you with anything until I see for myself that Amanda is safe and unharmed."

"Well, that is going to be hard considering that she has been taken," Ky said.

"Taken?" Oshen slammed his hands against the door separating them, his tail lashing from side to side. "By who?"

"We are not sure, but we believe it may be one of the males you refer to as the Grutex."

Oshen's body began to shake violently, his fushori pulsing. "She was supposed to be safe here!"

Ky gasped, stepping back as Oshen's body began to enlarge before their eyes.

"By the goddess," he heard her whisper. "The legends..."

Gulzar watched with fascination as the Venium's body reformed itself, bones cracking and snapping into new positions, flesh tearing and knitting itself back together. The clothing he had been wearing tore, falling to the floor beneath him as his hands twisted into massive paws with deadly claws. He was an Allasso, one of the legendary beasts from their books of lore, guardians and warriors of old who had the power to change forms in times of need.

He had never believed that the stories were true, but as Oshen lifted his head, eyes glowing brightly above a mouth full of long, pointed teeth, Gulzar counted himself a believer. Glowing golden stripes raced down the beast's back and sides while six long spines arched skyward, pushing up through the skin of his back. They too pulsed with light and Gulzar took a step backward as the beast roared. The spikes on his neck rattled together like a warning and he came forward, all recognition gone.

"Oshen," Gulzar spoke calmly, hoping the male was still in there somewhere. "Come back. Leave this form and come back. Amanda needs us. For her sake and for both your younglings, I am asking you to return."

The beast cocked his head to the side before throwing it back and letting loose a heart-stopping howl that Gulzar felt rattle through his bones.

CHAPTER 28

AMANDA

The sound of trickling water would have given her hope at one point, but not at the moment. She was slung over an alien's shoulder, staring at the ground, and feeling like she might puke every time he took a step.

Keep it together. You've got this, she told herself over and over as she pinched her eyes shut.

They had gotten out of the village without anyone noticing, slipping through a hole that had been dug out of one of the outer walls. She had wanted to fight him, to kick and scream when he released her mouth, but she was terrified of what he might do. There was no way she was going to risk the life of her baby by provoking him. There was madness in his eyes, and it seemed to grow every time he looked at her.

Her captor stepped up and over a large rock, jolting her and causing her stomach to roil violently. *Don't be sick. Don't be sick!* She slapped a hand over her mouth, trying her best to push it back, but she knew she couldn't. In fact, maybe she didn't even want to try after being taken by *him*. She finally lost the fight when he rocked her again and emptied her stomach's contents all down his back and legs.

The male stopped, jarring her again as he pulled her away from his body. Her feet touched the ground and she wobbled unsteadily.

"What have you done?"

"Sorry," she murmured, but she didn't really mean it. "You really shouldn't have been jostling me around like that."

When the male stepped toward her, his hand swinging back like he meant to hit her, Amanda flinched, her hands cradling her stomach protectively. He stopped, cocking his head as he watched her. His nostrils flared as he drew in a deep breath before he dropped to his knees in front of her, pressing his face into her rounded belly.

"You are carrying young?"

She swallowed the lump of fear that tried to lodge itself in her throat. "Yes."

His lips pulled back over his teeth in a snarl just before he let out something akin to a roar. The vines on his head writhed around his neck and shoulders as he slammed his fists into the ground near her feet. With lightning speed, the massive alien took hold of her arm and began pulling her through the woods.

"Hey!" she yelled, trying to pry his fingers from her. He was going so fast that she was nearly running in an attempt to keep up with him. "Cut it out!" She dug in her heels and bit down on his wrist as hard as she could.

Amanda collided with the back of his arm as he turned to stare at her, his head tilting. "Did you bite me?"

"You were hurting me." She shifted uncomfortably.

He looked down at where his hand was still wrapped around her arm and his grip loosened slowly. "Sorry."

The apology stunned Amanda for a moment and all she could

do was stare. The alien who had attacked her at the lab, who had stalked her not just on Earth, but all the way across the freaking galaxy to steal her away from her mates was apologizing for hurting her arm?

She kept her eyes on the woods around them as they continued at a much slower pace. Now that she knew what was out there, she wasn't going to risk getting caught off guard by another nightmare animal. With Oshen and Zar, she had felt safe and protected, but the Grutex wasn't from Venora. The sounds of rushing water grew louder and louder, drowning out all of the other noise around them. When they reached the river, the male turned his red eyes on her and pointed.

"Stay."

"I'm not a dog." Amanda crossed her arms over her chest when he released her to step into the rushing water.

Her eyes searched the shoreline for anything she might be able to use as a weapon. She wasn't fast enough to run from him, but if she could knock him out then she figured she stood a better chance of making it back to the village before he woke up. As luck would have it, there was a large, twisted branch just off to her right. Amanda crouched down, stretching her arm out.

Ignoring the tiny thorns that pressed into her skin, she wrapped her fingers around it and approached the edge of the water. When the male rubbed his hands over his face, she pulled the branch back before swinging it with all of her might. The force of the blow splintered the wood, vibrating up through her arms. She stumbled to the side as she lost her footing, scrambling across the sandy bank to get away.

Instead of falling into the water like she had hoped, the male threw his head back and laughed loudly. The sound made her blood run cold.

"What the fuck?" she stammered, crawling backward in an attempt to escape when he started out of the water toward her.

"What sort of crazy ass chitin do you fuckers have? You're like crabs on steroids!"

He picked up the broken branch where she had dropped it and flung it into the river. "I was right."

"Right about what?"

"You really are stronger than she was."

A shudder wracked her body as she watched his eyes roam over her as if she were something delicious he was intent on devouring. Revulsion surged through her as he pulled her up, cradling her against his wet chest like a child.

There was nothing left in her stomach, but that knowledge did nothing to keep the bile down. The bitter taste filled her mouth as she gagged, praying that he would just stop and let her rest or eat something to clean the taste off of her tongue.

The sun was just beginning to light up the sky when she felt his steps slow, and she looked up to see a ship wedged between two large trees. The ship had a triangular frame and four long arms equipped with multiple weapons on the front. It was daunting in size, even with some of the arms damaged and missing sections. Judging by the condition, Amanda assumed they had crashed.

The soil was upturned, and several of the coral shoots that littered the ground had been thrown from the impact. Exposed wires poked out from an open panel and lights flickered on and off beside it. The Grutex set her down, lifted his hand, and placed it beside the door before leaning forward and speaking in a growly language. The ship spoke and then the door disappeared.

Amanda frowned at the empty space, looking up at the Grutex, but he ignored the look and pulled her through behind him. They passed through a series of hallways, each one looking just like the next with no distinguishable features. The ship was like a maze.

A cold, daunting maze.

Anxiety began to curl in her stomach, and she felt like she was going to be sick again. "What's your name?" she asked, attempting to dissipate the growing terror she was experiencing.

"Xuvri."

"Zoofree?"

"No. Xu-vri."

Amanda worked her lips around the word drawing it out in her mind. "Xuvri?"

"Close enough," he murmured.

He hadn't been much of a talker during their trek here so she shouldn't have been surprised when he didn't volunteer anything further. The room he brought her to looked like some sort of mad scientist's lab, but that wasn't what made her breath catch in her chest.

Standing in the middle of the room with its head bent over a table full of vials was the strangest alien she had ever seen. His green skin reflected the dim light, and his black eyes were compound, made up of tiny hexagons. The long mouth that protruded from his face reminded her of a mosquito, and a shiver ran through her. Mosquitos were practically Florida's state bird, and the life-size representation was even more terrifying than she had ever imagined.

"You have come back!" the thing buzzed. Like a fly. The sound skittered across her nerves and she shivered again.

"Are you cold, human? Get me a blanket, Tachin," Xuvri ordered as he placed her onto a table.

"Why does she need a blanket?" the Tachin sneered. His feet didn't even touch the floor as he floated over to them. "She will be uncovered during the examination."

"She is carrying offspring," Xuvri said matter-of-factly.

"Already?" The alien turned toward her, and she felt the weight of his gaze.

Amanda looked away, scanning the room as she tried to block

out their conversation, but their voices rose as they began to argue.

"And the ship is still not ready for travel. Why is that?" Xuvri was demanding.

She felt herself sag in relief. If it wasn't ready for travel then at least they would be staying put for a little bit longer.

"I cannot produce supplies from thin air, Grutex."

"Then find them. Remember, I am not the only one risking everything here."

When her eyes fell on the large tank filled with liquid across the room, Amanda gasped, her mouth dropping open in horror. The woman she had seen Xuvri take six years ago floated within. Her long blonde hair had been shorn, but the choppy ends of it drifted softly around her face. Bile rose in her throat when she saw that the woman's limbs had been replaced with ones that were clearly alien, most likely Grutex.

Was this what Xuvri had planned for her? Were they going to Frankenstein her together until they made her the way they wanted?

She didn't even know if the woman was still alive, but there were no wires or tubes connected to her, and Amanda feared that she was merely a specimen in a jar at this point.

"She was weak, but you are not."

She turned to stare at Xuvri, whose eyes were on the woman. "You killed her?"

The male's voice was detached, like he was lost somewhere in his mind and not with them at all. "You are going to live." He touched her stomach, caressing the bump. "You will bring me strong offspring." He looked back at her, his eyes clouded. "Where she failed, you will succeed."

"You did this to her? You mutilated her." Amanda could feel the tears choke her as guilt swarmed her. She and Jun had run that day. They hadn't even made an attempt to save the woman. *What if I could have prevented this?*

Xuvri shook his head, his vines falling forward as he leaned toward her. "You are perfect."

A tear slid down her cheek as the Grutex moved to cover the tank with a thin sheet, hiding the woman from her view.

"Bring me the scanner," he told the insect-alien.

The fly pulled a small sphere from a drawer that sank back into the wall before he flew over to them, his feet gliding just above the floor. He reached out his free hand to touch the tips of her hair but recoiled when a roar filled the room. Xuvri grasped the arm of the other alien and his tail thrashed behind him as he forced the male away from her.

"Do not touch her!" he snarled as he yanked the sphere from his thin hands. "She is mine!"

The walls felt as if they were beginning to press in on her, and Amanda struggled to draw air into her lungs as shadows crept into the edges of her vision. *Too much,* her mind screamed. A soft, rumbling purr began to fill the space and her eyes flew around the room. *Zar?* Large hands pulled her into a warm, firm chest as the purr grew louder and she began to calm down.

This wasn't Zar though. She looked up into Xuvri's face and his six red eyes stared back at her. There was a softness there she had never seen. He seemed almost lucid, like the madness that was normally there had vanished, and she felt like she was actually seeing him for the first time.

Just as quickly as it had gone, however, the madness returned, hardening his features as he stopped his purring. Xuvri laid her back on the table, pressing her shoulders down as he took the sphere from the insect alien. She watched as he moved it slowly over the material that covered her stomach. A moment later, a projection lit up against the wall opposite them and she felt her heart clench in wonder.

Two perfect little beings were curled around one another. *Twins!* They were going to have twins. The little ones looked somewhat human, but with tiny tails extending from the base of their spines and delicate pointed ears, it was obvious these babies were Venium. Amanda felt tears roll down into her hair as she tried to memorize every detail of her babies.

"A fine specimen indeed. The other female never achieved this," the Tachin whispered as he stared at the image.

Above her, Xuvri stiffened, glaring at the other male. There was something between these two that she wasn't sure she would ever want to find out about. She turned her eyes back to the images of her babies and she felt her jaw set.

These aliens would never get their hands on them, and she was going to do everything in her power to make sure of it.

CHAPTER 29

OSHEN

By the goddess, his mate was going to be the death of him. Never in his life had he met someone who caused his protective instincts to nearly take over, even over his need to create peace.

Oshen shook his head, rubbing his hands over his face as he tried to come to terms with what had just happened to him. He had transformed into a beast, something from the old tales. He had wanted to scream when he felt his bones snapping and his skin ripping, but nothing had come out. His thoughts had barely been his own, but the monster had responded to Zar as if it knew him.

"Oshen?"

His eyes snapped up to the other male's worried face. "I'm fine." Oshen stood, steadying himself against one of the wooden chairs they had placed in the room. The shredded remains of his clothing littered the floor beneath his feet and he sighed. Nudity wasn't something that bothered him, or any of the Venium, but that was his second uniform lost in such a short period of time.

A gasp caught his attention, and both he and Zar turned to see the female staring at his body, lingering unabashed on his closed slit. He growled low in his throat as he felt his skin ripple uncomfortably.

"Enough, Ky. Find him some clothing," Zar hissed, shoving the female gently.

She smiled up at him, blinking innocently as her fushori glowed. "Forgive me. I have never witnessed the transformation. It was … exciting."

"He belongs to Amanda."

"I have no intentions of trying to lure him away." She looked back over her shoulder with a smirk as she turned to leave the room. "I was just curious."

The female laughed as she raced down the hall, leaving him alone in the small room with Zar. He began to pace, his long legs eating up the floor as he tried to figure out just how Amanda had managed to disappear in a village full of people.

"How did this happen?" he asked, his eyes narrowing as he turned to look at Zar.

Oshen felt his fushori pulse self-consciously as the other male's gaze lingered on his body in the same way Ky's had before all four of his eyes snapped up to his face. He frowned as his mating glands swelled painfully, threatening to extrude as he stood there unclothed within the room.

Stay in the slit. Stay in the slit. Don't come out!

Why was he having this reaction now? Couldn't this have happened in the woods where no one else would have been around to witness him behaving like a pup? They had been so focused on keeping Amanda safe that they hadn't actually noticed one another. His mind drifted to the stories of the goddess and her mates, and for the first time, he realized that it hadn't just been Una who Nem and Ven loved. They had loved one another as well. Zar stepped forward, his mouth opening as if he were trying to find the right words.

Ky cleared her throat from the doorway, a grin tugging at her lips as she looked on. "Have I interrupted? I could come back later."

"Quiet," Gulzar grumbled, snatching the pile of clothing from her hands before giving them to Oshen.

The garment was soft and white, but the shape confused him. He turned it this way and that, trying to figure out which side he was supposed to step into.

"Let me help you." Zar stepped forward, taking the garment from him and slipping it over Oshen's head.

He cinched the middle around his hips, and Oshen tried not to laugh when he looked down at himself. While Zar managed to look intimidating in his tunic, Oshen had somehow come out looking like one of his younger siblings playing dress up in his dam's clothing. It wasn't that different from the Venium's more traditional clothing, but this one was rather ill fitting.

"If you become hot, these unclasp at the shoulders." He pointed to the small metal pieces on the tops of the straps. The hanging vines around his head moved gently as the tips of his protrusions began to turn a deeper shade of black. "You can just allow it to hang as mine does."

Oshen nodded, clearing his throat as he brushed his hand over the cloth on his torso. "Thank you for this." His mind felt clouded, and he drew in the scent of Zar's pheromones.

Goddess help them, they needed Amanda.

"If you are ready…" Zar gestured toward the open door.

The three of them rushed down the hall, encountering no interference, but when they reached the steps that descended out into the street, Oshen recognized one of the raised voices in the distance. When they reached the courtyard, he caught sight of the familiar red glow of his sire's fushori. Calder was speaking agitatedly in their native tongue, his finger jabbing against the plated chest of the chief. He had never seen his sire lose his calm before and he stared for a moment in surprise.

"Thank the goddess!" his sire shouted when he turned and saw them approaching. "I have been trying to explain to them that I am your sire and that you are being held illegally, but they don't seem to know any of the common languages."

"They've learned English, one of the human languages." Oshen frowned, glancing at the chief. "I'm not entirely sure how."

As far as he knew, these people had little tech, and the idea that they had all learned the language so quickly just by listening to Amanda was something he couldn't imagine.

"Well then," Calder sighed as he turned back toward the rainbow-colored male. "I am Ambassador Calder and I come here on behalf of the Venium. This male is my son, Oshen." He gestured at him. "You have kept him and his mate here in your village and I have come to retrieve them."

"Yes. The female is also my mate," the chief smiled.

MINE.

A snarl was ripped from Oshen's throat and he found himself crossing the courtyard, his clawed hand wrapping around the throat of the other male as he struggled to contain his fury. He heard Zar's low, threatening growl behind him.

"Listen to me closely: you are not and will never be our third."

The male squirmed in his grasp, his lips pulling back from his teeth as he clutched at Oshen's arm.

"Zar is *mine.* Amanda is *mine.* I belong to them and you are not welcome."

The chief fell to the ground with a thud, gasping for air as he scrambled backward.

Kill him, he heard the beast whisper in his mind.

"Gulzar the Damned is not worthy of a triad," one of the elder males growled as they stepped between them.

Kill them all.

"Why don't we take a moment to talk this out?" His sire placed a calming hand on Oshen's shoulder. Oshen watched as the other elders assisted the chief, pulling him to his feet and leading him back toward the place they had kept him during his time here. He felt his sire's arms wrap around him and relaxed into the comforting embrace, letting the rage of the beast slip just enough to clear his mind. "Your siblings are waiting for you outside the village gates. Slip out while I speak to those in charge and go after your mate."

As he stepped back, Oshen struggled to remain in control, to not lose his temper and destroy something. Amanda was gone. He had done what he thought was best, thought that she would be safe here among others, but he had been wrong. Not only was he worrying about her, but now he had to worry about controlling the monster that felt as if it were trying to take him over. He looked down at his hands as they began to morph, his claws extending and his skin darkening.

A mauve-colored hand covered his, and Oshen looked up to see Zar watching his face intently. "Do not let it consume you."

"This rage belongs to the beast, Oshen. Use it, but do not allow it to use you," his sire whispered as he stepped away to follow one of the guards into the building.

"Allasso is a gift," Ky murmured as she watched his hands change back slowly. "This must be a sign of your blessing."

At that moment, it felt more like a curse. He felt the gentle tug of Zar's hand as he turned him.

"Oshen, focus whatever the beast has given you and use it to find our mate. She and both of your young are in danger."

"Both?" He frowned at the other male.

"Yes."

Two pups.

Goddess help them. *Mikra.* Little ones.

"We need to leave." Oshen took Zar's hand, pulling him along down the street as a crowd began to form at the doors his father had walked through. No one paid them any mind. "My family is here to help us."

"I know a less obvious way out of the village. Follow me." Zar ducked into the shadows, moving between the houses until they came upon a section of the outside wall that seemed to have been neglected over the solars. It was uneven, part of it sinking into the softer ground. "We used to climb it when we were younger. It is not as tall here."

Oshen jerked his chin toward the barrier. "You first."

"You are worse than our mate," Zar scoffed, shaking his head as he crouched down.

With more grace than most beings half his size, the other male leaped into the air, landing with ease on the top of the wall.

Mine, the beast within him growled as Oshen watched Zar steady himself and then spin back toward him.

"Are you coming?"

I braxing wish. "Yes." His feet dug into the stone as he propelled himself up and over to the other side. It was getting harder and harder to ignore the instinct to bond.

"Mouni, locate Evafyn and set route," he said to his AI as he scanned the woods in front of them.

"Gladly, Meatface. Offering you as a sacrifice to the more worthy sibling would be my pleasure."

As soon as he was within the dome, he was going to find someone to wipe Mouni's programing and then he would murder Brin.

The pair followed the AI's directions to a large stone shelter, much like the one Oshen had found Zar and Amanda in. A loud, ominous rumble shook the ground, sending some of the small animals running. The sky above them swirled with dark clouds, and Oshen cursed as they stepped inside just as a bright bolt of lightning lit up the dim interior. A second crack of thunder followed closely and he looked up to see three of his siblings standing in the corner, staring at them curiously.

"Just in time," Evafyn said.

"Braxing storms," he grumbled. The weather on the surface was unpredictable at times, which was one of the reasons his people preferred to make their homes in the water.

Big, fat drops of liquid began to pour from the sky as the wind picked up speed, howling angrily through the trees. If he were quick enough, he might be able to catch up to whoever had taken their mate. They had less than a day on him.

"Let's go. We can push through." Oshen turned to head into the rain, but Luz caught his arm.

"Brother, stop. These surface storms can turn deadly." He looked to his siblings for backup. "We will need to wait this one out."

"Wait it out?" Oshen shook off his brother's hand with a growl, the light-colored male stepping back as he advanced on him. "My mate and my pups are out there somewhere! They could be caught in this."

Luz's purple fushori pulsed as he clenched his jaw. "We do not wish to leave them out there either—"

"Then why would you even suggest it?" A snarl of pure frustration left his mouth as he scrubbed his hands down his face.

"She was taken by someone, yes? I doubt whoever has her is just sitting out in the woods with no shelter at all." Evafyn snorted. "That's assuming she was taken and didn't wander off on her own."

The golden light of his fushori reflected off of the walls. "Are you really suggesting my female would do that? That she would willingly leave the safety of the village knowing who waited for her?" He glared at his sister, not amused in the least by her comment, but she only crossed her arms over her chest.

"I was not suggesting that. I was merely—"

"It's what you said!" Evafyn's eyes narrowed dangerously as he yelled.

"She is not familiar with whatever danger our mate is in, Oshen. None of us truly are," Zar spoke softly.

"You were not even supposed to exist!" The words were out of his mouth before he could even think to stop them. Regret slammed into him at the look of shock on the other male's face and the way his eyes lowered in shame.

"What an awful thing to say to a mate!" Evafyn gasped, her claws extending as her golden fushori flashed. "He is your third. You should be ashamed of yourself."

"That's enough from all of you!" A frazzled Luz glared, wedging himself between his angry siblings before they could come to blows. Although he was naturally a peacekeeper, Luz stood at least a hand taller than Oshen and he was positive his younger brother outweighed him by a decent amount. Oshen had no doubt the male could have easily subdued them if he felt it was necessary. "Are you going to help me?" he asked Lief, who was standing propped against the far wall.

"I thought I might just let them kill one another, honestly."

"That's very helpful." Luz sighed. Lief shrugged a dark shoulder, his bright green eyes roaming the faces within the shelter. "Listen to me. We do not have mates so we cannot say that we know what you are feeling at this moment, but we all care for Amanda and the pups she is carrying. We want them home with everyone else. Fighting amongst ourselves will do nothing to help."

It took everything inside of him to step back and take a deep calming breath. "Has Brin sent any word?" Oshen turned to his sister.

She averted her eyes and shook her head quickly. "Nothing."

Oshen's brow furrowed as he peered through the opening out into the torrent that raged beyond the walls. There should have been something by now. He would check in with his brutok once they had recovered his mate.

What if she was injured, unconscious, abducted, and taken offplanet? A snarl ripped from his throat just at the thought. He would tear apart any creature that dared to keep his gynaika away from him. Once it was safe to return to the search, Oshen was going to find her and this time she was never leaving his sight again.

~

"*O*shen?" Something pressed against his shoulder, shaking him roughly. "The storm seems to have passed. We should go now." Oshen's eyes shot open and he bolted upright, glancing around the dim interior. Gulzar was crouched down at his side and a hand rested against his leg. "Are you all right?"

"I'm fine." He tried to keep the agitation from his voice. Zar wasn't the enemy, but he was still having a hard time admitting he had feelings for the male. The storm had almost completely stopped at this point, dark clouds gradually replaced by a clear sky. They had all agreed to follow Zar to the section of the wall closest to Kyra's home, hoping this was where the captor had decided to flee.

Zar growled when they came upon the hole in one section of the wall. There were claw marks, as if someone or something had dug straight through it. Evafyn ran a slender hand over the jagged edges and grimaced. The ground was soggy beneath his feet as he stepped away from the wall and he spun in a circle, inhaling deeply as he searched for Amanda's scent. Only the smell of the damp forest reached him and he frowned, trying again to catch even the faintest hint.

"It's not here," he murmured.

Beside him, Luz flared his gills as he gazed around at the windswept forest. "I do not know which direction they would have gone, brother."

To his right, Fyn inspected a tangle of branches near the barrier, kicking the pile in frustration. "The rain and wind have destroyed any signs that we might have followed." Her hands rested on her hips as she tipped her face up toward the sky, her eyes closing as she huffed out a breath.

"I believe they may be in this direction." The siblings turned to where Gulzar stood among a cluster of trees that had taken a decent amount of damage. "I can feel a pull this way."

Oshen narrowed his eyes on the male. "Pull toward what, exactly?"

"Our mate." Zar frowned. "Who else?"

Luz let out an exhausted sigh. "For two males who are supposed to share a mate, who should share a connection to one another, you seem to butt heads an awful lot."

Oshen knew he should apologize. "It's still new," he grumbled instead. "We should stay close. Since we have no other leads to go off of, we should investigate whatever pull Zar is feeling."

The group picked their way slowly through the woods, stopping every now and again to try and catch Amanda's scent, but nothing remained after the rains. Luz and Fyn walked on ahead, scouting for any tracks or clues that they were headed in the right direction. Beside him, Lief squinted, his eyes scanning the distance.

"What is it, brother?"

Lief was built similar to Oshen, tall and lean with broad shoulders, but the male was a warrior. Scars crisscrossed his black skin, and he could tell you the story behind each and every one of them. Long white hair hung loose down his back instead of being twisted into the more traditional braid. The male turned his green gaze on Oshen.

"Something just doesn't feel right about this. Why chase your female when there are so many humans on Earth to choose from?"

Oshen had wondered that himself. If this was indeed the male from solars before who had caused her to have such horrible dreams, what was it about his mate that attracted the attention?

"I do not know, but I plan to find out."

Zar led them further into the woods, his head cocked this way and that as he followed whatever he was sensing. When they caught up with Fyn, she was frowning and whispering to her wrist.

"What is it?"

Her head jerked up. "Nothing."

Oshen narrowed his eyes. His sister was keeping something from him. "You are an awful liar, Fyn."

The female turned to scoff at him, her breathing huffing out as she laughed. "I am not."

"You are absolutely Daya's daughter. Confess."

"You are her son."

"You keep secrets just as she does—horribly." Oshen blocked her path when she attempted to move past him. "I have been there for almost every moment over our shared thirty-four solars of life and you think I wouldn't know when something was amiss?"

"You do remember I am the older one, right?" she scoffed.

"Only by eight months!"

"Eight blissful months of being an only pup." Fyn flipped her golden braids over her shoulder. "Best eight months of my life."

"Here we go again." Lief's gills flared in annoyance.

"There is never a moment of peace with the two of you." Luz stopped walking and turned toward his bickering siblings.

"You're as truthful as a braxing Grutex." Oshen pulled his upper lip over his fangs in a snarl.

A gasp had Fyn rocking back on her feet as if she'd been physically wounded, her fushori bright with indignation. "You dare?"

"Your wit is as dull as your fushori."

"Our fushori are the same color, you stone skull!"

"Enough from you two!" Luz commanded, moving to stand between them.

"It is getting stronger," Gulzar whispered.

Oshen spun toward the other male, meeting his gaze as hope flared within his chest.

We are going to find you, he promised his pups as he rushed to catch up with Zar. *We will bring you and your dam home safely, mikra.*

CHAPTER 30

AMANDA

*X*uvri paced the room, his hands running over his sloped head as he mumbled incoherently to himself.

His eyes fell on her and he huffed, "You weren't supposed to be pregnant yet. This means things have to change."

"What things?" Amanda asked quietly from her position atop the exam table.

"You were supposed to be mine," he whispered to himself as if he hadn't heard her question. "I can hear you. I hear you in my mind—I *feel* you in my head. That must mean you are mine."

"You hear me inside your mind?"

He turned to look at her, stepping closer. "Right here." He pressed a finger to his temple before running his knuckle gently down the side of her face. "You were the first one… the only one to ever speak to me in such a way." Amanda watched his gaze fall on the covered tank across the room.

"But I'm not your mate."

"Lies. They have told you wrong," he insisted. "They bred what was mine."

Amanda shook her head, her throat tightening. "I'm not yours. You hurt me. People don't hurt the ones they care about."

"Hurt?" Xuvri huffed and shook his head. "Claim, not hurt."

His sentences were short and choppy, and Amanda could see he was slipping deeper into whatever madness had hold of him. "You chased me, knocked me to the ground that night at the lab."

"Yes. The claiming hunt. The chase. It excites."

"Excites you?"

Xuvri shook his head. "Excites the females." He looked at her like he couldn't believe he was having to explain it. "Females want it, want to run. We prove ourselves worthy of them."

"But I didn't run because I wanted you to prove yourself to me. I ran because I was afraid of you."

"Not true. Humans fight the hardest because they want us to be better, to be stronger."

"I don't belong with you though. I have two mates already."

Xuvri shook his head as he stepped away from her, continuing his pacing of the floor. "That's not possible." Even the fly alien was watching him now. "You are my mate. You are my strong, perfect female."

"Why are you taking humans in the first place?"

"The Grutex are dying out. We need mates, and humans are compatible."

Amanda swallowed thickly, looking back at the tank. "Did you have children with her?"

Emotion flitted over his face. "She was not strong enough to carry them."

Maybe she wasn't looking at someone who had set out to terrorize her. Maybe this was a male that had gone mad from loss. It didn't excuse what he had done to her or the mutilation she had seen, but it tugged at something deep inside her.

"Xuvri, I'm sorry for what happened to her, what happened to your children, but you can't just use me as a replacement." He frowned down at the floor, closing his eyes and shaking his head as if he didn't want to hear her words. "My babies have fathers who are worried about them. You're taking their children away. You're going to take their fathers away."

"No. *I* will be their father. *I* will raise them." A shudder racked her as he approached. His eyes were glossy again, his movements erratic. "It doesn't matter who created them because I will be here for them."

"I am not yours!" she yelled in frustration, her fists slamming into the hard plates of his chest. "I will never be yours!"

Xuvri snarled, snatching her hands up painfully and pulling her into him. "Enough—"

His face went slack as he grunted, releasing her hands and falling to his knees with a loud thud before he toppled over sideways. Behind him stood the alien Xuvri had called a Tachin. He held an empty syringe in his clawed hand and stared down at the Grutex's body.

"I could not listen to another word from that brainless, shell-skulled idiot," he grumbled. "He was wasting precious time."

Amanda felt his gaze shift to her and she barely stopped the whine that tried to escape her lips. She doubted this alien was going to have anything better planned for her.

"I tried to help him, but he brought me faulty products. You, however, are already proving to be far better quality." He stepped to the side, grabbing a vial and another syringe. "I may not even need to take you apart like I did the other female. I replaced limbs and organs, tried to get her to function correctly, but she was weak. I told him she would not survive, but you—" The needle pierced the covering on the vial, filling with the dark blue liquid. "You have given me not just one but two chances to test this theory."

My babies. This monster was going to not just experiment on her, but her unborn children as well. Amanda felt tears well up in her eyes as he advanced on her.

"Please don't do this," she whispered.

"Oh, none of that. This will not hurt you. We will simply attempt to override the genetic makeup of your offspring, to change them, make them better. They have the chance to be more, to be Tachin."

"Why wouldn't you just find your own female?" Amanda scrambled backward on the table, but there was nowhere to run.

The male's wings buzzed in apparent irritation at her questioning. "Infertility. It is perhaps the one thing we have in common with the Grutex."

"If the Grutex are infertile, then why are they still taking people?"

"Not all are infertile. This one did manage to impregnate the other female multiple times, but none were viable." If flies could sneer, she was sure that was what she would call the expression on his face. "The Tachin, however, do not reproduce in the same way. Our females cannot incubate our young so we must come up with new ways to further our species." He reached for her, sliding a hand over her stomach. "The data I can collect from you will no doubt prove useful for the home hive."

"You're insane if you think I'm going to let you do this to me," Amanda hissed.

"It will be a quick procedure, female. You will survive."

"You're damn straight I will," she growled as she brought her hands up and jammed the tips of her fingers into one of his large black eyes. Something warm and wet ran down her arms as the alien screamed. He twisted away from her, stumbling as he clutched the wound with both hands.

"*You!*" he shrieked. "You stupid, filthy—"

A dark hand shot around to grab his face, snapping his head to the side with an audible crack. She watched Xuvri stand and toss the lifeless body aside, his eyes focusing on her.

"Shh." He rushed to her as she began to cry, dropping down in front of her and pressing his face close to her stomach. "I will not let him hurt you. Not like last time." He began to rattle softly in the same way Zar had done, and although it took the edge off of her nausea, it repulsed her.

"Please, let me go, Xuvri."

He shook his head, the vines flying wildly around his face. "You are mine. I searched for you."

"You stalked me! You terrorized me! I don't find you worthy and I never will!" She brought her leg up between them, pushing away with all the strength she had.

Although the drug the Tachin had used hadn't served its intended purpose, it was still obviously affecting him. Xuvri stumbled backward, glaring at her as he fought to right himself. With a snarl, he lunged forward, knocking Amanda back onto the table as he climbed up on top of her.

"No. No, no, no!" he roared as he stared down at her.

The babies within her kicked and squirmed, no doubt disapproving of all the commotion, and the change that came over Xuvri's face was so sudden and unexpected that she wasn't even sure she was seeing the same male. It was almost as if someone had pulled a mask away and revealed the terrified creature beneath. He dropped his forehead to hers and took a deep breath.

"Leave."

She heard the whispered word, but she hardly believed it had come from him. "Xuvri—"

"I said leave! Go!" he roared again, slamming his hands down near her shoulders.

Amanda wasn't going to wait around for him to change his mind. As fast as she could, she slipped from beneath his body, nearly falling as her weakened legs tried to support her. She was barely across the room and when the door crumpled in on itself, falling with a metallic ring against the floor.

In the hall stood Zar, his violet eyes glowing as he stared back at her. Beside him stood a literal beast. It was nearly as large as he was, with skin that looked like black leather stretched over a steel frame. Its eyes and parts of its body glowed a shimmering gold, and she couldn't help but think it was the most beautiful and terrifying creature she had ever seen.

If hellhounds existed, this must be one.

The beast roared when he saw her and she felt her heart stop when it lunged, sailing over her head and slamming into Xuvri, who had apparently found his footing.

"Wait!" she screamed as three Venium raced into the room after it. "Stop! Please, stop!"

She felt strong arms wrap around her, pulling her away from the carnage and chaos that was unfolding before her. Amanda knew, logically, that she shouldn't feel anything aside from hatred for the Grutex male who had caused her so much pain and worry. Watching this creature close its mouth around his body shouldn't have made her want to cry, but somewhere inside of her, she had understood his grief.

"Zar, stop it! He let me go!" She struggled against him. "He let me go!"

"Oshen!" Zar growled over the commotion. "That's enough! Amanda is safe now."

The beast turned with a snarl as Zar's hand reached out to yank on one of the glowing ribbon-like spines on its back. Its muzzle dripped with blood and it growled so low and deep that Amanda swore she could feel it move through her. This beast couldn't be her Oshen. The smaller spines on his neck began to rattle as she rushed past him, dropping down to check Xuvri's broken body. He hadn't even tried to fight back.

His chest heaved with every labored breath he drew in. Deep

punctures from Oshen's fangs marred his body. She brushed her hand over the skin near his mangled eye.

"I am sorry," he whispered, his lips covered in his own blood. "I am..." His throat worked as he tried to speak again, but his face went slack, his arms sliding from his chest to the floor at her feet.

Amanda stared down at his face as tears welled in her eyes. Strong arms pulled her up, hoisting her into a comforting embrace. Zar leaned his head down to press a kiss to her hair when she rested her head against his shoulder. She was so grateful and relieved that the nightmare was over, but her heart was torn.

"I want to go home."

CHAPTER 31

GULZAR

"*H*e tried to force himself on you, stalked you, abducted you, and nearly got you and our pups experimented on! He doesn't deserve your tears, gynaika." Oshen was snarling as he paced in front of them.

"I don't know what you want me to say. I know what he did was wrong, I know he put us in danger, but you weren't there. You didn't see him." Amanda raked her hands through her hair. "I'm not saying he wasn't wrong, but I think he deserved a chance to fix his mistakes."

"Did you see the female in there? Did you see what was done to her?" The Venium male scrubbed a hand over his face. "If we had found you like that…"

"But you didn't because he let me go. The Grutex have been lied to about what human females want, about what we expect from a mating. He had no idea we didn't mate the way he had been taught—and before you interrupt me, I'm not excusing him.

He had lost his female, lost his children, Oshen. I think something inside of him was broken."

"You're blinded by your emotions, gynaika." Oshen reached his hand out to touch her face, but she knocked it away.

"Seriously?"

"Gynaika—" Gulzar watched as Amanda sidestepped the other male as he tried to pull her into his arms.

"Don't 'gynaika' me, Oshen. You have every right to be mad at him, to never forgive him for what he did, but you don't get to tell me how I should feel." His mate folded her arms over her chest as her lip trembled. "I can't change what happened with Xuvri or the human woman who was in there, but we have the chance to help from now on."

They both watched as she stomped off in the direction Oshen's sister had gone, the tears she had been holding in finally spilling down her face. With a frustrated growl, Oshen spun toward Gulzar. "I was just trying to protect them."

"I know."

"He wasn't in his right mind. He had already tried to force her into mating."

Gulzar nodded, his eyes following their mate until he saw her sit down with the other female. "I am not blaming you, Oshen. There are stories detailing the mating hunts, but they have not occurred for many generations. It seems the tainted ones have continued the archaic tradition."

Luz stepped into the small clearing where they stood, eyeing them cautiously. "I've received word from our sire. He didn't get terribly far with the elders of the tribe, but he said Gulzar's family has requested sanctuary within the dome. I'm going to assist him, if that is all right with you."

"Of course." Oshen nodded.

Gulzar sighed in relief. He had worried about leaving them behind, scared of the repercussions they might face because of what they had done for him and his mates. "Thank you for your help, Luz."

The male smiled warmly. "It is my pleasure."

"Oshen." Gulzar turned at the sound of Lief's voice. "Fyn and I are going to the dome to prepare everyone for your arrival."

"Prepare them for our arrival?" Oshen asked.

"You are bringing not just one alien back with you, but two. We don't need you causing a panic in the streets the moment you exit the pod."

"As long as he doesn't go full beast on anyone else, I think we'll be fine." Evafyn grinned as she walked up to Oshen, placing a hand on his shoulder. "Behave yourself, little brother." She nodded toward Gulzar. "We will see you all soon."

Gulzar stood, moving to lean against one of the larger trees as he watched Oshen's family depart. His little goddess was still sitting on her own, her arms wrapped around herself as she stared off into the forest.

"She hates me," Oshen whispered as he came to a stop beside him.

"She has been through so much lately, Oshen. Give her some time and she will forgive you."

"I hope you're right." He sighed, his hands rubbing at the soft material of the tunic. "She needs something to eat. Carrying two pups looks like it has sucked the life from her."

They watched as their mate lowered herself on to the log she sat on, her eyes closing as the sun played across her skin. She seemed exhausted, and the weight loss had been painfully notice-able as he carried her through the woods away from the carnage of the crashed dome. The little ones within her were growing, sapping what little strength she had.

"You find her something to eat and I will watch over her. We can find shelter for the night so we don't need to move her too far." He could see the reluctance to leave her painted on the male's face. Gulzar placed a hand on his shoulder and squeezed. "Our mate will be fine. Take a moment to clear your head."

With another glance in Amanda's direction, Oshen turned to begin his search, leaving Gulzar alone with their mate for the first time since he found her on the beach. Crouching down in front of her, he let his eyes roam over her face. As if sensing his presence, their young began to call out, reaching along the fragile bond as they sought comfort from him. He pushed air through his crest, releasing a soft rattle to calm their wild movements so they wouldn't disturb their sleeping dam.

"Settle now and let your dam rest. You will be well fed soon."

He sat there with them for a time, calming the younglings and rattling to soothe his mate's palpable anxiety. Sunlight filtered down through the leaves and he tilted his face up to feel the warmth.

Thank you, goddess, for all of your blessings.

Gulzar wished he could give her younglings as well, that he could experience the same thing she and Oshen would feel when these two were brought into the world, but the thought that he might lose her during birth like his own dam was enough to stop that dream in its tracks. He had been a large youngling from what Kyra had told him, and his dam had struggled. His little goddess was so much smaller than any of the females in his tribe, and he couldn't imagine her carrying a youngling that size.

"I will love any young you bring into my life," he whispered as he turned his face into her hair. "My blood or not, I will hold them in my heart as I hold them in my arms."

He stretched his arm back to lay his hand on her belly, marveling at how much it had grown. This was his family; this was the ultimate blessing. He couldn't ever see himself consummating this union out of fear she might become pregnant, but it wouldn't matter. Being with them, being allowed to love them all, meant more to him than anything.

"Thank you, Zar."

Oshen's voice startled him and he looked up to see the other male standing at the edge of the small clearing, fruit piled high in his arms.

"For what?"

"For always being here for her, for the pups. You watched over her, loved her, before I even knew of her existence."

Gulzar looked back at Amanda's face. "She was one of the only reasons I had to live," he said. "She has been a part of my soul for as long as I can remember."

"I'm sorry for what I said before."

"Do not think on—"

"No, let me finish, please." Oshen sighed wearily. "I lashed out at you because of my own insecurities and it was wrong. I am happy to have you as part of our triad."

"I am grateful to be included."

Oshen stepped forward, depositing the fruit on the ground at his feet. "Mouni informed me that these were nutritious and that they should be safe for her to consume." He picked up a galging fruit, inspecting the purple skin.

"They are popular among the tribe. And this one here," Gulzar plucked one of the ripened kelpora from the ground and held it up, "is one of Kyra's favorites. I can almost guarantee our mate has had one."

"Is that one of those lumpy green things Kyra loves?"

They both looked up in surprise at Amanda, who was eyeing the bounty Oshen had brought. "It is."

"Oh, thank you, merciful gods. I'm starving." She sat up and snagged the fruit from Gulzar's hand. "How do you open this thing? I never saw Kyra do it. I just ate what she gave me."

A laugh rumbled through Gulzar's chest as he held his hand out. "I'll show you." With little effort, he cracked the fruit in half, flipping it quickly so that the juices were not wasted. "Scoop the meat with your fingers."

A low moan tumbled from her lips as she dug in, popping small chunks of the meat into her mouth. "It's like guilt-free steak." She sucked the juice from her fingers. "So damn good."

Gulzar felt his body tighten as he watched her finish off the first half and start on the second. He felt his length harden within its sheath, pressing against the slit, begging to be free, but he pushed against it with his palm, willing it to go away. Even Oshen seemed to be coming undone by the way she devoured the food, his eyes never leaving her mouth and his breath quickening.

She wiped her chin as she set the fruit aside. "Thank you." Her eyes swept over him, trailing down over his arm to the hand he had covering his slit. "Are you all right?"

"Yes." The word was little more than a breathy whisper. He swiped his thumb beneath her bottom lip, wiping away the juice she had missed. "You are so beautiful, little goddess."

She reached out with her hand, her fingers grazing his cheek before she leaned forward, pressing her soft lips to his. Gulzar rattled in surprise, his eyes going wide. His lips parted when her tongue ran along the seam, slipping inside to brush his own before running cautiously over the tips of his teeth.

His little mate pressed closer, her hands slipping to the back of his head, tugging at his xines. The tip of his cock slipped free from his sheath and he growled low in his throat as it rubbed against the palm of his hand. This was something completely new, and he wanted more.

Gulzar pulled away from her, his breathing ragged as his eyes narrowed on his mate. "What was that?"

Amanda blinked, her pink lips pursing.

"The kiss?" Her brows furrowed. "No one's ever kissed you before?"

"Not like that, no."

Oshen moved closer, crouching near his leg. The male's scent was nearly as overwhelming as their mate's. It clouded his mind and he growled as his cock pulsed beneath his hand. He watched as Oshen leaned forward, pressing his lips to Amanda's as his clawed hand caressed Gulzar's thigh.

Goddess, help him. This was torture.

Inhaling the combined scents of his mates, Gulzar let his eyes close, listening to Amanda's soft whimper.

Warm lips brushed his chest and he looked down to see Oshen drawing closer, his mouth moving up his throat to his cheek. When Gulzar looked at Amanda, she had her lip caught between her teeth and her fingers trailed gently over her breasts. As he turned his head back, Oshen's lips descended on his. He felt the sharp tips of the other male's fangs nip at his skin and rattled in excitement.

"This is pretty much the hottest thing I've ever seen in my life." Amanda's breathy whisper drifted over him, and Oshen pulled back with a soft chuckle, leaving Gulzar panting and aching for more.

When Amanda reached for the hand that covered his slit, he stopped her. "This is not permitted for me. Those who are damned should not consummate a mating. They should not mate at all."

Amanda frowned. "Zar, if this is something you really don't want to do then I'll respect that, but this whole 'damned' business is something we need to talk about."

Here it was. Here was the rejection he had been waiting for. He cast his eyes toward the ground, not wishing for her to see his pain.

"You're not in that village anymore." Gulzar felt her hands on his face, turning it toward her. "Neither of us gives a damn about their laws. You aren't responsible for what happened to your mother. Do you hear me?"

Gulzar's throat tightened with emotion. "I hear you, little goddess."

"Good," Oshen grumbled, his hand moving into Gulzar's. "You are wanted here. You belong with us in every way possible."

The male reached up to unclasp the tunic at his shoulder. Gulzar flinched as the fabric fell away, revealing the scars. Proof of his damnation.

Amanda gasped, her hand flying to her mouth as she pulled him forward, her fingertips brushing against the closed wounds. "What happened here?"

"These are lashings," Oshen growled. "Who did this to you?"

"They are punishment." Gulzar swallowed thickly. "They are lessons from the elders."

"Why were you punished like this?"

He could hear the tears in her voice and grimaced. "Because I touched you."

"Gods, Zar."

"It was worth every lash." He reached up to twist a strand of her hair around his finger.

"How long have they been doing this to you?" Oshen asked.

"Since I was old enough to withstand it. Lashings were part of my reeducation." He moved his hand up to stop Oshen's hand as he traced the old scars. The first ones I received were for speaking to a woman who was not Kyra or Kythea."

"I'll be glad to never see that place again," Amanda said as she slid her arms around his neck, pulling his face against her breasts. "I'm sorry they treated you so horribly."

The feel of her body against his was enough to reignite his desire and the way Oshen's fingers trailed over his xines had his eyes closing in contentment. This was his life now. Gulzar could feel his worry, his fear, slipping away from him as his mates touched his scarred body.

"No one will ever do this to you again," Oshen whispered

against his shoulder where his lips pressed. "Things will be different within the dome. The Venium are not perfect, but they would never do this."

Gulzar caught his bondmates' gaze and shivered with the force of the desire he felt. He had never imagined that he would find himself mated and he had certainly never thought he would be accepted into a triad, but here he was, surrounded by his mates.

"Is there anything we can get to help them heal? They look so painful." His female frowned.

"The Venium don't normally use materials found out here."

"I am fine. It would not be the first time they had to heal on their own," Gulzar told them, pulling back to look up at Amanda. She still had the headdress tangled in her hair and he reached up to touch the glowing stone that rested against her skin. "Do you know what this is?"

"It was something Kyra and Kythea gave me."

"This is a mating stone." He ran his finger over it, smiling as it shimmered in the light. "We collect them when we find or select our mates. Traditionally, a male will dive into the okeanos to search for one that matches our eyes, or as close as we are able to find. Once it has been retrieved, both mates eat the miliseed so that they are able to breathe beneath the waves. It is within the okeanos, within the waters that Una and her mates united, that our people become one."

"This wasn't from you though."

"This is the stone that my sire gave my dam on the day they were mated." Gulzar felt a smile tug at his lips. "Kyra knew the whole time who you were to me. She knew that this belonged to you." He took her chin in his hand, pulling her lips down to his for a gentle kiss. "You were worth every single strike, every single moment of pain."

"I hate that they hurt you." His little goddess swiped at a tear at the corner of her eye.

"I would take it all on again if it meant I could be blessed in this way. I may never have young by blood, but—"

"Wait." Amanda pulled back, frowning down at him. "What makes you say that? I mean, I know I'm pregnant right now, but these two are going to need siblings at some point."

Gulzar shook his head. "I could never risk your life for my own selfish reasons. I could not bear losing you too."

"There's risk involved with anything we do, but there are ways to lessen complications now."

"I ripped my own dam apart during my birth. I tore her from the inside when I became stuck."

"I'm sure that was just some sort of survival instinct, Zar."

"I was too big for her. Look at you." He took her hips in his hands, pulling her close. "You are so much smaller than she was." Gulzar felt his heart clench at the thought of her having to carry his young, of her suffering as his dam did. "I will not..."

"Your mother didn't have the same options I will," Amanda said, her fingers trailing up his arms. "There are things we can do during pregnancy, ways to monitor a baby's growth. We can prevent that."

"Tell us what we can do to help." Oshen brushed his shoulder.

Closing his eyes, Gulzar took a deep breath, asking himself that same question. What did he need? What did he want? His mates were offering him a life he hadn't even dared to dream of, and he wasn't going to let it slip through his fingers.

"Touch me." The words tumbled from his mouth before he had even realized he'd spoken them. "I have spent my whole life being told I was unworthy of something so simple. I want that from both of you. I want to feel equal."

"I'm sorry for what you went through, Zar." His female whispered as she ran her palm down the center of his chest, watching as his plates glimmered. "I loved you for so long and I'm so glad you're here with us." When the same light appeared beneath

Oshen's hand, Amanda smiled. "You belong with us and no one can take that away." She stepped closer, wrapping them both in a warm embrace.

Fear welled up within him as he allowed his mates to surround him with their presence. Was it really going to be this simple? Were they really going to allow him into their family, into their lives? He had spent his whole life on the outside and here they were, offering to bring him in. His emotions overwhelmed him.

When he pulled back, his breath rushing in and out of his lungs, Amanda shared a knowing look with Oshen. "Maybe you can tell Oshen where to find something to help your back and I can share something with you?" Her fingers brushed over his stomach, dropping down to the hem of the tunic he wore.

"The saku leaves," he rasped out. "They are the only blue leaves in the woods. You cannot miss them."

"Be safe," Oshen whispered into Amanda's hair as he pressed a kiss to her head, his hand caressing her belly before he stepped back with a smile.

When Oshen was out of sight, his little goddess knelt down in front of him, her hands sliding beneath the fabric of his garment, brushing over his hard length. With a growl, Gulzar reached down, pulling her into his lap so that her face was level with his. The xines on his neck reached out, stroking her face and hair, touching the tiny glowing stone that made his heart race.

"You are mine," he whispered the words as if he couldn't believe them himself.

"Yes."

"*Mine,*" Gulzar hissed, crushing his mouth to hers. He worried he was doing it wrong, that his lack of experience was going to make this awkward and unpleasant, but the way she moaned into his mouth sent a shiver of pure lust through his body.

His name tumbled from her lips as she pressed the front of her body to his, grinding against him, digging her fingers into his shoulders.

"Gods, Zar."

He was grateful Oshen had stepped back and allowed him this time with her. It wasn't that Gulzar wanted her to himself—he felt the pull toward his bondmate as well—but the thought that he would have to struggle to please both of them this first time had made it daunting. When his little goddess pulled back, shimmying down his legs until she was on the ground between his knees, Gulzar frowned and tried to pull her back.

"What are you doing?"

She tsked at him, sliding her hands over his thighs. "I want to show you my favorite kind of hug."

He frowned, not even aware there were different kinds of hugs. There was so much to learn. "What kind of hug?"

"It's a little something I affectionately call a mouth hug." Her mouth curled up into a sultry grin while Gulzar began to purr in excitement. "Let me show you."

He watched with bated breath as she slid the straps of her dress from her shoulders, letting the top part fall down to her waist. Her pink-tipped breasts hung free and he reached out to brush his thumb over one of them, growling when she shuddered. She untied the sash around her middle, tossing it behind her as the garment pooled around her feet.

His female was beautiful, and he told her just as much as she sank to her knees again. When her hands slid his tunic over his hips and closed over his cock, Gulzar growled deep in his chest.

"I was wondering what it might look like," she said, her fingers playing along the swollen head. "I've never seen one quite like it."

"Is it different from a human male's?"

"Very different." She laughed quietly, tossing the loosened strands of her hair over her shoulder as she pressed her lips to the inside of his thigh. "I read an article once that went into nearly terrifying detail on the penis of a bee, images and everything included, and I'm amazed at the similarities."

"A bee?"

"You know what? Forget about the bee." She touched the protrusion above his cock, swirling her finger around it as the stem began to vibrate, the small bumps on it wiggling in a circular motion expectantly. "Oh, gods help me. I'm in for it."

"You are going to drive me mad," Gulzar ground out from between clenched teeth.

She smiled, fisting his length as she slowly slid her hand up and down. She might deny her divinity, but right now, with her kneeling before him, his throbbing cock in her small hand, Gulzar couldn't help but see her as the deity he had spent his entire life worshiping.

Amanda pressed a finger to the tapered head before moving slowly down his length where the glands swelled, growing larger beneath her touch. Leaning forward, Amanda let her breath fan out against his flesh, running the tip of her tongue from stem to tip before taking him into her hot mouth. Gulzar's hips jerked up from the ground in surprise as he watched her use her other hand to pump his length while she tried to fit his girth between her lips. She pulled back with an audible pop before smiling shyly up at him.

"A little bigger than I thought," she said with a wink. "We'll just work with what we've got."

She gave him no reprieve, dipping her head and taking him back inside her warmth, pulling a groan from the darkest depths of his body. He had taken himself in his own hands before, but this wasn't the same at all. The sight of his female moving her free fingers along his sensitive slit almost had him spilling within her mouth. He was going to embarrass himself.

Goddess help me.

As if sensing how close he was, Amanda moved faster, swirling her tongue along the bumps and ridges she could reach and then using her hands to squeeze what she couldn't fit in her mouth. He felt her other hand glide over his stem, circling and pinching softly. He could hardly draw air into his lungs.

In a bid to distract himself and prolong the encounter, he ran his hands over her chest, pinching the hardened tip of her breast between his fingers. The moan he drew from her vibrated along his cock, and he hissed at the almost painful pleasure it gave him. His cock jerked, seed shooting from the tip into her mouth as his mate tightened her hold around him.

With a snarl, Gulzar buried his hand in her hair and yanked her off his length, pushing her onto her back as he crawled over her. She arched beneath him as her tongue swiped at her lower lip, her breasts pushing up toward his face as he moved down her body. Gulzar couldn't resist the urge to capture the pink tip, pulling it into his mouth and nipping it with his fangs. His hands moved over her skin, clutching at her legs as they tried to wrap around his midsection.

A breathy sigh fell from her lips when he trailed a finger over the wet folds between her legs. The sounds of her pleasure spurred him on as he explored her cunt, probing gently into the heat of her body. When he pressed a finger into her, she gasped, grinding her hips against his palm.

"Zar!" She clutched at his head and shoulders, grabbing at his xines as she writhed against the forest floor.

"Yes?" he asked, pulling his mouth from her breast.

"Please! Please…"

He wondered idly if a male could "hug" a female in the way she had shown him and he found the idea appealed to him. He pressed his lips to her chest, trailing them over the growing bump of her belly. He nibbled at the skin on her hips and he smiled when he saw her shiver. Gulzar moved down, following the potent scent of her desire, spreading her folds and growling low as he let his gaze roam over her delicate pink flesh.

His eyes swept up her body, locking onto hers as his tongue glided over her from the bottom of her sex to the top. The taste of her body was indescribable, richer than anything he had ever consumed. When his tongue hit the hidden nub, she arched again and he grinned against her.

Amanda gasped. "Do that again."

CHAPTER 32

AMANDA

*I*f she hadn't known Zar, if she hadn't been in the village to witness the way others had treated him, Amanda would never have believed this was his first sexual experience. His tongue, unlike a human's, was rough with tiny ridges running from one side to the other.

Just one swipe of it over her folds was nearly enough to push her over the edge of sanity. When she thought it couldn't get any better, his tongue began to vibrate gently and she sucked in a deep breath as her body tensed.

Butterflies filled her stomach as her heart pounded inside her chest, and she squeezed her eyes shut as she let the pleasure of his touch wash over her. There was movement somewhere to her side, but Zar renewed his efforts and her mind went blank. The vines around his head struck out at her thighs, making her hiss as the light sting heightened the sensations he was giving her.

When she felt a hand move over her breast, followed quickly

by a warm mouth, Amanda's eyes shot open, meeting Oshen's intense golden gaze. His hand moved to her other breast, kneading and pinching the tip as Zar worked her with his mouth. The feeling of both her males giving her pleasure was overwhelming and so much more than she had ever imagined it would be.

Amanda moved her hand beneath the borrowed tunic Oshen wore, sending up a silent thank you to any and every deity that she wasn't going to have to struggle with his usual uniform pants. She found him hard and extruded, the glands at the base already swollen and pulsing with need, his fushori glowing with a fierceness she hadn't seen before.

"You are so beautiful, gynaika," he breathed against her.

The heat she saw in his eyes raised goosebumps along her skin, and Gulzar chose that exact moment to caress her clit with that fantastic tongue of his. Amanda arched up as a moan tore out of her throat and the sweet bliss of her orgasm crashed over her. Shudders racked her, and she felt her toes curl as her body tensed. Gulzar continued to lap at her sensitive flesh, swiping his tongue across her opening as he growled.

"Oshen, please," she whispered, tugging at the braids that hung over his shoulder.

"What is it?"

"I need you. I want you." She whimpered at the loss of Gulzar's heat, but Oshen was quick to take his place, nudging her legs apart as he moved over her.

She shivered when Gulzar reached down to take Oshen's cock in his large hands, stroking it a few times before he angled it toward her sex. The sight of them together made her breath catch. As Oshen pressed himself into her cunt, Zar trailed his fingers up to rub against her clit. Amanda could feel each ridge, each inch as he pressed deeper inside of her, and just when she felt like she couldn't take any more, he bottomed out inside of her. Oshen pulled his hips back slowly before thrusting himself forward in time with the movement of Zar's fingers.

She felt his mating glands swelling inside of her as their hips collided. Gulzar moved up to kiss her, but she tilted her head away, pressing her lips close to his ear, his xines moving up to caress her face as she spoke breathlessly. "You want Oshen?" She could only smile when he growled. "Show him," she whispered. "Show him you want him too."

Zar turned and, with a snarl, reached forward to bring Oshen's mouth down to his for a kiss that turned her on more than anything she had ever seen. She worked herself on Oshen's cock as she watched them with hooded eyes. Her hand stroked Zar's cock, and she smiled when she noticed it was already hard and throbbing, ready for more attention. Oshen hissed when her body tightened around his.

"I need..." Her words ended on a groan.

"What do you need, little goddess?"

She felt Zar's fingers trail over her arm. "I want both of you. I want my mates."

The realization that she could have died in that ship slammed into her and she felt her emotions choke her. She would have never had this opportunity, would have never been able to share her love with both of them. Oshen pulled her up into his arms, flipping them so that she straddled his hips. He looked up at her and touched her cheek, smiling as if he could read her mind.

She turned her head to watch Zar as he moved up behind her, his tongue running along her shoulders and the back of her neck as he got down on his knees. Oshen's cock jerked within her as Zar's hands ran over his thighs, guiding her forward until she was lying on top of Oshen. The tip of Zar's cock pressed into her and she gasped.

Oshen pulled nearly all the way out and she felt both of them thrust together, gently working their lengths inside of her body.

She whimpered at the fullness, at the way her body stretched almost painfully to accommodate them.

"Oh fuck," she breathed, groaning as they moved against one another within her.

Beneath her, Oshen's eyes slid closed and he arched his back, snarling as his glands pressed against her walls.

The small protrusion above Zar's cock pressed against her ass as he sank into her, drawing a moan from Amanda as she met his movements. Oshen's fingers played with her nipples as Zar thrust forward again, grinding her clit against their mate's pelvis. When the vibrating protrusion slipped into her, Amanda's head fell forward.

"You feel so good," Zar groaned as he gripped her hips with his claws, his mouth moving down to kiss her shoulder. "Mine," he growled as he opened his mouth and then dug his fangs into her skin, causing a haze to fall over her vision.

Oshen hissed, and she glanced down to see Zar's claws sinking into the dark skin on his thighs just before she felt his mating glands expand within her, locking the three of them together. Hot seed bathed her walls as they came together, all three of them coming with a moan of pure bliss. Amanda sighed as Zar's tongue stroked the wound he had made, and she clutched at Oshen's arms as they turned onto their sides. For the first time in her life, Amanda felt complete.

❧

"*I*s this the only way to get to the dome?" Amanda narrowed her eyes on the sleek pod Oshen stood in front of, her feet shifting restlessly against the stone platform they stood on.

"It's the fastest and safest way to get you there." Oshen held his hand out to her. "I don't know how long the leaves are going to keep infection from Zar's wounds. I would like for them to be checked by the healer as soon as possible."

"They have never failed Kyra." Zar frowned as he stepped up behind her. "I do not like the idea of being surrounded by the wayward offsprings' technology."

"Well, you happen to be mated to one of them, so I suppose you will get used to it," Oshen drawled, motioning to the pod with his chin. "Let's go, you two."

Amanda bit her lip, shrugging at Zar as she stepped forward into the pod. Her big mauve mate climbed in hesitantly behind her, pulling her into his lap as he sat down on the cushioned bench. His hands cradled her belly and she rested her head against his shoulder as Oshen closed the door.

"Welcome back, Ambassador Oshen."

"Set coordinates to the main dome."

"Setting destination. Please be seated." The pod lurched as it began to move across the ground toward the beach.

Amanda glanced around in wonder as she took in her surroundings. She was finally getting her first good look at Venora without her life being in danger, and it was more beautiful than she had realized. She had once thought it might look like Earth, but she had been wrong.

Red leaves peeked at her from outside the window of the pod, curling black trunks reaching for her as if to welcome her to the new world. She eagerly absorbed everything around her as she looked for any sign of creatures she had encountered over the last few days, but only plant life and terrain were visible.

"Why aren't there any animals out here?"

"The transport emits a high-pitched noise that keeps them away for our protection."

"Interesting," she mused as she turned this way and that in Zar's arms, trying to get a better look.

Oshen leaned forward, plucking a pad from a pocket in the

wall. She watched him as he scrolled, frowning down at whatever it was he was reading. He'd been quiet most of the morning, and she wasn't sure if it was because of what had happened between them the day before or if it was something else entirely. He would tell her eventually. For now, she was going to take in as much as she could. Gulzar shifted uncomfortably beneath her and she squeezed his hand gently.

The babies wiggled in her belly and she felt Zar rattle softly, stopping the nausea that being in the enclosed space was causing. Zar pointed out some of the plants she had seen on their journey, telling her their names and what his people used them for. She recognized the porous rocks they had taken shelter in on their way to the village and again yesterday after they had finally pulled themselves away from one another.

Excitement pulsed through her body, the hairs on her arms standing on end as the first waves licked at the edge of the pod. She was finally going down into the ocean her mate had bragged about. A new world was opened up to her as they sank farther into the surf and she gaped in utter amazement.

"Ooh, look! What's that one? It's like a fish-eating anemone but way longer and translucent!"

Oshen only grunted in response as he continued to scroll, his brows pinched as he chewed at his lip.

"Hey, Meatface! Your mate is talking to you," Mouni announced, ever helpful.

Oshen looked up, a guilty expression flashing across his face. "My apologies, my heart. I'm sincerely glad you find my world interesting. I was just reading the article the healer sent Mouni."

The AI had stolen the words straight from her mind and she could have kissed her for calling Oshen out.

"Article about what?"

"I had inquired while you were sleeping about your sickness and he found a problem that humans have during pregnancy called hyperemesis gravidarum. It is very rare, but he says with the weight you have lost and your symptoms, you qualify for the diagnosis. He said he could confirm at the clinic and talk about a treatment plan to keep you healthy."

"That's good, but I prefer Zar's rattle." She grinned back at Zar before looking around once more. Medical talk could wait until her appointment.

A creature swam near the window and she nearly jumped out of Zar's lap to get a better look. Its body was long and slender, like an eel, but it was transparent and the head looked more like the exoskeleton of a crustacean.

Whatever the eel thing was, it didn't stay around long, dashing off as a reptilian beast drifted too close. This new one was even more extraordinary, with its massive horned shell and the long mermaid's tail that trailed behind it.

Amanda itched to throw on her gear and dive right in, but that would have to wait at least until the little ones arrived. Taps on the glass above her had her looking up to see four claws scooting along the surface. A long, fleshy tether connected the crab-like critter to a large buoyant balloon with flowering at the top.

"Does the noise not keep the sea life away like it did on land? I would think the sound waves would travel better under the water."

"It keeps the larger ones at bay, but some can withstand the noise."

"So it ripples away from the pod then? I can't imagine how many miles out they must scatter considering how far sound waves can carry. I wonder if these are similar to the octopus in that they have limited hearing." Normally, crustaceans like the common prawn were sensitive to higher frequencies. Though she supposed that instead of the statocyst, these could have sensory hairs that made them less sensitive. "I would kill to learn more about the inhabitants you have here! It's all so fascinating."

Oshen smiled as he leaned forward to cup her face, tenderly kissing her forehead. "You don't have to kill anyone to get that chance. I will talk to a few acquaintances and see if I can get you a position with our scientists, my love. Maybe get you diving again," his hand caressed her stomach. "Whenever it is safe again."

"Maybe I could snorkel in the meantime?" She pursed her lips, glancing back into the depths. She hadn't really considered what she might do once she got here. "Do you guys have something similar I could do?"

"Maybe we could look into the miliseeds?" Gulzar supplied.

"I'll ask around. Perhaps, for the time being at least, we use the pods to explore the open water? The city within will have more than enough for you to explore."

"Yeah." She sighed as the pod came to a soft stop. Bouncing her leg anxiously, she looked for something to distract herself from her thoughts. Despite the fact that she would have her mates beside her, meeting new people wasn't exactly something she looked forward to. Zar set her on her feet gently, but he caused the entire craft to shudder as he stood, making Amanda fall into Oshen as she stumbled to the side. He caught her with ease and gave her a gentle smile as he brushed her hair from her face.

"You'll do great. They will love you, not just because I do, but because you are so very worthy of it." He looked over at Zar. "Both of you."

The fact that he knew her so well made her heart ache. Maybe it was the hormones talking, but she really loved this male so much more than she could ever explain, more than she had ever thought possible.

"Get down here, big guy," she whispered as she grabbed his borrowed tunic and pulled him to her level. Soft lips pressed against her own as her fingers tangled into his braids.

The swoosh of the door barely registered in her mind as his

tongue swept into her mouth and explored with a hunger she was more than ready to sate. Tendrils of desire rushed through her, overwhelmed all her senses as a fire burned in her lower belly. A soft, feminine gasp had her rearing back and blushing feverishly when she locked eyes with an older Venium female who stood on the platform outside.

Gulzar's deep, rumbling laugh didn't do anything to cool her heated cheeks.

"I decided to meet you here when the pod sent word that you were coming. I do hope I didn't intrude," she said, not even trying to hide her knowing grin.

"Busted, Meatface," Mouni chimed in.

"Of course not, Daya. We appreciate your thoughtfulness. I had thought to just go to the house. I didn't know you would be looking for us." Oshen squeezed her hand as he addressed the female. "Excuse the AI. She is in need of an adjustment. Amanda, Zar, this is my dam, Nyissa."

Nyissa had a look of noble bearing, her back perfectly straight and hands folded primly in front of her. Five small, tight braids ran along the top of her head into a long ponytail, making the slick sides look as if they had been shaved. Around her slender neck hung a glowing red gem, which Amanda recognized as a glowing stone like the one on her headdress.

The female's fushori flared a bright white when her eyes landed on them, making Amanda squint against it. Her flowing white dress was nearly sheer against her gray skin. If she hadn't known better, Amanda would think she wasn't a day over thirty. Her face showed no hint of age except for small smile lines at the corner of each eye. She held out a hand with artfully painted, dainty claws to her son.

"Come here so I can see you, my pup."

"Daya..." Oshen groaned but took hold of her hand just before he pulled her up into a bear hug.

A giggle of surprise escaped her, and she stared almost reverently down at her son.

"I have missed you so much." He set her back down on her feet and stepped away. "Do you really find me that much of a threat?" she asked with a playful grin, nodding to his hands as he tugged them from her grasp.

"You know I don't. I told you I haven't been able to retract them since I found Amanda. Her body is so vulnerable that the beast seems to constantly be primed to defend her."

"In time you will find control." She smiled wistfully. "You are your sire's son."

"Is he back already?"

"He returned from the village early this morning." Nyissa turned her attention toward Amanda, moving to wrap her arms around her, giving her a small squeeze. "Welcome, daughter of my heart."

When she finally turned to Gulzar, her smile didn't falter. Instead, it grew bigger as she tugged him down into another firm hug. By the look of surprise on his face, Zar hadn't been expecting her to give him such a warm welcome. "Welcome to you as well, son of my heart."

"Thank you," he whispered, swallowing thickly.

Nyissa's smile was knowing as she spun on her heel, winking over her shoulder and moving forward with purpose. The air around her seemed charged with the power she exuded, as if the world bowed to her very presence. Actually, Amanda swore she saw a couple of people bowing their heads as she walked past them.

Glowing plants were strategically placed along the hall to light the way, giving off a soft, natural glow. The walls were made of glass, which made feeding her obsession for the ocean life quite easy. She could lose herself for hours just staring at the underwater world around her.

A few people grabbed their children when they looked Zar's way and hurried inside the nearest buildings as if they thought he was some sort of pariah. What could it possibly be that made them act this way just at the sight of him? Was it really so strange to see aliens here? Oshen had told her about the diversity of the underwater city so a couple of aliens shouldn't have caused such a commotion.

A beautifully ethereal woman with pale gray-blue skin and bright green stripes stood beside a residence that looked like it was made of something akin to obsidian. She had two horns that held up red hair and ears that looked like Venus flytraps. On her shoulders, three mushroom-like ruffles curled up, tipped in blue, and she wore a form fitting black suit. Her black eyes watched Amanda as she passed, a smile working its way across her lips.

Despite the fact that there were other species here, the fleeing onlookers didn't stop. It was starting to make her rather uncomfortable. She reached her hand out and curled it around Zar's when she saw that he had begun to notice as well. Warmth filled her belly as his gaze found hers, his xines, as he called them, wiggling lightly as he drank her in.

"It doesn't matter what they think." Amanda whispered to him. "We love you. We accept you."

The walls of the dome arched high over her head, the curved sides meeting above the city center where the light seemed to be brightest. Towering buildings, higher than anything she had seen on Earth, stretched upward, glinting in the sunlight that filtered in from the surface of the water. There were smaller domes that branched in all directions from the main one. Amanda assumed they were the family pods that she had been told about. She felt overwhelmed by all the sounds and new visuals, yet she wanted to explore more. She wanted to see everything this place had to offer.

Instead of heading off toward one of the family pods like she had expected, Nyissa led them farther into the main city. To her absolute delight, there was a street market or bazaar of some sort set up in the center. Many different species were milling around, trading goods, speaking in strange languages.

"What is that?" some whispered.

"Is that one of the humans the Grutex talked about?"

"What is one doing here?"

"Why is there a Grutex with them?"

"I heard Ambassador Oshen is mated to it."

Nyissa cleared her throat, sending out a few venomous glares as they came upon the gossiping people. She swore the love she felt for her mother-in-law grew tenfold, even as it made her heart ache for the mother she lost years ago.

"We will be stopping by the house to wash up before we check everyone in."

"Check in?" Oshen asked. "Since when do we have to do that?"

"Oh, new procedure. You know how they are constantly changing everything," she replied airily.

If Amanda had known her better, she might have thought that something was up. Maybe this was just how Nyissa was. She saw Oshen arch his brow but he didn't question her. The house she brought them to was downright majestic. It was made of the same black material as the building she had seen when they left the pod, but this one had a more pearlescent appearance with blue and green hues.

There were balconies at nearly every window of the massive home, and it was taller than any of the other ones she had seen on her way through the city. Amanda's stomach clenched anxiously as she craned her neck to gaze up at the very top floor. It was an incredibly daunting sight. She was really interested in seeing the child proofing measures they had to take with as many children as they had living in the home.

"Nyissa." Her voice came out a little shaky even to her own ears, but before she could continue Oshen's mother interrupted.

"It would bring me great honor if you would also call me Daya." She looked at Zar briefly. "You as well."

The anxiety that had been gripping her eased with the words, and her shoulders sagged with relief. "Absolutely. Thank you, daya."

"Now, you were saying?"

"There are so many windows. What happens if someone falls from one? You haven't ever been afraid one of the children—pups, I mean, would fall and be killed?"

"Killed by the fall?" Nyissa tilted her head in curiosity. "Do you not have a tasi on your homeworld?"

"Tasi?"

"Yes, it prevents injury when falling from heights. If the sensor picks it up, an anti-gravity force field will activate and make the landing softer."

"Wow. Fewer broken bones that way, I suppose..." She trailed off as she considered how great that would have been for so many unlucky human children who had ended up in emergency rooms from falling off of trampolines or slipping out of tall trees.

Did kids even climb trees here? She saw some along the way, though they were different from the trees she had first seen on land. These stretched up like acacia trees but were topped with beautiful translucent parachutes that held a whole rainbow of colors. It seemed that each residence in this area had at least two of these planted nearby.

"You have a beautiful home, Nyissa," Amanda said, unable to hide the awe in her voice as she attempted to take in every detail. Gulzar gently squeezed her hand.

"*Daya*." Nyissa stroked a gentle hand down Amanda's hair "I'm glad you like your new home."

"Sorry. Her cheeks heated as she moved through the door that

Oshen held open for her. The ceilings stretched and arched high above her in crescents. The floor was made of a white tile that looked cool and smooth to the touch.

"Same room, Daya?"

"Of course, my pup. It will always be yours."

"Up the stairs, gynaika. The uppermost room is for our use." He looked at his mates with a grin. "I liked to be as close as possible to the okeanos."

"I find that completely unsurprising." Amanda smiled knowingly. "It sounds amazing. Show me?"

He reached out and cupped her elbow as they ascended the stairs, like he was afraid she would fall. She wouldn't hold his fear against him; even Gulzar was holding onto her. She had been feeling weaker than usual from her last few days within the village. Today had been good, but she was thankful for their support. Nyissa called up from the bottom of the staircase that she would wait for them in the viewing room, wherever that might be, until they were ready to leave.

CHAPTER 33

AMANDA

*O*shen led them higher and higher until they reached a single door at the very top of the stairs. He swung it open and ushered them both inside. As if the babies knew they were finally alone again, they kicked furiously and Amanda's stomach roiled. She smacked a hand over her mouth as she rushed to the bathroom only to realize she had absolutely no idea where it was in here.

Before she could even try to ask Oshen to point her in the right direction, she lost her battle to keep down the meager contents of her stomach. Vomit pooled on the floor at Amanda's feet as she doubled over, and she felt hot tears burn the back of her eyes as her face flushed with embarrassment.

"I'm so sorry, Oshen!" She wiped her mouth with the back of her hand. "I couldn't hold it in anymore."

Gulzar soothed his hand down her back, rattling softly. "I apologize, little goddess. I did not feel the little ones until it was too late to calm them."

"It isn't your fault." She swallowed before drawing in a deep breath.

"It is all right, gynaika. No need for tears." A button on the wall lit up with a wave of Oshen's hand and he pressed a finger to it. A large, round disc creeped out of a slot in the bottom of the wall, sweeping over the mess she had made and completely removing it before rushing back to hide within its nook. "Easily fixed."

"Where's the bathroom?"

He moved further into the room, waving his hand at a certain point on the wall so that a hidden door was revealed, opening up to a smaller chamber. On the inside wall, he tapped a small button and then held down another as an object looking pretty similar to an Earth toilet appeared next to him. He gestured at it with a grin. "There, now it will stay out for you, my heart."

"Thank you," she said, sighing with relief.

"No thanks needed. We should all wash up anyway."

He and Zar helped her to undress, and she didn't bother to hide her interest as they did the same for themselves before carrying her to the shower. They all washed their bodies, scrubbing away the grime from their travels. When they had finished and dried off, Oshen slipped a beautiful dress over her head, made from a wonderfully soft material that was a dusty rose color.

"Be kind to your dam, mikra," he whispered against her slightly rounded belly. She smiled down when she felt him nuzzle his face into her, stroking his braids while he continued talking to their babies. "She needs all the strength she can get. Behave today."

It was moments like these, when her big warrior showed such tender emotions, that she understood why she had never had a lasting relationship with any other man. She had always been meant for him and Zar. No one but her mates could have loved her this fully.

"Where did you get this dress? It's gorgeous," she said, giving it a little bit of a twirl so she could watch it twist around her legs.

"I had it made for you. I asked Daya before we left for Venora," he replied, his fushori lighting up and his cheeks flushing a darker gray. "I wanted to give you something you could grow into for when you conceived. I admit I hadn't thought it would be so soon."

Could he be any more perfect? Goosebumps swept over her body as she smiled. Gulzar crouched down, rattling out a soft purr and nuzzling her stomach.

"We can do this together," Zar whispered.

When they were all ready and she was feeling well enough, Oshen led them back downstairs and they left the family home, following Nyissa down the street. Each building they passed seemed to sit a little higher than the next in a rainbow of colors. If she didn't know better, she would think they were made out of pearls. It seemed fitting for an underwater community.

The dark depths of the ocean above her called, and she tilted her head back to try and center herself. They beckoned to a part of her she hadn't been able to indulge in for months. A shadow passed overhead, belonging to a creature larger than any ocean dwelling animal she had ever seen. The thing looked like a bug with ridges along its exoskeleton, fins flared from its dragon-like face and tentacles spread out from its body. It was a brilliant blue and looked to be the size of two passenger planes put together. Describing it as massive seemed inadequate.

"What is that?" A loud roar shook the dome around them as it passed overhead. She had to get her hands on that thing! What was it made up of? Was it a predator? She had to know more.

"That's a plokami. They are notoriously hard to kill and one of the reasons we have the soundwaves to scare off predators."

One long tentacle dragged against the glass of the dome, and a loud sound vibrated through the enclosed space, making her wonder how she hadn't heard it at all during her stay. "Are we in any danger? Could it break through the dome?"

"No, my love. They are actually incredibly rare. Seeing one is considered a good omen." Oshen pulled her into his arms. "We are only in danger if we are outside the dome."

The thing reminded her of a terrestrial crustacean called pill bugs, or rollie pollies, back on Earth that she had grown up playing with. Only where rollie pollies had legs, the plokami had tentacles that flared out.

"You know, the tentacles of many species mainly work like muscular hydrostats. Meaning they have no skeletal system and work like hands to grab things and propel its host along. Many have sensory receptors so they use them to not only feel, but to see, smell, and taste too. It's their best form of defense. Maybe that's why you guys have such a hard time hunting them." Oshen's eyes had grown round and glassy as they usually did when she found she had been on a tangent. He had once told her he had no idea where she kept all of these random facts stored because every episode contained something he had never heard before. A blush colored her cheeks as she shut her mouth. "I'm babbling again, aren't I?"

"It's all right. You're adorable. I love hearing your voice." Oshen tilted his face down to nuzzle into her hair, purring deeply. "Let's catch up."

She hadn't even realized they had fallen behind.

The streets seemed less crowded as they made their way over to what looked like a large courtyard. Little plants that looked like blue bulbs were strung from tree to tree, which were now lit with their own luminescence. Groups of people milled about talking among themselves, going between tables that were filled with unfamiliar foods. Some looked like oranges but had spikes, while others looked like blocked cheese but were sickly green in color.

The aromas that met her nose were enticing but yet her stomach roiled again.

Zar pushed a rattle through his crest and a calmness took her over once again. She smiled up gratefully at him.

Was this kind of meal normal for their people? Oshen gave her lower back a gentle nudge, reminding her to keep walking, but she moved forward with hesitant steps. Something felt off, and it was making her nervous. She had grown up with such a small family that she had never really gotten used to having so many others around her like this. Social anxiety had been a real problem for her for many years. Jun had been the first person to really put her at ease and not judge her for her interests and insecurities. She accepted Amanda, quirks and all.

Just the thought of Jun made her heart ache. How was her best friend? They had so much to catch up on. A large Venium male with red eyes stood near one of the tables, holding a small baby. He stepped forward with a smile when he caught sight of them. Right away, she could see the likeness that made it impossible to miss the fact that this male was Oshen's father.

They shared the same broad features, and even the flare of their gills when they got emotional was nearly identical. His tail reached forward hesitantly, but he snapped it back to rest around his feet. One of his fingers trailed over the white braids on top of the small head that rested on his chest. The baby in his arms opened her bright pink eyes and locked onto Amanda, just before she parted her tiny black lips and let out the softest of sounds. Her heart swelled at the overabundance of sheer cuteness the little one exuded.

Soon she would have two of her own, but her hands itched to soothe the little one. She stepped forward at the same time as the red-eyed male.

"Oshen." He nodded toward her mate, who wore a wide, excited smile before he turned his attention to her again.

"Daughter and son of my heart." His head bowed as if to show them the greatest respect. "I am proud and so very honored to have you both here on this day."

His attention on her seemed to draw every eye in the courtyard directly to their small group. All at once, every voice in the crowd gave a loud shout. "Happy Shower Day!"

"Shower day?" Amanda turned to Nyissa with a questioning arch of her brow. She knew Oshen's mother had to be behind this.

"Is this not what your people call it?" She frowned, her hands going to her hips. "I spent a lot of time in the viewing room looking up how humans celebrated bringing a new pup into the world..." Her lip quivered. "Did I get it wrong?"

"No, not wrong!" Amanda looked around, swallowing dryly. "It's perfect."

She had never thought that Oshen's mother would set up a whole baby shower for her, especially with everything that was currently going on. It wasn't that she wasn't grateful, but she was starting to feel overwhelmed. When they began introducing the family and friends who had gathered, it didn't do anything to calm her nerves. The only thing that made her feel like she wasn't adrift in this sea of new faces alone was the fact that Zar looked just as lost as she felt.

There was no way on Earth—or Venora for that matter—that she was going to remember any of these names or even their faces. She knew the baby was Ina from Oshen's stories, and his father introduced himself as Calder. Then there was Vac, Nalah, Kolt, and Dolass... or was it Solass? Lief, Luz, and Evafyn she had met the day before. Amanda thought back to the day she saw the family photo in Oshen's room on the ship and smiled. She hadn't been wrong when she had told him she wasn't going to be able to remember.

"Don't worry, Amanda. You will learn us all with time." Evafyn put a comforting hand on her arm. "We understand and will remind you when you need it. None of us will hold a forgotten or mixed up name against you." She looked so much like her mother, but her fushori glowed a softer yellow than Oshen's. "Even we sometimes get confused."

Arms wrapped around Amanda from behind, and when she looked over her shoulder, she wasn't surprised to find Ky grinning like a fool.

"You made it." Amanda turned to throw her arms around the taller female.

"Of course I did. I could not just leave you with my arrogant brother." Ky laughed before pulling away. "Come now, tell me you are well."

"I will be." Amanda sighed as she allowed herself to be pulled away with Ky from all of the commotion.

"Who was he?"

It took Amanda only a moment to realize what she meant. "He was a Grutex who followed me from Earth."

"Why follow you all the way here?"

"I don't know." She shrugged, her fingers playing nervously with the material of her dress. "He said he could feel me. I'm not sure what that means exactly, but I think it must be in the same way Zar has described."

"That makes some sense, actually."

"How so?"

"The Sanctus were able to read the minds of others. This is why it is assumed they were taken away. These were the children who most closely resembled Una. Those who share this trait normally have a small part of the original ability. They can connect with their mates and others who share it." Ky frowned. "There have been stories of such people going mad when they cannot find the ones they connect with. Zar was lucky to have you. We had feared for him, feared he had finally gone mad when he confessed that he was seeing a goddess."

"What do you mean?"

"Zar found you before he went insane, but can you imagine what it must be like to never find the one you are connecting with or someone who shares the same ability? I imagine after a life-time of having not found this person that when he found you, someone who had a bond with another like him, he broke. Perhaps he latched onto you because he feared he might never find what he was actually looking for."

Amanda sighed again. It was just another sad layer to Xuvri's story.

"Go, have fun. Enjoy your new family. You deserve it." Ky gently pushed Amanda back to the party. "We will catch up more later."

The "little party," as Nyissa called it, was going better than she had expected. His family had welcomed her and Zar with open arms and they all seemed to be very happy for her and the promise of not just one new baby, but two. All wished her and her "pups" good health. Oshen's maternal grandmother, Cassya, was one of her favorite relatives so far. She looked to be barely older than Nyissa and was so straightforward that she left little room for worry.

"May I rub your belly for luck?" Cassya smiled, an eyelid twitching as if she was exerting great effort to not move her hand. "I read in many Earth cultures that it is considered rude to touch, but here, it is considered the closest one can get to the gods outside of a triad," she said as she looked at Zar with a grin.

Amanda laughed. "Of course. Feel free to give them a rub whenever you want."

"Gia!" she quickly scolded when Amanda forgot to use the term for grandmother. But the woman's face held nothing but warmth as her light blue fushori lit with obvious pleasure. Her hand reached out to caress Amanda's stomach reverently as she began to mumble words that Amanda couldn't even hope to understand. Cassya's hand moved in circular motions as she spoke, crossing over her abdomen at the end of each sentence.

Oshen spoke up beside her in a gentle whisper. "She is asking that the Goddess Una and her mates, Ven and Nim, watch over you. That they give you as many blessings as they have bestowed Daya, and place over you all of the protection that is within their power. She prays that the moon gods will shine their light on our mating."

Amanda nearly jumped when the woman bent down and pressed her forehead to her stomach. "May the gods see fit to bestow mercy on you and ease your sickness so that you may enjoy the lives you are forming." Cassya pulled back, standing as she leaned her forehead against Amanda's as if closing the prayer. "I will try to travel to the mainland and search for the plant my own gia used for sickness. Perhaps it will help you as well, my little daughter."

"Oh no, please don't trouble yourself, Gia." Her eyes burned with tears that she couldn't hold in.

Cassya's hand cupped her cheek as Oshen wrapped his tail around her leg. "You are a delight. I am glad my grandpup found such a worthy mate."

"Thank you for everything, Gia."

Her heart felt so full. This was where she was meant to be.

CHAPTER 34

OSHEN

$\mathcal{T}$he early morning light that filtered down through the dome and into his room woke Oshen. He knew that this was artificial light and not really the sun since they lived so far beneath the surface of the Okeanos, but he still reveled in its warmth. He turned his face to look at Amanda, who was curled up between both him and Zar, sleeping soundly.

Her hair was tangled around her face, her lashes brushing her cheeks as her mouth hung open just slightly. The cutest little sounds came from her in her sleep, making his heart flutter. She was his everything. Seeing her wrapped protectively in his bond-mates arms made his kokoras swell with need.

His beast rumbled within him as Oshen ran his hand up her thigh. A moan fell from her lips as she turned onto her back, causing her breasts to spill from the shirt she had insisted on wearing. He had never been so glad that they were able to retrieve her luggage from the crash site. He ran his hand up her body and slowly down her arms until he grasped her wrists, pinning them above her head.

A gasp caught in her throat as her blue eyes flew open, looking up at him with unabashed desire. *Mine.* His hips pushed against hers, grinding steadily as her scent grew more potent from the delicious friction. Her knees closed against his hips when he tried to pull back. He felt the bed dip gently, but paid no mind as he leaned down to nip at the top of her exposed breast.

"Oshen," she whimpered.

Hands gripped his hips, pulling him back against the heat of a hard, throbbing kokoras. Fangs pricked at the skin on his nape, causing a shiver to run through his body.

"Good morning," Zar growled against his ear.

His own kokoras swelled almost painfully as his bondmate pressed himself into him from behind, reaching around to grab the swollen base of his mating glands. Oshen ran his tail up Zar's thigh before wrapping it around the male's hard member. The other male reached around Oshen's hip, his claws extending from his nail beds so he could shred the thin shorts she wore. She giggled, watching as they worked together to toss aside the fabric.

"Take her, Oshen," Zar said. "Show her she belongs to us."

He didn't need to be told twice. As Zar lined the tip of his cock up with her soaking slit, Oshen pushed forward slowly. He wanted her to feel every ridge, to need more, and to beg for his glands. Pulling back from her breast to meet her eyes as he watched the pleasure wash over her face. *Ours. Always ours.*

Zar moved his hands to either side of Oshen's hips again, pulling him back before pressing him forward into Amanda. The sweet pain of Zar's fangs sliding into the flesh of Oshen's shoulder only made his need spike, and he thrust his hips forward, harder into their mate. The nudge of the vibrating cock against his ass spurred his desire.

Yes. Take me, the beast growled, making its lust for his bondmate known. His claws extended, and the skin on his hands began to darken. *Goddess help me.* Now was not the time to shift. Oshen closed his eyes, trying his best to concentrate on Amanda as he moved within her and his bondmate as Zar pressed against his back.

"Do you want me, Oshen?" Zar asked, his breath warm against the back of Oshen's neck.

"Yes," he growled, pistoning his hips faster as excitement coursed through him.

"Oh gods, yes," Amanda whimpered, a grin spreading across her face as she panted beneath him.

"Not yet," Zar teased, pulling away from Oshen as he slipped from the bed.

He moved up next to Amanda, pressing the tip of his kokoras against her cheek. Oshen watched as she turned her head and eagerly opened her mouth for him. The sight of his bondmate sliding into her tight mouth nearly had him spilling inside her warm walls. The beast pushed against him, willing Oshen to let him rise to the surface, but he couldn't afford to lose control. Already, he could feel his teeth elongating within his mouth and the sting as the spines poked through the skin of his back. Oshen moved her wrists into his left hand, sliding his right down to steady her hip so he could thrust harder against her. He pulled back before pummeling into her channel again. His head filled with the sound of their hearts beating in thunderous roars as one, pleasure shared equally between them as they loved one another.

With a whimper, his mate arched beneath him, her mouth sucking their bondmate as both males worked themselves into her. Oshen plunged deep, his mating glands swelling painfully as they slipped into her tight cunt, locking him in place.

Then he felt it, the rippling of her walls as her orgasm hit, clamping down on his kokoras as she cried out around Zar. His bondmate pulled out of her mouth, moving behind Oshen as he grabbed him around the middle and pressed his smaller stem into his body. Zar's kokoras rubbed between his and Amanda's bodies, sliding through the slick they had created. He worked himself faster in and out of Oshen as an explosion of pleasure was ripped from him.

Immersed deep in his own pleasure, Zar clung to Oshen, pounding into him with total abandon. Oshen gritted his teeth, the beast hissing and growling in pleasure as he felt himself spill into Amanda just as Zar grunted and pressed against his backside, bathing the outside of her cunt in his warm seed as he came between them.

"You are both mine," Zar whispered, his hand gripping Oshen's braids so that he could turn his face for a firm, but gentle kiss.

The beast within him purred with satisfaction. *Yes.*

~

"You seem to be doing well," Oshen commented as he looked down at Vog.

"The sooner the healers let me out of this bed, the better," Vog said, annoyance flashing across his face. "I have things to see to."

"Like what?"

"Like explaining to the council why we took a human female from Earth before speaking with their government first." Vog's frown deepened. "As an ambassador, that was supposed to be your job."

Oshen felt there was more he wasn't being told, but after years of serving with the commander he knew better than to prod.

"Amanda was in danger. We could not leave her on the planet."

"They won't care about that Oshen."

"Earth's government or our council?" he asked, arms crossing over his chest.

"Both, most likely. You know how this all works, ambassador." He added when Oshen grunted. "This wasn't your first assignment. You were well aware of what could happen when you took the female without any communication with–"

"There was a deranged male after her. You didn't see what he did to the other human female he had taken!"

"Lower your voice, Ambassador," Vog warned.

"Amanda is my mate," Oshen said once he had collected himself. "I was not going to leave her as a captive, no matter what you all think."

"I never said I disagreed with your actions."

Oshen stared at the commander for a moment before shaking his head. "You are the most impossible being I have ever met in my life."

The other male shrugged his shoulder. "Have you found your mate's little beast?"

"Hades?" Oshen shook his head. "No. We saw no signs of him on the beach or in the woods."

"We should look again."

"We?" Oshen asked.

"You. I meant you should look for him," Vog amended, his eyes refusing to meet Oshen's.

"Of course. You have important matters to attend to, after all."

Oshen excused himself when the healer arrived to change Vog's bandages. He stopped in with Brom, Amanda's healer, to confirm his mate's next appointment before leaving the building and heading home.

As frustrating as Commander Vog could be, he had been right about one thing: Hades needed to be found, and soon.

The cat had already been out in the wild for over a week. Amanda missed him and would burst into tears anytime she saw something small and fluffy within the dome. His gills flared in annoyance as he walked through the door of his family home.

"Zar," he growled as he pushed his way into his personal quarters. The sight of his mates curled around one another on the bed made him want to forget about everything so that he could join them. His little gynaika was so beautiful when she slept.

"You are going to wake her," Zar whispered, his large hand caressing her belly.

"I'm sorry." He sat on the edge of the bed. "I have an idea for a mating gift."

His bondmate slowly untangled himself from Amanda, climbing out of bed. Oshen led him out into the hall, his eyes going bright.

"What is your idea?"

"We are going to find Hades."

~

$\mathcal{F}$inding the ball of fluff was a lot easier said than done, he realized. They had practically scanned all of Venora in search of the little beast, but they hadn't found even the smallest clue as to where he might be. Oshen stared into the distance, his eyes roaming over every tree, bush, and small rock. Rubbing at his neck as his skin prickled, Oshen darted a glance behind him. He had the strangest feeling he was being followed.

"What did you say the beast looks like again?" Zar asked, ducking his head into a small, hollow log.

"Like a tigeara, but smaller. He is about the size of one of their cubs."

He nodded in agreement before he turned to Oshen with a smile. "Good luck on your hunt today."

"To you as well." Oshen laughed, watching as his bondmate departed, following him with his eyes until he was just out of sight before continuing on for the day. With any luck, they would be able to find the elusive cat soon, or he hoped so anyway. His patience was starting to wear thin. This felt like the one thing he and Zar could do for their female to bring her a little happiness. They hadn't been able to get through to Earth since returning to the dome so he couldn't even reunite her with Jun. At least the time he had spent looking for Amanda on the mainland had been useful during this hunt.

If only he had thought to put a tracker on the beast before leaving Earth. That would be the first thing he did when he recovered him.

One uur passed before he heard the sounds of someone, or something, coming toward him. Oshen braced himself, extending his claws as he scanned the area.

"Oshen!"

He frowned, tilting his head at the sound of Zar's voice.

"Oshen! I found him!"

Oshen groaned, rubbing a hand over his face. The male had already brought him more than one animal over the course of their search that looked nothing like the cat. The thought that he could be bringing another such beast did not excite him in the least.

"Are you sure this time?"

"I am sure," Gulzar said, panting as he pushed through the brush.

Like before, this wasn't Amanda's cat he held; it was something much, much worse. Gulzar stood with a tigeara cub trapped in his big hands. The little black and gray beast was clawing and biting at Zar's arms, trying its best to get free as it hissed its displeasure. The only thing they could be grateful for was that the outer fangs, which were the strongest, had yet to grow in. The little creature was gumming his arm to death. Deep gouges lined his flesh from where the cub's claws had dug in.

"Zar, that is not what you think it is."

"Sure it is, and he is just as mean as you said he was!"

The beast sprang free of his bondmate's grasp. It lunged at Oshen, catching his face with its claws as it growled. When he thought things couldn't get any worse, another fluffy body latched onto the first as a loud yowl filled the space, both creatures toppling to the ground as Oshen was left staring in shock. Hades had the cub pinned to the ground and was hissing angrily. Hades must have been following them the entire time. Oshen leaned down, scooping the dirty beast into his arms just as Zar caught the cub by the scruff of its neck.

"This," Oshen muttered, "is Hades."

"Oh." Zar looked disappointed for a moment before he looked again at the beast in his arms. "She would love this one as well, no?"

"We cannot gift our mate a braxing tigeara."

Zar frowned, cuddling the hissing beast to his chest. "I found him all on his own. A female will never abandon her cub, which most likely means he is orphaned." When Oshen merely blinked at him, Zar sighed. "You are right. I will simply leave him here to die. Alone."

For the love of the goddess...

"It's not going to stay small forever."

"I am aware of this. I have hunted these woods since I was a youngling."

Oshen sighed in frustration. "Do you want to die? If you bring that home, it will grow up and eat you."

"It loves me." The cub swatted at Zar's face as he leaned in to kiss its head. "With time, it will love me."

"It already wants to eat you!" Oshen grumbled as the beast gummed his arm again.

"It will be fine."

How had he managed to mate the two most soft-hearted beings in the universe? "Just keep it away from our mate."

"I will keep it in the spare room and train it every day." Zar's grin seemed to stretch from ear to ear.

How they managed to make it back into the dome and all the way to their home without anyone stopping to ask what the brax they were doing with the animals was nothing short of a miracle.

Instead of trying to slip in through the front door, Oshen led Zar through the back garden into the side door. When the other male shut the door behind them, Hades panicked, sinking his tiny fangs into Oshen's arm and fleeing down the hall.

"Wonderful. Now the hunt begins again," Zar muttered.

"No, it does not," Oshen said calmly. "First, we need to get this thing put away." He stared at the tigeara in Zar's arms.

Zar narrowed his eyes. "Its name is not 'thing.'"

"Oh? Then what is it?"

"Mister Fluffy Paws."

Oshen couldn't stop his groan. Amanda had been writing little books for their pups, stories about a cat named Mister Fluffy Paws who goes on crazy adventures. She had started reading the first of them to his youngest siblings nearly every night and he had caught Zar sitting among them, completely enthralled.

Oshen stared into his bondmate's face. "Mister? Do you even know if it is a male?"

"No." He looked away before trying to flip the thing in his arms as he examined its underbelly. "I have never been this close to one. Is it male or female?"

It didn't seem to have any features that would give them a clue as to which gender it was. "Mouni, how do you tell a male tigeara from a female tigeara?"

"The males have two bright stripes of color down their bellies, while females do not have these stripes."

Oshen looked at the belly as the tigeara wiggled around in an attempt to get free. He didn't see any stripes. "I think this is female, Zar."

Gulzar nodded his head with conviction. "Right. So... Miss Fluffy Paws."

"Go put *Miss* Fluffy Paws away, and I will look for Hades."

A few ure later, when Oshen still hadn't found Hades, he considered conceding defeat. Even using his beast's heightened sense of smell hadn't helped.

"Oshen?"

He froze in place as Amanda called out to him. *Not yet!*

"You're home!" she exclaimed as she rounded the corner but stopped in her tracks when she saw his face. "What the hell happened to you?"

"Food is finished!" Daya yelled, saving him temporarily from having to answer.

Oshen grabbed Amanda's hand, pulling her down the stairs and into the gathering room where they took their meals.

"Daya! Dele and Tashal aren't sharing!" Kherelan, his youngest brother, ran into the room, a pout set firmly on his little face.

"Share what, my pup?" Daya turned to look where he was pointing as the girls walked through the doorway.

Dele, his sister who was only six solars, carried a disgruntled-looking Hades covered in bows and ribbons. Amanda stared as her cat was hauled in by the two younger females, who looked incredibly proud of their newest playmate. All of the Venium in the room jumped up, grabbing the smaller children and hiding them behind their bodies.

"Drop that!"

"Where in the world did you find that?"

"What are you thinking?"

The voices all meshed together in the chaos as everyone shouted.

"*Brax*! Put it down!" Lief jumped to the front, claws extended and fangs bared. His fingers brushed the holster on his side as he crouched, looking ready to pounce.

Amanda stepped forward quickly, putting herself between her cat and the family. "He's just my pet! He isn't dangerous!"

"You have a tigeara as a pet?" Dolass, his brother who was only fourteen solars, gave a toothy smile. "That is so awesome!"

"His name is Hades, and he is not a tigeara. He is an animal from Amanda's homeworld called a *cat*, pup. They are companions." Oshen laid a hand on his father's shoulder. "I am sorry I haven't had a chance to introduce him. He ran as soon as I got home."

"It's not dangerous?" Calder asked as he eyed the cat his daughters were fawning over.

"No, the worst he will do is protect you from your visitors." Oshen laughed. Maybe he shouldn't tell them what Gulzar brought home just yet.

His father nodded. "No scales lost, Oshen." He gestured to Amanda, who was trying not to laugh at Hades' predicament. "If it makes your mate happy."

So maybe it wouldn't take much to talk them into not tossing Zar's pet back up on the mainland. The younger children ducked out from behind the adults, begging to have a turn petting the ferocious beast. They cooed and fawned over him as he rolled onto his back on the floor.

EPILOGUE

AMANDA

A COUPLE MONTHS LATER...

"Are you sure this will work?" she asked, worrying her lip between her teeth.

"The healer says you will be okay." Oshen ran a hand down her back.

"The healer can go suck a dick." Pregnancy was not making her feel very nice.

Zar's dark, velvety laugh tickled over her skin, sparking along her nerves like electricity from an eel. Just enough shock to get her attention, but not enough to hurt. She hummed, running her hand down his chest as she licked her lips. They had spoken with the healer about the miliseeds, had run all of the tests, and even though they had been told it was perfectly safe, she still felt doubt tug at her.

"It is our mating ceremony. If we weren't sure, we wouldn't

risk it." Oshen smiled down at her, twirling a lock of her hair around his finger.

"Okay…" Amanda held her hand out for the seed. "Hand it over."

The seed looked odd, but she hadn't ever seen one that was so perfectly star-shaped before. With a shrug of her shoulders, she popped it in her mouth and swallowed the pill-sized seed with a grimace.

Oshen reached a hand forward and touched the wall beside the door like she had seen him do at home. There was a daunting number of buttons, and she felt like she would never remember which one controlled what. He pressed a large red one and the door in front of them opened with a soft woosh.

Why is it always the red buttons?

With a deep breath, she stepped into the airlock chamber with her mates, watching as Oshen closed the entrance that led back into the dome. There was a slight hiss and a click before a light over the outer door lit up green.

"Ready?" he asked.

"As I'll ever be," she muttered.

Zar's hand slipped into hers as it shook and he let out a gentle purr. "You will be just fine."

Oshen pressed another button and water began to fill the room. Anxiety curled deep in her stomach as it rose to her calves and then her waist. It made it to her chin before her heart began to pound hard enough that she could feel her pulse in her neck.

She was going to die. Not really, but it felt like it.

Despite the beauty as the outer door opened, Amanda held her breath, worried about whether the miliseed would actually allow her to breathe underwater. It was her mate's gentle touches and reassuring looks that made her breathe in deeply. Okay, maybe it was also her burning lungs.

To her surprise, she had no difficulties. Her eyes went wide when something moved on her neck. *What the hell?* Amanda reached up to touch her skin and nearly choked when she felt three horizontal slits. She had gills. Her marine biologist heart was singing with the endless possibilities this presented her with.

Her worries were soon swept away by the gentle caresses of her mates. The way they were unafraid to touch each other, to show one another affection, brought her so much happiness. Amanda looked pointedly at Zar, glad that their bond had grown stronger over the months of them being aware of what it was and how to use it. Ky's knowledge had helped tremendously.

I want to watch you with each other, she concentrated as hard as she could, hoping he could read her.

Her only answer was Zar sweeping Oshen up into his arms, into a spin that made the water shimmer and blur around them. His mouth descended on Oshen's, licking his lower lip until he opened for him before delving inside. They kissed each other like each stroke was a breath of fresh air, like nothing mattered but the next touch of their tongues.

She watched as Zar's hand trailed down between them, teasing their mate's slit, growling as Oshen's cock extruded into his palm. Her cunt pulsed with need as Zar ran his hand over Oshen's length, pumping him as if it were his own cock. On Earth, this might be looked down upon, but here with her, this was everything she craved.

Amanda pushed her way over to her mates, smiling as Oshen wrapped his tail around her waist and pulled her close. She reached her hand down to where Zar was partially extruding himself and began to gently tease his tip until he fully pushed through. They would forever be her males, and she would never discourage them from loving each other as well. It was the most beautiful and exotic thing she had ever witnessed, and she couldn't wait to see more.

~

*E*ven as heavily pregnant as she was, Amanda raced toward the daunting but familiar ship. They had gotten the call this morning, and she hadn't even been able to brush her hair before she was off to the landing pad. Jun was here. After months of not being able to get in touch with her, Jun was finally here. That she had shown up on a Grutex ship instead of a Venium one didn't surprise her at all.

The port was in complete chaos when they finally reached it. People were yelling at one another, toting plasma shooters—which Oshen said was a very rare occurrence—and there was a huge Grutex ship sitting directly in the middle of the landing pad.

A weight she hadn't realized she had been carrying around was lifted from her chest as she realized what this meant. Where there was Jun, there was a very enchanted Brin. Oshen wouldn't have to worry anymore. He looked better than the last time she had seen him. Better, but very angry. The male was standing toe-to-toe with a beautiful Venium female who also looked like a warrior, both snarling and yelling hotly.

"Brin's dam," Oshen whispered.

Brin's blue fushori was pulsing, and his tail whipped behind him as he spoke. What the hell was going on here? The moment her feisty best friend met her eyes, she began tearing a path through the crowd toward her.

"Amanda! Hey, Fishboy! Someone who will fucking listen!" Amanda's heart soared at the sound of Jun's voice. "Fishboy! I need your help…" She stopped in her tracks as her eyes met Zar's. "The rumors are true then? Venium have teamed up with the Grutex?"

Brin snickered behind her, his tail wrapping around her calf. "She called you Fishboy."

"No, they haven't. This is my mate, Zar." Amanda grinned, happy to see them.

"Shut up, Glowworm," she mumbled at Brin as she looked over her shoulder before her gaze settled back on him. "Oshen, something is wrong."

Oshen automatically stood at attention. "Tell me what is going on."

Jun narrowed her eyes, suspicion clearly setting in. "Well, here's the short version: we were kidnapped. We escaped. Now we're here, and *your* people have detained some of *our* people." Crossing her arms over her chest, she tapped her foot on the ground impatiently. "And you're going to help me get them back."

"You were missing?" Oshen asked.

Why hadn't they been told? Evafyn, who had met them there, looked away guiltily.

"You knew, didn't you, Fyn?" Oshen accused.

"We did not want to worry Amanda and risk her losing the pups," she replied.

A blonde woman slipped out of the ship and ran straight for the forest. "Uh, Jun, someone is escaping."

"Goddamn it! That infuriating woman! I don't have time for this."

"What is it?"

"She doesn't trust us because my other mate is one of the Grutex scientists." Jun shook her head.

"A what?!" Had she heard that right?

"No time to explain. He's in trouble."

"Don't think you're getting away without telling me, Junafer," Amanda warned. "When this is cleared up I want the entire story."

"I'll get a search party together and join in myself," Ky said before taking off toward the group of men.

Not only had Jun made a scene on the landing pad, she sent the members of the council into a full-blown panic when she burst through their doors. Even the Venium guards outside the building hadn't tried to stop her. In all honesty, Amanda thought she'd seen Jun at her angriest already, but she was so very wrong.

Her friend's murderous rage when Oshen told her that the council had refused to provide aid in the search for a very pregnant Amanda when she was stolen by a Grutex had been a truly terrifying sight to behold.

As luck would have it, the councilmembers were already gathered due to the newest alien arrivals, and their displeasure at being interrupted didn't deter her in the least. She faced down the entire room, including the ornery head councilman, with a fervor that would rival even the fiercest Venium warrior. Meanwhile, Brin beamed with pride, watching her diatribe with adoring eyes.

The shouting faded in her ears as the room slowly began to spin.

"We didn't warn Earth just to turn our backs on them now!" Jun screamed.

"Warn Earth? We did no such thing," the councilman sneered.

"You didn't, but I did," Brin glared at the council. "They needed to know Galactic Law so I took over where Oshen left off."

"You lied to us. There is a Sanctus female statue in the middle of Zar's village. She is Una." She could hear the distress in Oshen's voice.

"That is a lie! They lie!" the councilman yelled.

"We have no reason to lie." Zar growled.

She pressed a hand to her stomach as she felt her muscles tighten. This had been happening often over the last week or so. She closed her eyes, taking a deep breath to calm herself. The realization that this wasn't merely braxton hicks hit her when a trail of warm water dripped down Amanda's thighs. She grabbed Oshen's shirt and let out a pained cry.

"I think the babies are coming."

~

*G*ulzar

Gulzar looked down into the face of the little Venium female he held in his arms. This was his daughter. Her eyes opened, and the violet orbs that stared back at him tugged at his heart. The color matched his own.

Gulzar turned to the healer. "How?"

"Perhaps your bond with the pups before they were fully developed? It has been hypothesized before."

A little cry drew his attention across the bed to the tiny male Oshen cradled in his arms. They were both hybrids, but their Venium side was far more dominant.

"They're perfect..." Amanda whispered as she looked back and forth between them both.

"What are their names?" Jun, Amanda's human friend, asked as she stroked his mate's hair.

"This is Rydel." She brushed their son's soft head. "And this," she smiled, turning toward their daughter, "is Zenah."

Gulzar felt his heart constrict with emotion as he stared down at his little goddess. She had named their young after his parents.

"Thank you," he whispered, but he knew he didn't need to thank them. They loved Gulzar just as much as he loved them.

This next scene is a bonus epilogue/sneak peek into what we plan to write in the future. The book is complete without a cliffhanger without reading this scene. We hope you enjoyed our book. Continue on to learn more.

BONUS EPILOGUE

XUVRI

A soft touch along his chest plates pulled at his consciousness as the sound of a woman's voice filled his ears. The voice sounded seductive and familiar. Another voice joined the first, only he understood this one.

"Is he dead?"

Xuvri opened all six of his eyes and looked up at the beautiful females who hovered over him. One was clearly human. Her blonde hair made his heart stop in his chest as he remembered the female he had lost. The other was *her*. He had finally found her. The hybrid female's fushori lit as she placed her hand on his chest. He looked down at the two hands that touched him, surprised when he lit up red beneath each of their palms.

My mates.

ALSO BY OCTAVIA KORE

Venora Mates:

Ecstasy from the Deep (short story)

Dauur Mates:

Queen Of Twilight

Seyton Mates:

Breaths of Desire (short story)

WORKS COMING SOON BY OCTAVIA KORE

Venora Mates:

Kept from the Deep

Kidnapped from the Deep

Seyton Mates:

Breaths of Desire (extended edition)

ABOUT THE AUTHORS

Born in the Sunshine State, Hayley Benitez and Amanda Crawford are cousins who have come together to write under the name Octavia Kore. Both women share a love for reading, a passion for writing, and the inclination toward word vomiting when meeting new people. *Ecstasy from the Deep* (*From the Depths* anthology version) was their very first published work. Hayley and Amanda are both stay-at-home moms who squeeze in time to write when they aren't being used as jungle gyms or snack dispensers. They are both inspired by their love for mythology, science fiction, and all things extraordinary. Amanda has an unhealthy obsession with house plants, and Hayley can often be found gaming in her downtime.

FACEBOOK:
https://www.facebook.com/groups/MatesAmongUs/
SIGN UP FOR OUR NEWSLETTER:
https://mailchi.mp/27d09665e243/matesamongusnewsletter
INSTAGRAM:
https://www.instagram.com/octaviakore/?igshid=1bxhtr1snonz4
GOODREADS:
https://www.goodreads.com/octaviakore
BOOKBUB:
https://www.bookbub.com/profile/octavia-kore
AMAZON:
https://www.amazon.com/Octavia-Kore/e/B0845YHRVS